FINDING SONNY

FINDING SONNY

STEVE LAZARUS

Boyle
&
Dalton

Book Design & Production:
Boyle & Dalton
www.BoyleandDalton.com

Hardback ISBN: 978-1-63337-889-6
Paperback ISBN: 978-1-63337-915-2
E-book ISBN: 978-1-63337-890-2
LCCN: 2025902338

Printed in the United States of America
1 3 5 7 9 10 8 6 4 2

TO SUSAN, FOR YOUR
UNWAVERING LOVE
AND SUPPORT.

PROLOGUE

DANIELLE NEWBERRY died two days shy of her thirteenth birthday. It would have been a week sooner if the decision was left solely to the doctors; Dani was gone and the only things keeping her alive were a ventilator and the hydration coursing through an intravenous lead. The glioblastoma that had wracked her young body since the age of four had been beaten back by modern medicine three times over the years. With each remission the Newberry family hoped, only to have that hope crushed with another diagnosis, each worse than the last. In the end, as it often does, the brain cancer won. After a week of keeping her alive through artificial means, the hospital sent word through its patient representative that they would pursue legal remedies to end Dani's life if her father didn't accept the inevitable and allow them to do what was necessary and right.

Joe Newberry asked the nurses to leave the room when they switched off the machines so he could be alone with his daughter and hold her hand as she passed. In his free hand he clutched pictures of Dani's mother and little brother, both of whom had preceded her in death, both victims of the same cancer cluster that was discovered at Griffin Air Force Base in upstate New York ten years earlier. For reasons unknown, Joe was clean, "healthy as a horse" in the words of his doctors. Instead of suffering the ravages of cancer, he was sentenced to watch the disease obliterate his family.

The Newberry home filled with friends, family, and too many casseroles to count after Dani's funeral. Everyone had words of comfort, scripture, and anecdotes of their own trials with the loss of a loved one; Joe heard none of it as he moved around the two-story house in a semiconscious fog of grief. He was on autopilot, responding politely to their commentary but with his eyes fixed in a thousand-yard stare and his ears hearing little more than white noise. They stayed for a few hours, alternating between showering Joe with sympathy and whispering in quiet corners about the tragedy of it all. Toward evening, the women began to usher away the hangers-on, clearing dishes and cleaning the kitchen. The last to leave was Joe's sister Andrea, and she went over the reheating instructions for a lasagna and a pan of chicken cacciatore before kissing her brother on the cheek, telling him she loved him, and driving away.

Joe locked the house, showered, and put on his pajamas. He padded downstairs in his stocking feet, fixed himself a glass of bourbon over ice, and downed it in one swallow. He poured another, then a third. He returned to the bedroom he once shared with his wife and sat on the edge of the bed, staring at their pictures on the dresser. Anna, Dani, and Nicholas. All smiling, happy, healthy, none of them knowing how close they were to the ends of their lives. And now, all gone.

He reached into the nightstand and pulled out a pistol. He laid back on his pillow, closed his eyes, put the gun in his mouth, and waited for the courage to do what he needed to do.

———————

Congress created the Base Realignment and Closure Commission, or BRACC, in 1991 to address the issue of bloated military spending in the wake of the collapse of the Soviet Union. Its targets were the large old-school military installations that were built to fight Cold-War-style engagements. None fit the bill better than Griffin Air Force Base, with its ancient fleet of nuclear-loaded B-52 bombers sitting on concrete alert pads, poised to return Russia and its allies to the Stone Age. In the era of Glasnost and Perestroika brought about by Mikhail Gorbachev, all such bluster was deemed passé, and Griffin joined the list of thirty-five military installations slated for closure by 1995.

Frank D'Angelo was having none of it. A personal injury attorney turned politician, he was New York's representative for the Twenty-Second Congressional District, and he knew his career in Washington would be over the moment his constituents lost their single biggest employer. Without Griffin, his district would dry up and blow away. It happened around the country after World War II, as ghost towns sprang up where thriving military communities once stood. It would not happen in his town on his watch.

As chairman of the House Appropriations Committee, Frank wielded a powerful gavel. He held the purse strings for nearly all government spending, including the largest piece of the federal budget, designated for the Department of Defense. Chairman D'Angelo decided which bills would be placed before the membership for consideration and which would later be voted on by the full House of Representatives. It gave him more power than the president, whose veto pen could only return a bill to Congress, where it faced the possibility of an override.

Frank D'Angelo could kill legislation in its crib, and it would stay dead.

And he made it clear he would do just that if Griffin remained on the BRACC's hit list. The modern military was focusing on smaller, faster, lighter ways to fight the wars of the future. Next generation fighter aircraft and stealth versions of everything from bombers to surface warships were all the rage, and the coming years' defense budgets were padded with trillions of dollars for research and development. It took months of backroom wrangling with the defense secretary and the shot-callers in the Senate, but Frank D'Angelo got what he wanted. Not only did Griffin remain open, it was remade into a DoD showcase for its "new look" military. A ten-billion-dollar makeover saw the Cold War relic transformed into an installation that was the first of its kind; a joint-service mega-base combining an army light-infantry division, marine and navy special-operations rapid-deployment units, and the most lethal stockpile of high-tech airpower ever assembled in a single location. Between 1993 and 2005, Griffin Air Force Base tripled in size and saw its combined force of military and civilian workers swell from 12,000 to 50,000. It became its own city and brought with it an economic boom that doubled the population of the surrounding area and increased the average household income by 50 percent. Congressman D'Angelo became a hero throughout the upstate, and when he ran for the United States Senate in 2006, he won his seat with an unheard-of 75 percent of the vote.

The first cancer cases began appearing around 2008, and it took two years for public health officials and the Environmental Protection Agency to connect the dots. When they did, what they found was the single worst abuse of hazardous materials disposal laws in United States history. At the center of the disaster was Earth Tech, the contractor charged with ensuring Griffin Air Force Base's compliance with federal laws governing the mitigation and removal of hazardous materials. Investigators uncovered levels of toxic substances in the base's drinking water at more than twelve hundred times the safe limit, a number that had never been seen before and left environmental scientists scratching their heads at how such a finding was even possible. The two main culprits were benzene, a widely used solvent, and an entire class of chemicals known as polyfluoroalkyl substances, or PFAS, which were found in firefighting foam.

A joint EPA/FBI investigation uncovered a staggering amount of malfeasance on the part of Earth Tech. A forensic audit proved that they disposed of less than half of the hazardous chemicals for which they billed the Department of Defense. The remainder was dumped at random locations around the thirty-thousand-acre military installation, where it leeched into the groundwater. Earth Tech became the national poster child for corporate greed and environmental recklessness, and the company's president, chief operating officer, and two vice presidents were arrested during a raid on their corporate headquarters. All four of them cut sweetheart deals with the government to avoid jail time. In return for their full cooperation, they were allowed to plead guilty to misdemeanor charges and enter the Witness Security Program. It was a rare but necessary concession, due to the non-stop barrage of death threats the disgraced executives endured after their names and faces were put on display to the public like so much red meat. Dozens of lower-ranking company employees were sentenced to prison terms ranging from two to fifteen years.

The entire base was declared an EPA Superfund site in 2010, freeing billions of dollars in federal funding to clean up the mess and compensate the victims. Personal injury and wrongful death attorneys descended on the area like locusts, blanketing the airwaves with ads offering free consultations and the promise of no-fee representation to their clients unless they collected an award on their behalf. Most of them were from out of town, and they were spinning their wheels. The law firm of Abbott and D'Angelo had been doing business in the upstate for nearly a century, and their name recognition won the day as they secured the rights to represent 90 percent of claimants in their suits against Earth Tech and the United States government.

By 2011, over five thousand current and former residents of Griffin Air Force Base, including Joe Newberry's family, were seriously ill. The first deaths were logged soon after. By the time Congress and the DoD decided to pull the plug on Griffin and shutter their crown jewel in 2014, more than a thousand had succumbed to various forms of cancer linked to the poisonous drinking water that had been piped into their workplaces, schools, and homes.

Earth Tech was bankrupted in less than a year, leaving the federal government to foot the remainder of the bill for cleanup and victim compensation. The attorneys at Abbott and D'Angelo, who by now numbered in the hundreds and were exclusively servicing the victims of Griffin Air Force Base, were overjoyed with the news. There were no deeper pockets than Uncle Sam's, and the average injury claim was projected to settle for between one and two million dollars. Death claims would start at ten million dollars. Abbott and D'Angelo stood to collect 40 percent of every settlement in attorney's fees, and the partners estimated their ten-year revenue potential to be between five and ten billion dollars.

Frank D'Angelo hadn't practiced law since his election to Congress in 1982, but retained his title and status as the senior partner in the firm his grandfather opened after returning home from World War II. His eldest son, Maxwell, ran the day-to-day operations of the firm, where a twenty-four-hour call center fed potential clients to paralegals who assessed the merits of their cases. If the client had a compelling case, they were passed to the army of attorneys who filed claims on their behalf. It was a massive operation, and the firm occupied six floors of the Herkimer Building in nearby Syracuse, a block away from the courthouse where the Northern Judicial District of New York oversaw the civil and criminal remedies due the victims of Griffin Air Force Base's negligence.

Maxwell, or Max to his friends, became the face of the firm, and he took pride in being more than just a figurehead. He was a details man who knew the particulars of every case his attorneys took on. When the Griffin disaster became the firm's primary focus, Max made it a point to learn everything he could about the effects of benzene and PFAS poisoning, the treatment protocols, and the levels of pain and suffering its victims would endure. He remembered the names of each of their clients and attended the funeral for every one of them who didn't live to see their settlement check. There was nobody on either side of the issue who knew more about the Griffin Air Force Base case than Max D'Angelo.

In fact, there was only one thing he didn't know.

CHAPTER 1

"THANK YOU for your service, sweetie."

The elderly waitress handed him the bill, though today it was a mere formality. If you were a veteran in Adairsville, Iowa, population 5,250, you weren't paying for your breakfast (or lunch, or dinner for that matter) on November 11.

And he was clearly a veteran. A baseball cap advertised his membership in the fraternity of the 101st Airborne Division, one of the United States Army's premier combat outfits. The black leather vest hanging off his shoulders was festooned with all manner of military memorabilia, including parachutist's wings, a Combat Infantryman's Badge, a Purple Heart, and a Silver Star, the nation's third highest award for valor under fire, only two rungs down from the Congressional Medal of Honor. An embroidered Vietnam banner sewn across the back of the vest completed the ensemble, leaving little doubt that here stood the distinguished servant of a grateful nation.

And in Adairsville, Rodney Coleman wasn't just another veteran. He was the most famous and decorated serviceman past or present in his adopted hometown, and the honors didn't stop with free omelets and home fries. Twice he was named grand marshal of the Adairsville Veterans Day parade, and a key to the city was displayed above his fireplace, alongside a framed local newspaper article proclaiming him "Our Hometown Hero." Six months earlier, a Des Moines news station had come to town to shoot a feel-good piece about the war hero living in their midst, and the reporter was able to coax a reluctant Rodney into sharing the details of how he had earned his medals of valor during the infamous Tet Offensive.

He stood from his chair, fished a couple dollar bills from his pocket, and left them on the table for the waitress next to the handwritten check that read *Thank you, Rodney* and had a line through the total with a large *0* inked underneath it. There were more acknowledgments of his presence as he made his way through the dining room and toward the door. Another waitress wished him a happy Veterans Day, and several patrons waved from their tables as he walked past. While some shied away from their celebrity status, Rodney reveled in his, and why shouldn't he? People adored him. He was a decorated combat veteran, all-around good guy, and Adairsville's favorite son.

He was also a complete fraud. He couldn't find Vietnam on a map, which was understandable given that he was ten years old when the Tet Offensive began. The closest Rodney Coleman (not his real name) ever came to military service was an aborted attempt to enlist in the Marines during his senior year of high school. The recruiter was able to work past his borderline test scores and even managed to wrangle a medical waiver for his flat feet and heart murmur. But when the details of his arrest for indecent exposure and enticing a minor to perform a sexual act were uncovered, it was game over for the aspiring Audie Murphy, and he embarked instead on the life's journey that would lead him here, the middle of nowhere, some thirty-five years later. One of life's great incongruences was that, in the midst of the information age, with public records more voluminous and accessible than at any other time in human history, an impostor like Rodney could live such a blatant lie and go about his sham life unchallenged. But his was a story people wanted and needed to believe, and so believe him they did.

He stopped at the local donut shop for a bear claw and coffee ("No charge—thanks for your service!") before heading home to walk the dog, rake a few leaves, and perhaps squeeze in a nap before resuming his gratis culinary tour of the town. He had it all mapped out in his head, his mouth watering as he drove. Ernie's Diner boasted the "best Rueben in the Midwest," and it was no idle claim. He would have one for lunch with sweet potato fries and coleslaw. As luck would have it, Veterans Day fell on a Thursday this year, and Thursday was better known as "steak and all-you-can-eat fried shrimp" day at the Hawkeye Grille. He could think of no better way to end the day, unless of course he was able to snag a free piece of their signature turtle cheesecake for dessert. Maybe he would bring along his cane.

Ten years of relative anonymity in America's heartland had made him complacent, so much so that when he opened his front door, he didn't notice his dog wasn't there to greet him. He heard a few yips from the back of the house and scarcely had time to wonder if he had locked the poor thing in his bedroom before he heard the voice in the shadows of the living room.

"Have a seat, Alvin."

His blood ran cold and his knees weakened at the utterance of the name he hadn't used or heard in so many years. He turned toward the voice and saw the intruder sitting in the recliner. He pointed toward the couch with the gun he held in his right hand.

Alvin froze, glanced toward the door he had just walked through, and turned ever so slightly toward his only possible escape route.

"Don't even think about it," the intruder said. His voice was calm and cold. "Now have a seat. And don't make me say it again."

He did as he was told and had no sooner collapsed onto the sofa than he began to feel the sweat breaking out on his forehead, the rapid heartbeat, the trembling in his hands and feet, and the involuntary spasms in his abdomen.

"I'm going to be sick," he pleaded, hoping against hope for a measure of sympathy that would not be forthcoming.

"Yes, Alvin, I imagine you are."

A moment later, he emptied the contents of his stomach into his lap, a free breakfast now gone to waste.

The intruder gave Alvin a moment to compose himself, then began the questioning.

"Do you know who I am?" he asked.

"N-no," he stuttered through teary eyes and quivering lips covered in vomit and spittle.

"Do you know why I'm here?"

Alvin paused, gathered his composure, and resigned himself to his fate. "Yes."

"Did you think they wouldn't find you?"

"I don't know. I didn't have a choice. If I had stayed in New York I was a dead man."

"You had choices, Alvin. You could have chosen to honor your commitment to the people who paid you. Handsomely, I might add. Now, this next question is very important, so I'd like you to make your answer genuine. Have you talked to anyone about what you did since 2012?"

"Of course not. Even back then, I never talked about all of it. If I did, they'd be in jail," Alvin pleaded. "All the FBI ever knew was that I cooked some books."

The intruder continued as if Alvin hadn't said a word. "Well, it appears some people see it differently. Back to the issue of choices. You could have chosen not to cooperate with the FBI at all. You could have gone to prison and done your time like a man. You could have done a lot of things differently, but you chose to become a rat. And this is how it ends for rats. Are you ready?" He stood from his chair, took two steps toward Alvin, and raised the suppressed .40-caliber pistol.

"Don't...please!" Alvin screamed as he held his hands in front of his face.

The first shot pierced his right hand and shattered his cheekbone, causing a gaping wound that, as grotesque as it appeared, would not be fatal. The killer fired another into the center of Alvin's chest, and a third for good measure into his forehead, centered between his eyes.

He holstered the pistol in his waistband, then went to the kitchen and rummaged through the cabinets, where he found two large Tupperware containers and a bag of dry dog food. He filled one container with food and the other with water, then took them both to Alvin's bedroom, where the small mixed-breed dog he had locked away earlier was cowering in a corner.

"Pace yourself, buddy," he said to the dog as he placed the food and water on the floor near the bed. He closed the bedroom door behind him, left the house through the same rear door by which he had entered, and retraced his steps a half mile back to where his car was parked.

As soon as he was clear of the city limits, he pulled out his phone, scrolled through his recent calls, found the number he was looking for, and hit the Call button.

The female voice on the other end was familiar, as was the greeting. "McNair Industries, how may I direct your call?"

"I need to speak to Mr. Jackson," he said.

"Hold, please."

He hummed along to Christopher Cross's "Sailing" while he waited.

"Jackson," the voice on the other end answered.

"It's done."

"Any problems?" Mr. Jackson asked.

"None."

"What about the other thing?"

"He said he never told anyone about it. And he made a good point: if he had snitched way back when, our client would be in prison. Maybe I'm going soft, but I believed him."

"Maybe. Hopefully we never have to find out."

"What about the other ones?"

"They've already been assigned. You can stand down." The line went dead.

He disposed of his gun and suppressor in separate dumpsters behind a couple of fast food joints between Adairsville and Des Moines. He showered and changed out of his clothes at a truck stop along Interstate 80, throwing them into a third dumpster before fueling the rental car and making his way to the airport for the short flight home.

After dismissing his caller, Mr. Jackson (like Rodney, not his real name) dialed the number he knew by heart. He never liked having to call the boss, but at least on this occasion he had good news to share.

"Yeah?" was the one word greeting.

"The first one's done."

"Refresh my memory."

"Alvin Donaldson. The accountant."

"Good. What about the rest?"

"The other three jobs have been assigned. It's up to the individual operators now. And Sonny—" Jackson sighed rather than complete his thought.

"What? Say it."

"Sonny, we went over this. Taking out multiple targets for the same customer just isn't good business. It gives the cops too many data points to connect. That's how they got onto us after the whole Travis Conway fiasco. We're repeating our mistake, and it's going to bite us in the ass."

"I hear your concerns," Sonny answered. "And we're not going to make a habit of it. But we're doing this job. The partners voted."

"The partners went your way because you persuaded them to. And because all they really care about is getting paid."

"And you don't?"

He had known Sonny long enough to know when further discussion was not only counterproductive but bordering on dangerous.

"You're right, Sonny. I'm still just a little spooked over last time. We'll get it done, and there won't be any issues."

"That's the spirit."

CHAPTER 2

IF THERE WAS a place on Earth where it felt like you were living in a Jimmy Buffett song, it was Key West. Once home to Caribbean pirates and Ernest Hemingway, the sleepy hamlet at the end of Henry Flagler's railroad had grown into one of the country's most popular tourist destinations. It was an island-sized tiki bar famous for its open-air drag shows, free-roaming street chickens, neon-painted cottages, and an overall air of trademark weirdness.

And for one long week every year, even by Key West standards, things got weirder still. Fantasy Fest was an adults-only extravaganza of costumes, parades, and parties that was part Mardi Gras, part Comicon, and part Rio Carnival. Over recent years, the police and chamber of commerce had taken steps to tone down the debauchery, prohibiting total nudity and restricting the drunken revelry and public displays of explicit behavior to designated "fantasy zones" along a six-block stretch of the city's iconic Duval Street. But the attempts to control the uncontrollable met with predictable results, and love it or hate it, Fantasy Fest became known as the week in Key West when "anything goes."

By no small coincidence, it was also the pimp's most lucrative time of the year. He waited for his customer in a nine-foot inflatable rubber dinghy parked among dozens of similar, barely seaworthy craft tied off to the pier outside the Anchor House Pub and Grill on Key West's north end. The john showed up on time, and even the pimp, accustomed as he was to dealing with all manner of humanity, was taken aback by his appearance. He looked to be in his mid-forties, and it had been forty-plus hard years. Rail thin and covered with tattoos, he walked with an obvious limp. His long hair was pulled back in a mangy ponytail, and the pair of tourist trap sunglasses perched atop his head might have served him better on his face, where they would have covered the disfigured left eye that stared to one side. He stepped into the boat and sat down facing the stern, opposite the pimp.

"Zeke?" he asked. His one-word inquiry sounded slurred.

The pimp nodded. "It's three hundred," he said in a thick Cajun accent.

He pulled a wad of twenties from his pocket and gave it to the pimp, his hand trembling not out of fear but more likely due to a neurological illness or injury. For a brief moment, the pimp felt a twinge of pity. *What a mess,* he thought. *It's no wonder this guy has to pay to get laid.*

He pull-started the twenty horsepower motor, backed the boat out of its slip, and idled through the harbor, past the hordes of tourists enjoying their happy-hour two-fer deals before they were due back on the cruise ship. When they cleared the harbor entrance, he turned north, opened up the motor, and made his way at ten knots through the maze of live-aboard vessels that dotted the shallow waters off Fleming Key. Ten minutes later they pulled alongside a dilapidated thirty-eight-foot Catalina sailboat that looked as if it hadn't moved in years. Mooring lines stretched from the bow and stern, holding the vessel in place four hundred yards from the nearest boat and a mile from the shoreline. The pimp had chosen his spot for privacy, and he had chosen well. He tied the dinghy off at the Catalina's transom, climbed aboard, then turned and extended his hand to steady his customer as he followed.

"She's down below," he said, gesturing toward the door leading to the boat's sleeping quarters. "You've got one hour, and my rules are simple: You can do whatever you want, but nothing that leaves her with any marks or bruises. Also, there's condoms on the nightstand. Use them." He donned a pair of Bluetooth headphones, grabbed a beer from a cooler, sat down near the stern, and piped in a classic-rock playlist while he waited. Years of victimizing young women had left him cold and indifferent to their suffering, though blocking out the actual sounds of their tortured existence made it a bit easier to sleep at night.

Those years had also made him complacent, and he never noticed the other dinghy, similar to his own, that had trailed him at a distance from the harbor and now sat anchored off his bow, some two hundred yards away.

Below deck, the boat was musty, dimly lit, and sparsely appointed. A queen-sized mattress was wedged into the bow space, littered with pillows and fitted with sheets that looked like they hadn't been washed in a month. She was sitting on the edge, facing him as he walked down the steps, dressed in a pair of too-short shorts, a halter top showing her bare midriff, and a pair of glitter-encrusted sandals. Her makeup was caked on, grotesquely aging a face that should have been finishing high school in Anytown, USA, not servicing perverts on a floating brothel in the Gulf of Mexico.

She reached for him, but he recoiled at the advance. "What's the matter?" she asked through glazed eyes. "Don't you like me?"

"I do," he smiled. "Just let me get a look at you." He pulled his phone from his pocket and scrolled through his photos, his eyes darting between the girl before him and the three pictures he had been given. They were from happier times, and she looked ten years younger, but the eyes, the nose, and the dimple on her chin gave it away. It was her.

He knew she would lie, but he asked anyway. "What's your name, sweetheart?"

"Misty," she replied.

"No. Your real name."

Her lower lip began to quiver, and tears formed in the corners of her eyes. "I'm not supposed to say," she whimpered.

"It's okay. He can't hear us. And I promise you, he's never going to touch you again. Now what's your real name?"

She whispered it. "Rachel."

He turned his attention back to his phone, texted a thumbs-up emoji, then put it back into his pocket and locked eyes with her.

"Okay, Rachel, listen up. In a minute or two, things are going to get a little crazy. I need you to do everything I tell you without any questions, so we can get you out of here. Do you understand?"

She nodded. "Who are you? Where are we going?" she asked.

"My name is Harley, and you're going home."

Bryce Chandler had halved the distance to the Catalina by the time Harley finished his instructions to Rachel, and thirty seconds later he killed the motor as he drifted the remaining fifty feet to the sailboat's bow. He tied off and swung himself aboard using the vessel's safety railings. The pimp never saw him coming, oblivious to his surroundings as he tapped his foot and strummed an air guitar to the strains of "Free Bird." By the time he felt the boat rock under Bryce's weight and turned to look toward him, it was too late. He reached for the sawed off shotgun he kept next to the steering wheel, but Bryce had already seen it. He drew a pistol from his waistband and pointed it at the pimp.

"Don't do anything stupid," he said. "And keep your hands where I can see them." He backed toward the cabin, where he picked up the shotgun, kicked the door with his heel, and called out, "All clear, Harley. Let's go."

Harley and Rachel emerged from the cabin into the blinding light of the afternoon sun. Bryce handed Harley the shotgun and told him to take Rachel to the dinghy and wait for him. She saw the man who had become her captor at a disadvantage, his hands in the air and a gun aimed at his face, and still her reaction was that of a beaten dog in the presence of its unrepentant owner. She began to sob as Harley put his arm around her shoulders and led her toward Bryce's boat.

"What are you, her daddy or something?" the pimp sneered. "Or one of those johns with a hero complex?"

"Give me your wallet," Bryce said.

"Are you kidding me? You're stealing my girl, and now you're gonna take my money too?" the pimp asked.

"Your wallet. Now." Bryce repeated. "Stay right where you are and toss it to me. Nice and easy."

The pimp scoffed, but complied. Bryce caught the wallet on the fly and rifled through it with his non-shooting hand. There was upwards of a thousand dollars inside. He fished a Louisiana driver's license from the folds and tossed the wallet and the untouched money back at the pimp's feet.

"Percy Lambreaux," he read aloud from the license before shifting his stare to the now-cornered pimp. "Do you mind if I call you Percy? Let me tell you what's going to happen next, Percy."

The pimp smirked. "Let me guess. You and your undercover partner are going to haul me in and lock me up for pandering?"

Bryce smiled. "I only wish I could, Percy. But today is your lucky day, because I'm not a cop. I'm just a private investigator who was hired by a worried-sick mother and father to find their little girl. And since returning her to them is what I'm getting paid for, this is where you and I part company. Now, on our way out of town, I'm going to take your driver's license to my friends at the police department and sheriff's office, tell them what I know about you, and make sure you can never get another night's sleep in the Florida Keys. You're going to want to find another line of work, somewhere far away from here."

It was a concocted and empty threat. While pandering was a felony in Florida, it was a low level one, and the standard of proof was far beyond what Bryce had in the way of evidence. He got the case less than a week ago, and his investigation consisted of showing Rachel's picture in the right places and having Harley leverage his relationship with the local prostitute community to track her down. There were no phone records, no surveillance logs, and no actual documentation of cash in exchange for sex, all of which would be necessary to build a case worthy of prosecution. Rachel was a runaway, one of hundreds who turned up in the Keys every year, got hooked on drugs, and made terrible witnesses. The police would wash their hands of this one without so much as interrogating Percy Lambreaux. Bryce had done all he could.

And the pimp knew it. "Sure thing," he said through a contemptuous smile. "Now get the hell out of here, take that little slut with you, and don't come back. You think I'm gonna miss her? There's a bus comes into the terminal twice a day full of fresh young tail. I'll have one back on this boat and turned out before you get this one home to mommy and daddy. And then maybe I'll come looking for you, mister private investigator."

Bryce had begun moving toward the getaway boat, but Percy's threat froze him in his tracks. "What did you say?" he asked, his eyes filling with anger as he turned to face the pimp again.

"You heard me. You probably think you accomplished something today, but all you did was give me a reason to freshen up my talent. Like I said, there's a dozen more like her headed this way, and Uncle Percy is going to take real good care of at least one of them. That one was used up anyway. And you? Watch your back, cowboy. You and your gimp friend. The Keys is a small place, and I know people too."

Bryce walked to the bow, where Harley had Rachel seated and ready to go. He looked down at them, then back at Percy, who was still seated near the stern, smiling as if he didn't have a care in the world.

Decision time.

"Harley, hand me the shotgun."

A look of trepidation crept over Harley's face. "Bryce, don't. We got what we came here for. Let's go."

Bryce was not swayed. "Hand me the shotgun," he repeated, more firmly this time.

Harley, knowing his protests were futile, did as he was told. Bryce gave the weapon a quick once-over and was satisfied with what he saw. It was a vintage Century Arms Old West Coach model, side-by-side .410 gauge, known as a "scatter gun" among enthusiasts. The twenty-inch barrel had been sawn off just past the gun's fore-end, and the buttstock had been removed and replaced with a homemade version half its original size, giving the weapon an overall length far shorter than its factory specifications. Grinding marks on the barrel obscured what would have been the gun's serial number. All the better for what Bryce had in mind. He opened the breech, confirmed a pair of unfired birdshot shells were in place, closed everything back up, and holstered his pistol.

Without a word, he walked back toward the stern, stopping a few feet short of Percy, who had not moved from his seat since first seeing Bryce. The shotgun was pointed at the pimp's head.

"You gonna kill me, tough guy?" Percy asked. "Out here on the open water, with all these other boats around?"

Bryce smiled. "I've been in the Keys long enough to know the code of the live-aboards, Percy. Everyone keeps to themselves, nobody calls the cops, and nobody talks to the cops if they come around. Half of the folks on these pieces of crap you call home are just as crooked as you are, and the other half only want to be left alone. I could hang you from the mast and nobody would so much as lift a finger to help you."

For the first time since he laid eyes on him, Bryce saw a twinge of fear in Percy's eyes. "So that's it, then? You're going to kill me? Over a piece of ass?"

Bryce shook his head. "You ever go lobstering, Percy?"

"Can't say as I have."

"Well, you can't just take any lobster you pull out of the water. There are rules. They have to be in season. They have to be the right size. They can't be too small, and believe it or not, in some places they can't be too large either."

"That's fascinating," Percy said. "Does your story have a point, or are you ready to get the hell off my boat and ride into the sunset with your little whore?" His tone, which had been contemptuous, now smacked more of anxiety.

Bryce kept speaking as if Percy hadn't said a word. "And then there's breeding females. You'll know when you see one, because she's covered all along her bottom side with hundreds, even thousands, of the most beautiful black lobster eggs. Those girls are the reason we don't run out of lobsters, so harvesting them is illegal. You have to throw them back. But once they lay all those eggs, how is the next fisherman supposed to know this is a lobster that needs to be left alone, to be treated specially? And that's where the v-notch comes in. Lobstermen have a special notching tool they use to mark the tails of breeding females. That way, the next guy who pulls her out of the water knows what she is and what to do with her."

Percy began to squirm in his seat. He was uncertain of the exact point of the story, but sure enough he wasn't going to like the ending. "Look," he said, his voice more contrite than at any previous point in the conversation, "you've made your point. Why don't you just take the girl and get out of here? I've got no axe to grind with you. You're just doing your job, that's all."

Bryce continued. "Now, you're no breeding lobster, Percy. No sir, you're nowhere near that valuable. In fact, you're a pox on society. But just like that lobster, you need to be marked. People need to be able to identify you on sight, to know what they're dealing with. To know who you are and what you are."

In a single motion, he lowered the barrel of the shotgun, pointed it toward Percy's right knee, and pulled the trigger.

Had the gun been loaded with a solid slug, or even a pellet round of a heavier gauge, it might have blown Percy's lower leg off, or at least caused a lethal loss of blood. But less powerful "varmint guns" like Percy's were intended for use on snakes and small pests not bigger than the average rodent. While the amount of force they delivered was deadly to gophers, rabbits, and the like, the effect on the human body was less severe. Still, Bryce's shot was well-placed and taken at the perfect distance for its intended purpose, and it folded Percy's leg in half in the wrong direction as his knee gave way underneath him.

"You son of a bitch!" Percy screamed as he fell to the deck, his voice equal parts shock, anger, and pain. Blood oozed from the mangled mess that used to be his knee, but true to Bryce's intent, it wasn't shooting or spurting from the wound, which would have indicated a life-threatening arterial injury. Percy would never walk right again, but neither was he going to die, at least not here and now.

Without a word, Bryce retreated to the boat's cabin and assessed his next task. The shot needed to be below the waterline, but also in a spot where the fiberglass was weak enough to allow the wimpy .410 birdshot round to penetrate. There was a closet on the starboard side, and when he opened the door, the light shining through the thinnest part of the hull gave him his answer. This was the spot. Mindful of the potential for back blast from splintering fiberglass, he extended the shotgun as far as possible from his body with his right hand, turned his head away from the target to protect his face and eyes, and pulled the trigger. The little varmint gun made a thunderous noise in the confined quarters of the boat's underdeck, and Bryce had to wait for the smoke to clear before he could inspect his handiwork.

The result wasn't all he had hoped for, but it wasn't bad, either. Rather than a gaping hole in the boat's hull, there was a quarter-sized fracture just below the waterline, through which water was streaming at a rate Bryce guessed to be ten gallons a minute. At that pace, the boat had an hour, two at best, before it gave way and sank. He dropped the shotgun on the cabin floor and returned topside, where Percy, who had not moved, was now staring at him through murderous, tear-filled eyes.

Bryce stared down at his broken adversary. "Percy, the pimp with a limp," he taunted. "It's going to be tough to outrun that nickname, no pun intended. You know what?" he added, pointing toward the mangled remains of Percy's right knee. "That's bad enough the doctors might not even be able to save it. Wouldn't that be something? 'Percy, the one-legged pimp.' I think I like that one even better. In any case, consider yourself marked, just like our lobster friends. No more hiding in the shadows for you. From now on, you're going to be famous."

"Fuck you. This isn't over," Percy threatened, staring into Bryce's eyes.

"Well, it is for today, Percy, and I'm afraid I have to go. You should get moving yourself. That leg isn't going to get any better, and you've got an hour or two before your office is underwater. Do you need help getting into your dinghy?"

"Go to hell," Percy replied.

"I'll take that as a no." Bryce retreated to the bow and lowered himself onto his rented boat. Harley and Rachel stared at him, mouths agape, as if he had just disembarked from an alien spaceship. They rode in silence back to the marina, turned in the rental, and made their way to Bryce's truck in a nearby parking lot. Before leaving Key West, Bryce ducked into a t-shirt shop and purchased a pair of sweatpants and a two-sizes-too-large Salty Dog Café sweatshirt for Rachel to wear for the ride to Marathon, where Mr. and Mrs. Lyle Wyndham were awaiting the return of their only daughter.

CHAPTER 3

THE FBI DIRECTOR'S conference room was filled to capacity, and everyone stood when he entered and took his seat at the head of the table, facing the giant monitor on which the day's briefing content would be broadcast.

Marcus Angiulino was known throughout the bureau as "an agent's director." He valued the hard work of his field investigators above all else, and particularly over the careerist bootlickers who self-promoted by moving from one desk job to another at the J. Edgar Hoover building in Washington, DC. He was only the second special agent to ascend to the top job in the bureau, and the first to do so without serving as a federal prosecutor, a district court judge, or both. He had a well-earned reputation as a stickler for details and a man who did not suffer fools.

Less than a month earlier, Director Angiulino had publicly fired four of his most senior executives, including an assistant director, his deputy, and a pair of field-office bosses known as special agents in charge, or SACs. The dismissals came in the wake of a botched investigation into a murder-for-hire network. It was an embarrassing breakdown of leadership, which had allowed the network to find and murder the government's star witness along with one of the deputy US marshals assigned to protect him. In a terse conference call, the director admonished the disgraced executives' replacements to "get your collective shit together" and report back to him on the status of the investigation within thirty days. Their report would be delivered in the day's briefing.

Supervisory Special Agent Donnie Morris stood at the podium, chosen by the assistant director of the criminal investigative division as the primary speaker due to his familiarity with the case. Assigned to the FBI's Atlanta division, SSA Morris was the first in the bureau to recognize similarities between a string of seemingly unrelated murders, which he tied to a subject in a decades-old Atlanta street gang case. The screen behind him was emblazoned with the FBI seal and "MC-455" written below it in bold red letters.

"Good morning, Director Angiulino. I'm SSA Donald Morris from Atlanta, and I'm here today to bring everyone up to speed on the status of major case 455, codenamed 'Finding Sonny.'" As he spoke, he used the remote in his hand to advance to the next slide in the presentation, and a photograph of a smiling young man in a dark blue uniform appeared on the screen.

"This is Andrew Pittman, a Bureau of Prisons correctional officer who was murdered at his home earlier this year. The killer used an explosive device that detonated while Officer Pittman was backing down his driveway."

He advanced the slide deck again, and a picture of an attractive woman in her thirties, clad in conservative business attire, flashed on the screen. "Julia Martinez was a former assistant United States attorney for the Northern District of Georgia. One week after Officer Pittman was killed, she was murdered by a gunman while out for her early morning jog in the Buckhead section of Atlanta."

A third click and another photo, this one of a distinguished, stern-faced man with gray hair, wearing a black robe and seated in front of an American flag. "This is retired United States District Court Judge Wendell Branch, also from the Northern District of Georgia. Two weeks after AUSA Martinez's death, he was attacked in his home in the Georgia mountains just outside of Dawsonville, but he was armed and managed to shoot and kill his attacker."

The fourth photo was of a middle-aged man in a coat and tie, also seated in front of an American flag. "Bryce Chandler is a retired FBI agent from the Atlanta division, and in the interest of full disclosure, he is also my former partner and a close personal friend," SSA Morris said. "He lives in the Florida Keys now and works as a private investigator. He was targeted by the same group responsible for the attacks on Officer Pittman, AUSA Martinez, and Judge Branch."

Bryce's picture transitioned to one of a man in his late forties, clad in an orange jumpsuit. "This is Robert Charles Petty, the hit man we believe was targeting Agent Chandler. Due to a sequence of events we are still trying to piece together, he encountered a pair of drug dealers in Agent Chandler's home, and a gunfight erupted. When it was over, the two drug dealers were dead and Mr. Petty was seriously injured. At present, he is in custody at the Miami-Dade Pre-Trial Detention Center."

Sullivan "Sully" Caine, the CID assistant director who had chosen Donnie to lead the briefing, chimed in. He was an imposing figure, six feet six inches tall with an athletic build and a full head of gray hair that he wore in a crew cut. A former organized crime investigator who cut his teeth as a new agent in the Las

Vegas division in the early 2000s, he had a reputation for a quick temper and an abrasive management style. He got results and was respected among the FBI's special agents, but it was a respect born of fear. "Dare I ask what a pair of drug dealers were doing in a retired FBI agent's home?"

"We believe they were there to either assault or kill Agent Chandler, who wasn't home," Donnie answered. "One of his private investigations stirred up a hornet's nest and heaped law-enforcement attention on a Miami drug dealer. That drug dealer sent a pair of his enforcers to deal with Agent Chander."

"So Agent Chandler had a pair of drug dealers *and* a hit man after him, and they all show up at his place while he's not there? That sounds mighty convenient to me."

The director shot his assistant a disapproving glance. "Let him finish, Sully."

"Sorry, sir. Continue, Agent Morris."

Another photo, this one also a mugshot, popped up on the screen. "This is Travis Conway, deceased, and it's where the pieces of the puzzle begin to come together. Agent Chandler arrested Mr. Conway in 2007 on a gun trafficking charge. AUSA Martinez was the prosecutor, and Judge Branch heard the case and sentenced Mister Conway to twenty-five years in federal prison. He went away to the federal correctional institute at Edgefield, then for disciplinary reasons was moved to the United States prison at Terre Haute, Indiana, where Officer Pittman was a guard. We are still investigating the details, but it appears that Officer Pittman was corrupt and tried to get Mr. Conway killed for running a smuggling ring inside the prison that conflicted with his own interests."

"So this Conway fellow set up four contract hits from inside the walls at Terre Haute?" the director asked. "How was he able to do that?"

"Actually, sir, Terre Haute wasn't his last stop," Donnie replied. "During the attempt on Mr. Conway's life, he killed one of the prisoners who attacked him in his cell. He was convicted of murder and sentenced to life at ADMAX in Florence, Colorado. Again, we are still piecing the details together, but it appears he paid off a guard there, and that guard was able to summon an Atlanta attorney to ADMAX to meet with Mr. Conway in person."

Travis's picture was replaced with one of a smiling James Todd dressed in a dark pinstripe suit, his hair perfectly coiffed, smiling through teeth that had been whitened several shades beyond nature's intent. It was the same photo that graced his business card, web page, and the ads he took out in the Yellow Pages before the internet and word of mouth accounted for most of his business.

"Like Mr. Conway, Mr. Todd is deceased," Donnie continued. "The marshals had him in protective custody, but the Network was able find him in a safehouse, and the hit man they dispatched killed not only Mr. Todd but one of the deputy marshals assigned to protect him."

"And it was right after that briefing that your ASAC got involved?" the director asked.

Atlanta's assistant special agent in charge, Gregory Peoples, had done more than just "get involved." He had suspended Donnie, taken over the case himself, claimed credit for solving a pair of murders that were anything but solved, and orchestrated a press conference that led to a double murder and an enormous black eye for the FBI.

"Yes, sir. But before Mr. Todd died, Agent Chandler and I debriefed him for over twenty-four hours, and he gave us a tremendous amount of information about the Network, as we are calling it, and how it operates."

Sullivan Caine interjected again. "How did this become a major case? Sure, we've got some murders for hire, and I get that the victims were all members of the federal law enforcement system, but at the risk of sounding callous, so what? Individual field offices work these cases all the time. Why are we making a Hollywood production out of it?"

The director took over. "You weren't in the room when I got my ass handed to me by the attorney general. The deputy's murder made the presidential daily brief. The media had a field day with it. And it was all our fault, from the idiot ASAC in Atlanta to everyone up his chain who should have been keeping him in check. We broke this, and we're going to fix it. Agent Morris, give me the broad strokes. What do we have to work with, based on James Todd's statements?"

Donnie replied, "Nothing that's going to lead us directly to anyone. We learned the Network was formed in the mid-1990s by Travis Conway and someone Mr. Todd knew only as 'Sonny.' They hired a dozen or so former military special forces types as hit men and started doling out assignments from a client base Sonny had when he was a contract killer himself. As the Network grew, they brought on a few partners to help them manage the workload and provide managerial oversight. The idea was to keep the organization and its operators from going off the rails or doing anything stupid to draw attention to themselves. Ironically, in 2007 Travis Conway did something stupid when he sold a batch of military rifles to an FBI undercover agent, and that's what got him locked up and on his way to ADMAX."

"Correct me if I'm wrong—nobody has actually laid eyes on this 'Sonny' character, have they?" Sullivan Caine asked.

"Not in the flesh, no sir," Donnie replied. "But several sources, including Mr. Todd, have reported on him, and we assess that, although we've yet to fully identify him, Sonny does in fact exist."

"Yeah, color me skeptical," the assistant director scoffed.

"Jesus, Sully, what's with you today?" the director asked. It was a rare rebuke of a senior executive in front of a room full of subordinates. "From what I've seen, Agent Morris's assessment is sound. And not only that, but it appears this 'Sonny,' whatever his real name, is the head of the snake and needs to be brought to justice. I don't understand all this resistance coming from you, but it's not helpful. Agent Morris, other than Robert Petty, what other Network members have we identified?"

Donnie winced. "None, sir. And I should add, we are all but certain that Robert Petty isn't his real name."

"Was he fingerprinted? Swabbed for DNA? That should clear up any identity issues, right?"

"Yes, it would. But I'm afraid I have some bad news in that regard."

The director laughed out loud. "Agent Morris, from start to finish this whole mess has been one big piece of bad news. I hate to ask, but what could you possibly say to make it any worse?"

Donnie hesitated, then ripped off the bandage. "There may be an FBI employee on the Network's payroll, sir. A mole, if you will."

"I beg your pardon?" the director asked.

"Well, after Judge Branch killed his attacker, the dead man's fingerprints and DNA were sent to NCIC, and everything came back as 'no match.' The same for Robert Charles Petty."

The National Crime Information Center, part of the FBI's Criminal Justice Information Services division in Clarksburg, West Virginia, served as the nation's primary repository for fingerprints and, more recently, DNA samples from anyone who was ever arrested in the United States. In its century of existence, countless crimes had been solved by comparing biometric data from new cases to known samples on file at CJIS.

"So?" the director asked. "Maybe they'd never been arrested."

"True," Donnie said. "But still, we found it odd that a professional hit man never had a brush with the law, so we asked James Todd about it. He said the Network had one of our people at CJIS on their payroll. Whenever the Network brought on a new operator, they sent their biometrics to their contact in Clarksburg, and he or she checked it against the database to see if there was an existing record. If there was, the mole's job was to make it disappear. So if the dead hit man from Judge Branch's house or Mister Petty ever had a set of prints or DNA on file, it had been erased from the system by the time the law enforcement agency sent their inquiry," Donnie explained.

The director was fuming. "I want a name. And I want them dragged out of the building in handcuffs, kicking and screaming for everyone to see."

"That's assuming there really is a mole, sir," Assistant Director Caine offered. "All this information—the existence of Sonny, this so-called 'mole,' all of it came from the mouth of a scumbag attorney who was facing life in prison. Who knows what he tried to sell Agent Morris to save his own skin?"

The director had heard enough from his assistant, and the outstretched palm and the daggers in his eyes told Sullivan it was time to stop talking. His expression softened as he turned and addressed Donnie.

"Find the mole, Agent Morris. And if there's one, there are probably more. Watch your back."

"I will, sir. And we're working on the West Virginia problem. Whoever it is, we'll find them."

Donnie continued on with his prepared briefing, detailing what they knew about the Network, what they didn't know, and how they planned to fill in the gaps. He explained the organization's use of attorneys to communicate with incarcerated operators, including the coded greeting that identified the attorney as a trusted representative of the Network.

"So let me get this straight," the director said. "I walk into a jail's visiting room, tell some hit man I've never met my name is Marcus, but call me Mark, and I'm your attorney—and from that he knows to trust me?"

"Yes, sir," Donnie replied. "I know it sounds simple, but it's effective. It was all Travis Conway needed to trust James Todd when he visited him at ADMAX, and they had never met."

"All right, let's wrap this up," the director said. He was intolerant of meetings that lasted longer than an hour, and this one was approaching the limit. "Where do we go from here?"

Donnie spent another five minutes outlining the investigative plan. As the meeting concluded, the director pulled Sullivan, Donnie, and Rex Simpson, Donnie's SAC, to a corner of the room for an impromptu huddle.

He was brief and to the point. "This was the biggest gut punch of my career. The attorney general is questioning our investigative ability. The director of the Marshals Service feels like we got one of his deputies killed, and I can't say I disagree with him. I want updates weekly. Your case is aptly titled, Agent Morris. We need Sonny found, and we need it done yesterday."

Donnie nodded his silent understanding of the charge.

The director extended his hand, gripped Donnie's, and pumped it. "Donnie, I appreciate all you've done, and I want to apologize for the way you were treated by your front office. Without you, there wouldn't even be a case. Keep at it, and you let me know if there's anything you need. Anything at all."

Donnie stared straight into the director's eyes as a smile spread across his face.

"Anything, sir?"

CHAPTER 4

"YOU GOTTA BE kidding me," Bryce said. Donnie spent the first ten minutes of the phone call bringing Bryce up to speed on the details of his meeting with the FBI director, and he had just delivered the money shot.

"Nope," Donnie replied. "He said anything I needed, so I asked, and he didn't even blink. You're back in if you want it."

"Donnie, I'm too old, I'm too tired, and I've been out of the game for five years. What am I supposed to do, just quit my job, pack up my life down here, and move back to Atlanta?"

Donnie countered, "You're fifty-five, Bryce. Mandatory retirement is fifty-seven, and you can get an extension to age sixty. The director grants those, and he wants you back on the team. Your current job sucks, and you know it. And you won't have to move anywhere."

"How's that going to work?" Bryce asked. "Last time I checked, the bureau wasn't big on its agents working from home."

"There's an extra desk at the Key West RA," Donnie replied. Resident agencies, or RAs, as they were called, were small sub-offices under the control of a major field office, which served to extend the FBI's investigative reach in remote areas and keep agents from having to travel hundreds of miles to work a case or cover a simple lead. The Miami division had several RAs in its territory, the furthest of which was in America's southernmost city.

"Not that you'll be spending too much time in the office," he continued. "We're taking the fight to the Network, and we're going to hunt them down wherever that leads us. I don't need you sitting at a desk pumping out paperwork, but when you need to take care of some administrative chore, you can use the office down there. Also, there's supposed to be some hotshot intelligence analyst in Key West who we could use to track leads and stuff."

"There's the other thing, you know," Bryce added.

"Are you talking about the drinking stuff?" Donnie asked.

"You're being kind. I'm an alcoholic, Donnie. It killed my marriage and got me put out to pasture early. I've been sober for a few years, but it was the stress of the job that landed me in the bottle to begin with. I'm not sure I want to jump back into that world again."

"You have stress in your job now," Donnie countered. "A hit man and a pair of cartel goons came after you. Did that make you start drinking again?"

"No."

"You've grown, Bryce. Even old dogs like you can learn new tricks, and you've learned to deal with your triggers without turning to booze for help. You can do this."

Bryce's resistance waned as he mulled the idea in his head and admitted to himself that it sounded right. He offered up one final, feeble protest. "I don't know, Donnie. My security clearance is expired. Those things take months to reinstate, sometimes longer. I have a DUI on my record now that wasn't there five years ago."

"Way ahead of you," Donnie responded. "At the risk of repeating myself, the director himself has OK'd you coming back on board. That makes the hard things easy. He knows about the DUI and doesn't care. Security Division has orders to fast-track your clearance, and it will be a couple weeks at most. You drive up to Miami, have the SAC swear you in, grab your new set of credentials, a gun, and a bureau car, and it's like you never left. Then you and I get to work."

Bryce sighed. "All right. Let me sleep on it, and I'll give you an answer in the morning."

"Fair enough. Before you decide, let me sweeten the deal a bit. After you leave the Miami office as a born-again FBI agent, don't go anywhere. You and I are going to Miami Pre-Trial Detention to interview Robert Charles Petty."

"The asshole that tried to kill me?"

"One and the same."

Bryce smiled. "Okay, partner. Give me overnight to think about it. And I need to run it by someone."

CHAPTER 5

THERE WERE ONLY two people to whom Bryce felt obligated to explain his decision. Harley was disappointed but understood. The Ashley situation was a little more delicate because their relationship had progressed beyond the casual dating phase, and they were referring to each other as boyfriend and girlfriend. Both had been scarred by long-term relationships that had ended in flames, and accordingly, they both were gun-shy about taking matters to the next level, that involving formal commitment and the L-word. But they were exclusive, and more nights than not Bryce slept at Ashley's condo in Marathon, some thirty miles from his own house. Ashley remained firm in her aversion to sleeping over at Bryce's place, citing the double murder there almost a year earlier. Bryce assured her all traces of the massacre had been cleaned or removed from the premises, to no avail. "Until you find a way to clean away the creepiness," she insisted, "it's a hard no for me." It was impossible to argue against such logic, and Bryce quit trying.

He decided to broach the subject over dinner at the Sundown Grille, which had become their go-to place since their first social meeting there just before the murders. Through the meal they chatted about other things, including a cruise to Grand Cayman and Cozumel they were planning for Ashley's birthday. Over coffee and dessert, he hit her with the news. Bryce watched her mood change before his eyes, going in an instant from carefree to distressed.

"I didn't think the FBI would allow something like that," she said.

"Neither did I. Donnie had the director's ear at the right time, and when you're the director of the FBI, you can pretty much do what you want."

"Well, I'm sure they have their reasons. And it's just for this one case?" Bryce had told her there was a major case involved, but other than that hadn't offered any details. Ashley knew a hit man from his past had come to his house to kill him. She knew that he had instead run into a pair of Mexican cartel enforcers who were in Bryce's house on unrelated business. And she knew it all had happened while she and Bryce were in bed together for the first time. Bryce had drawn the line at filling her in on the details of the Network investigation. He felt a show of trust and good faith was in order.

"Yes, but it could be a long, drawn-out investigation. I've never told you this—the hit man who came looking for me wasn't some lone wolf. He was working for an organization that puts out contracts on the dark web. They call themselves the Network, and they—"

Ashley held up her hand, palm toward Bryce. "Are you sure you should be telling me this?" she asked.

Bryce shrugged. "It's sensitive, but not classified. I'm not exactly spilling state secrets."

Ashley smiled. "Okay, then."

"Basically, they're an internet-based group of professional hit men. We don't know exactly how they're organized. We don't know the true names of any of their members, including their leader. We don't know exactly how they communicate other than through some site on the dark web. We were making progress with one of their people, but they found out about it and had him killed."

"That's terrible. So what *do* you know about them? And how do you move forward?"

"We're starting with the guy who came after me. He's locked up in Miami, probably under a fake name. Donnie and I are going to see if he's willing to talk."

"And if he won't?"

"We'll try to identify his attorney."

A quizzical look came over Ashley's face. "That shouldn't be hard. Isn't it a matter of public record?"

"Not his actual attorney. The one the Network sent. I forgot to mention it, but that's one of the things we do know about how they operate. When one of their hit men gets locked up, they dispatch a messenger, in the form of an attorney, to establish a communications link and make sure their guy knows to keep his mouth shut. The source Donnie and I were working with, the one who got killed? He was a Network attorney. And they found him even though he was being protected by the United States Marshals. They set fire to an apartment complex to get to him, and they killed one of the marshals protecting him as well."

Ashley gasped, and covered her hand with her mouth as if stifling a scream. Her eyes filled with fear and she began to tremble.

Bryce saw her reaction and knew he had shared too much. He reached across the table and took her hands in his. "Easy, baby. They're not after me anymore." He smiled. "Or at least, I don't think so."

His attempt at humor fell flat. "Don't make jokes, Bryce," Ashley admonished.

"I'm sorry," he replied. "Let's change the subject."

"Yes, let's."

They spent another five minutes over their coffee and pie, trying to get back to the carefree place they'd been half an hour earlier, before Bryce brought up his return to the rolls of the FBI. But the date-night mood was gone, replaced by the weight of the Network conversation. Bryce knew it, and so he paid the bill and they drove in silence back to Ashley's place.

When they got to her apartment, she led him to the bedroom, took off his clothes, and made love to him with a sense of detachment Bryce hadn't felt in any of their previous encounters. She wasn't cold, but she wasn't warm and engaging, either. It was mechanical, perfunctory, and, Bryce sensed, meant to take his mind off all things related to the FBI and murderous hit men. And it worked.

———————————

After Bryce fell asleep, Ashley took her phone and slipped out of the bedroom. She scrolled through her contacts, pressed the Call button, and waited.

"McNair Industries," the female voice answered.

Ashley replied in a lowered voice, sans pleasantries. "Mr. Jackson."

She didn't have to wait long. "I was wondering when I'd hear from you," came the gruff male voice from the other end.

"They're going to go see your man in Miami," she said.

"Who's 'they'?"

"The FBI."

"And who told you this?"

"Bryce. He's rejoining the FBI."

"That's great news."

"No, it isn't. Their first order of business is to identify the Network attorney. And we both know who that is."

"Did you do what I told you?"

"Yes. I wore a wig, signed in with a fake name, all of it. But still—"

He cut her off. "Stop worrying about being found out. Worry instead about keeping your end of the deal. That's what we're paying you for. I expect a full report after your boyfriend gets back from Miami."

The line went dead.

CHAPTER 6

THE SECURITY CLEARANCE took less time than even Donnie predicted, and within three weeks of their phone call, Bryce was standing in the office of the Miami FBI special agent in charge, retaking his oath of office. True to his word, Donnie made the trip from Atlanta to witness the occasion, and afterward they caught up and strategized in the car during the ride to the Miami Pre-Trial Detention Center, where their best and only lead, the so-called Robert Charles Petty, was locked up and waiting.

"How's the management gig treating you?" Bryce teased. "Did they give you a key to the executive bathroom at the Hoover building yet?"

"Funny. It's okay. I miss being a street agent, but some of the big picture stuff I've been exposed to is fascinating. AD Caine is a pain in the ass, though."

"How so?"

"Don't get me wrong, he's involved and really knows his stuff, more so than most senior executives. He worked OC for a long time, so he's smart on how criminal enterprises operate."

"Well, that's a plus, isn't it?" Bryce countered. "Think of all the know-nothing bosses we had to school every time we opened a new case."

"Yeah, it's okay. It's just that sometimes he's a little too involved. Like a micromanager from hell. He wants to see every piece of paper that goes in the file. He's approving memos at his level that should never go higher than the desk of a field office supervisor. I'm on orders to call him and debrief the results of today's interview once we're done. He doesn't even want to wait for the 302 to be written. The guy's an assistant director, for crying out loud. He's got bigger things to worry about."

"Speaking of today's interview, do you think he'll even talk to us?" Bryce asked.

"Your guess is as good as mine. We do know Robert Charles Petty is almost certainly not his real name, but thanks to whoever scrubbed his file in West Virginia, his DNA and fingerprints aren't showing up in any databases. His address in Kansas City comes back to a Mailboxes Plus store, and the credit card he used to book his flight and rental car was opened a week before he showed up in Miami. He's trying pretty hard not to leave a trail."

"So what's the goal?"

"I'd like to break him," Donnie replied. "But that's not going to happen, at least not today. Right now he thinks everyone is buying his fake identity, and even though he knows they have him for the murders in your house, we're the only ones who know why he was really there. So I want to feed him a few bits of closely held information that he doesn't think we have, and gauge his response. Try and find his weak spot and work from there."

"Should we quiz him about the visit from the Network attorney?"

"Let's keep that close-hold for now," Donnie replied. "I'm sure they have an intelligence unit in the jail. We'll see if they have a visitor log or video that would be useful."

They pulled into the visitor's parking lot at the detention center, where they locked their guns in the trunk of Donnie's car, made their way inside, and announced their presence to the Miami-Dade deputy manning the front desk. After a ten-minute wait, another deputy showed up to take them to the interview room.

"So you two are here for the mystery man, eh?" the deputy asked, smiling as they made their way through a maze of seafoam-green cinderblock corridors.

"Is that his nickname?" Bryce asked.

"Sure is. He's been here almost six months and hasn't said two words to anyone that we're aware of. He just sits in his solitary cell reading all day. Refuses to go out to the yard for exercise. They've got him pegged for a pair of murders down in the lower Keys. Rumor is he killed a couple of goons who were working for a local drug dealer. You guys ever heard of Chase Worthing?"

"Is he the one that owned the fancy car dealership?" Bryce asked, playing dumb. It was his investigation into Chase Worthing's business dealings that set in motion the series of events culminating in the double murder in his home on Big Pine Key.

"Yep, that's him. He's the most famous inmate in this place. They've got him in isolation over in the west wing. Word is they've tied him to two tons of coke and a pair of murders. Which, if true, means he's never getting out. Or worse."

"Sucks to be him," Donnie said as they arrived at the interview room. The deputy led them inside and gestured toward the small rectangular table with two chairs on either side.

"Have a seat, gentlemen. I'll go get your boy. When we bring him in, you want him cuffed or uncuffed?"

"Uncuffed," Donnie replied.

"All right then. Give me five minutes."

Vincent wasn't expecting company, but then he never really knew when another in the endless stream of visitors would show up. They had been relentless during his first month in the jail, peppering him with questions he refused to answer and displaying the mountains of evidence against him that he refused to acknowledge. He gave his public defender the same silent treatment, despite the counsel's repeated pleas to assist in his own defense, negotiate a plea, and stave off the death-penalty trial the government said it was planning to seek.

About two months into his stay he had occasion to speak with the Network's attorney, but only to acknowledge receipt and understanding of the contents of the sealed envelope she delivered. The instructions inside were clear: He was expected to honor his vow of silence, and in return the Network would honor their responsibility to protect his identity and his safety while he was incarcerated. Vincent knew the Network's reach extended into the vast framework of state and federal prisons across the country, and theirs was no empty threat.

The note was typed on a single page of bond paper, and no signature was necessary. There was one other item in the envelope, a computer-printed photograph of Vincent's daughter, Shayna. It appeared to be a screen grab from one of her several social media accounts. If it was meant to be a threat, it was an empty one. Vincent knew enough of the Network's business model to know that family members, especially children, were off limits. The founders of the organization were old-school Mafia types, and when they had a problem with you, they dealt with you. If they wanted him dead, there were people on the inside who could make it happen.

On this day, the deputies found Vincent immersed in *American Prometheus*, the biography of J. Robert Oppenheimer of Manhattan Project fame. His failed attempt on Bryce's life left him with a bullet in his abdomen and resulted in the resection of his lower intestinal tract, meaning he would carry a colostomy apparatus for life. And then there were the headaches, which had increased in both frequency and severity since his incarceration. Between the two afflictions he was in almost constant pain. He was able to walk, but found it easier to move across distances with the aid of a wheelchair. The deputies strapped him in and cuffed his hands in front of him for the five-minute ride from his cell to the interview room.

Once inside, they removed the cuffs, placed him opposite his visitors, and left the room. There were two of them, one several years older than the other, and they were both dressed in dark suits, white shirts, and conservative ties. They had their badges and credentials at the ready for the introduction, but one of them was no stranger to Vincent.

"Good morning, Mr. Petty," the younger one said. I'm Special Agent Donald Morris, and this is Special Agent Bryce Chandler. We're with the FBI."

Vincent glared in silence at the pair, trying not to focus his attention on the one he had stalked in the Lower Keys; the one whose house he shot his way into and stumbled out of minutes later, almost fatally wounded. It was only six months ago, but it seemed like a lifetime.

"They told us you wouldn't talk, but that's okay," Donnie continued. "We'll do the talking. You do the listening."

The older one spoke up. Chandler. The one Vincent was sure he had killed, until a pair of Mexican drug cartel goons ruined his plan and his life.

"You'll have to forgive me if I don't call you Mr. Petty. Not because I don't respect you, but because you and I both know damned well that isn't your name."

Ah, the bad cop. Okay, smart guy, what is my name then?

"And for the record, I haven't taken any of this personally. I know why you came to my house, and this is business for me, as I'm sure it was for you."

Vincent watched the agent's eyes as he spoke and saw Chandler mapping his body, scanning his face, his hands, and his legs, his posture in the wheelchair. It wasn't the FBI agent's first interrogation, not by a long shot. When Chandler's gaze paused near his torso, Vincent shifted in his seat and tugged on the bottom rear side of his t-shirt, drawing the neckline upward until it touched his Adam's apple, then easing back against the wheelchair to hold it in place.

"We know you were sent by the Network," Chandler continued. "We know who took out the hit, and we know why."

Vincent stared, expressionless, and folded his hands in front of him in his best "Do I look like I give a shit?" pose.

"What we don't know is where the leadership of the Network hang their hats. The ones like Sonny, who made all the money on this deal, while you get to spend the rest of your life in a prison cell, crapping in a bag. Until, of course, they serve you your last meal, walk you into the death chamber, and pump you full of Pentobarbital. This is Florida, after all. They have a reputation to uphold, and they hate it when Texas gets all the headlines."

Fuck you, joker. I had your ass. You should be rotting in the ground right now.

"Another thing we don't know is what you want. Only you know that. But I've been in this business a while, and there's always something the guy sitting across the table wants or needs. Maybe it's a deal. Maybe it's a change of location. Maybe you want some commissary money so you can eat ramen and beef jerky every day instead of that slop they push through the door in your cell."

Vincent didn't flinch, didn't open his mouth, didn't shift his dead-eyed stare.

"But I don't think it's any of that. Here's what I do think: You went under for this job, so deep you can't have any reach-back to your former life. I'm sure the Network sees to that. And so if there is anyone you care about in your real world, you're cut off from them. Might be your wife, your girlfriend, your kid—"

It was just a twitch in his hands as they tensed at the mention of family. She was the only person in the world he cared about, the daughter he hadn't spoken to since leaving Arizona for the last time on his ill-fated mission. She was a grown woman, but she would be worried sick, and she needed her father. As little as he cared for his own well-being, the thought of her not knowing whether he was dead or alive was his main source of torment. He regained his composure as quickly as it failed him, and hoped the agents didn't notice the break in his stoic facade.

Chandler continued. "Now, since this is our first meeting, I'm not expecting much in the way of cooperation, or communication, or even acknowledging our presence. I can see that 'eat shit and die' look in your eyes, and that's fine. You're a professional, and I respect that. But you also know you're not walking out of here, ever. And since the Florida authorities have you dead to rights on a double murder, Agent Morris and I are the only two people with whom you might still have some bargaining power. So we'll let you ruminate on it for a while, and we'll check back in a couple weeks if we still need anything from you."

You dangle my kid in front of me and then play "fear of missing out" head games? You motherless prick.

Vincent knew they could see the contempt in his face, and he remained laser-focused on them until they left, refusing to break eye contact as men often do when asserting their dominance. Once they were gone, he waited alone for the deputies to return him to his cell.

"Thoughts?" Donnie asked as they made their way back toward the visitor's intake area.

"He's as stone cold as I imagined he'd be," Bryce replied. "But he had a couple tells. When I mentioned family, he couldn't help himself. He flinched, and his eyes darted away for a split second. There's somebody somewhere he cares about. And there's one more thing."

"What's that?" Donnie asked.

"He saw me looking him over, and he got squirrelly. At one point he pulled his shirt up like he was covering his chest. I don't think it was modesty. More like he's got a scar or tattoo he didn't want us to see. Let's add it to our to-do list at the intel unit."

The deputy escorting them led them back through the maze of hallways, depositing them in a pair of folding chairs outside a door marked *Lieutenant Raymond Childress, Chief, Intelligence Division.*

The door opened, and a tall, lanky deputy in a coat and tie stepped into the waiting room, extending his hand to Bryce and Donnie as they stood.

"Ray Childress, gentlemen. What can I do you for?"

"We just came from interviewing Robert Petty," Bryce replied. "We'd like to have a look at his file, to see if your unit logged any scars, marks, or tattoos during his intake process. We'd also like to see if you have any record of an attorney's visit other than his attorney of record."

"Well, you've come to the right place," the lieutenant answered with a smile. "Step into my office." Childress showed his guests to a pair of more comfortable padded chairs while he brought up the inmate's file on a laptop computer.

"Let's start with the attorney," the lieutenant said as he typed away. "Says here he's represented by Skylar Barnes out of Fort Lauderdale. I know of him. Longtime public defender but experienced in death penalty cases."

"Any other visitors?" Bryce asked.

"Hang on," Ray answered, continuing his furious pecking at the keyboard. "Here we go. About a month after he arrived. It's classified as an attorney visit, but it's not with Mr. Barnes. That's odd."

"Is there a name?"

"Rebecca Flaherty. That's another name I know. Strange though. If it's the same one, she was a divorce attorney here in the Miami-Dade area. I thought she was retired."

"Is there audio and video of her visit?" Donnie asked.

"Video, yes. Audio, no. We're not allowed to tape conversations with counsel," the lieutenant said. He spun his laptop around. "Have a look."

It looked like the same room they had just come from. Robert Petty was seated at a table facing the camera, and the attorney sat facing him, limiting their view to the back of her head. She had shoulder-length blonde hair and wore a bulky coat that looked out of place in Miami, regardless of the time of year.

"It's just fifteen minutes of this," the lieutenant said. His tone was apologetic. "The video starts when he enters the room and stops when he leaves. She got there before him and left after him, so there's no view of her face. If I'm being honest, we do a terrible job tracking the attorneys who visit this place. We don't even make copies of the identification documents they use to get past the guards. We got sued years back by some lawyer who was denied access to his client, and some good men lost their jobs. Ever since then we've treated defense attorneys with kid gloves."

"Okay," Bryce said, clearly disappointed. "We'll work with what we have. How about scars, marks, and tattoos?"

Childress flipped the computer back toward himself and started anew with the typing. "Scars he's got plenty of," he said from behind the screen. "Looks like a couple of knee replacements, some sort of back surgery, and of course the zipper he had installed when he got shot up right before he was arrested. Nothing in the way of birthmarks."

"What about tattoos?" Bryce asked.

"He's got a few of them, too. Let's see—a Guns & Roses logo on his upper left arm, part of the twenty-third Psalm on his upper right arm, and something on his chest he tried to have removed. I hope he didn't pay too much; they did a shitty job of it."

"What do you mean?" Bryce asked.

"Here, have a look." Childress spun the laptop around again so Bryce and Donnie could see.

The lieutenant was right: Whoever wielded the laser had done more harm than good, and the skin was now discolored and heavily scarred. The image was almost gone, but Bryce could make out a few details, including the faintest outline of a human skull, the handle of either a knife or a bayonet, and portions of a few words that appeared to be in a foreign language.

"Can you zoom in on the letters?" he asked.

Childress magnified the photograph to the point where it just began to lose clarity and turned the mouse over to Bryce to continue manipulating the image. Bryce scanned over the remnants of the inked letters embedded in the scar tissue, jotting down in his notebook what he could make out:

3 S G E P ESSO IB R

"What does it say?" Donnie asked.

"It's missing some letters, but the skull and the knife give it away," Bryce replied. "De Oppresso Liber. 'To Free the Oppressed.' And 'Third Special Forces Group.'"

"Where's that?" Donnie asked.

"Fort Bragg, North Carolina."

"Okay, so what does all this mean?" Childress asked.

"It means our mystery man was a Green Beret."

CHAPTER 7

KHOST PROVINCE, AFGHANISTAN
OCTOBER 13, 2006

The CH-47 Chinook set down at 2300 hours. It was a hot offload, so the rotors kept spinning as the twelve US Army special operators and eleven Afghan commandos disembarked the helo and moved to their staging area. The planners picked a moonless night for the operation, giving the team the best chance of advancing on their objective undetected. As the Chinook lifted off and flew away, the team leader, Captain Thomas Delaney, and his right-hand man, Master Sergeant Tom Kraft, conducted a final briefing with their men. They waited as the interpreter repeated everything to the commandos, then set off on foot toward the village some seven kilometers away.

The PC, or "precious cargo," for the operation was Mohammed Abu Ramsi al Kuwaiti, but the planners had seized on his initials and dubbed him MARK. In a war being decided by the use of improvised explosive devices, military leaders had put a premium on capturing or killing bomb makers, and MARK was among the most respected and feared members of that deadly fraternity. His specialty was the design and construction of a class of devices known as explosively formed penetrators, or EFPs, and the ones he built had killed or maimed hundreds of American and coalition soldiers.

EFPs were invented to overcome armor plating on every-thing from lightly buttressed personnel carriers all the way to main battle tanks, and they did so with devastating effects. The device consisted of a dome-shaped copper liner that the bomb maker packed with high explosives and aimed toward the tar-get at a predetermined height and distance, usually on the side of the road. When the target passed, the bomber used either a command detonator or a sensor to fire the main charge, which turned the copper liner into a slug traveling near Mach-6 speed. Once the EFP breached the armor and entered the passenger compartment of its target, it brought with it not only the ballistic damage caused by the slug itself, but residual heat and explosive energy from the main charge. The results were catastrophic and included multiple amputations, concussive-shock injuries, and major burns. To live through an EFP attack was both blessing and curse.

MARK was a suspected terrorist actor well before his emer-gence on the bomb-making scene. An electrical engineer by trade, he was rolled up by Army Rangers during a raid on a Sadr City compound in Baghdad in 2003 and spent a year at Abu Ghraib prison before being released in the wake of the infamous 2004 prisoner abuse scandal there. He made his way back home to Kuwait City before being recruited by Taliban sympathizers in early 2005, and since then his fingerprints and DNA had been recovered on triggers from two exploded devices and a pair of copper liners recovered during raids on a bomb-making factory. A million-dollar bounty went unclaimed for six months, until a Pashtun tribal elder walked up to an American forward operating base near Kandahar and gave intelligence officers the location of their most wanted terrorist. Drone footage over the village near the Pakistan border confirmed MARK's presence at the compound, along with thirty military-age males. The lack of women or children during the reconnaissance overflights might have made MARK and his cohorts perfect targets for a missile or bomb strike, but military brass decided there was valuable intelligence to be gained from capturing him alive, and the ticket went to the Third Special Forces Group.

Vincent cinched the straps on his pack as he set out on the long, slow march toward the objective. His load wasn't very heavy by Special Forces standards, but it wasn't light either. Between his basic ruck, M4, ammunition, water, and ballistic gear, he was carrying fifty pounds of equipment, or a little less than a third of his own body weight. At twenty-seven, he was the team's second youngest member and shared status as its lowest ranking soldier with his best friend, Bobby, who was one of the team's two demolition specialists. The pair had both joined the army after 9/11, met in infantry school, and crossed paths numerous times before being paired together again at the infamous Special Forces Q course, the grueling year-long selection and assessment crucible that all aspiring Green Berets were required to endure and which 75 percent of candidates would not complete.

The team paused for a final rest and equipment check at phase line Brooklyn, five hundred meters short of the objective. It was the last position of available cover before they would enter the village and begin a house-to-house clearing operation in search of their target. When they began moving again it was with purpose and renewed emphasis on noise and light discipline. The element of surprise hung in the balance.

The village sat at the base of a small mountain range, and they reached the outer walls as planned at 0400. There were a dozen or so individual huts within the compound, and the source told his military interrogators they would find MARK in the largest of them, the only one with double wooden entry doors. On the signal from his team sergeant, Bobby moved forward to plant a breaching charge while his teammates stood overwatch and prepared to storm the house.

Vincent saw it first. A tiny thin line at ankle height, stretched three feet in front of the doorway and anchored on one side in a massive concrete cistern. It would have been invisible to the naked eye, but through his night vision goggles the monofilament string caught just enough ambient light to cast a faint glow, and its purpose was clear.

Tripwire.

"Bobby, no!" was all Vincent could get out before the cistern exploded and the EFP it was hiding launched across the doorway, severing the breacher's legs at the knees in a microsecond. As he fell to the ground, Vincent and the rest of his team came under a barrage of fire from the village's inhabitants, who had abandoned their village and taken up fighting positions on the mountainside. It was an ambush.

The team was pinned down and they knew it, even as they emptied their magazines toward the sight and sound of the incoming fire. A rocket-propelled grenade whizzed past Vincent's head and exploded thirty meters away, killing three Afghan commandos who had taken cover in the doorway of an adjacent hut. Vincent sprinted across an open courtyard to where Bobby lay, a hail of bullets following him in the dirt but none finding their mark. When he got to his friend he grabbed the loop on the back of his ballistic vest, dragged him through the doorway of the hut, and turned him over to assess his condition.

He was beyond saving. Still, Vincent pulled a pair of tourniquets from his medical bag and applied them to the mangled remains of Bobby's upper legs, tightening the windlasses down until the flow of blood stopped. In his earpiece he heard the team's radio operator calling for fire from the AC-130 Spectre gunship that was turning circles in the sky ten miles away, waiting for the chance to unleash its airborne arsenal. The reply came back from the gunship: Three minutes.

The team hunkered down and waited for their only salvation. As promised, three minutes after the acknowledgment from the aircrew, the mountainside above them lit up in hellfire as the AC-130 blanketed every square meter of the enemy's position with twenty- and forty-millimeter rounds from its Vulcan and Bofors cannons. For good measure, the gunners added a few 102-millimeter Howitzer rounds, and when the gunship departed the area, not a Taliban fighter was left alive. DNA analysis of scattered body parts confirmed that MARK, or at least what was left of him, was among the dead.

Three MH-60 Blackhawk helicopters set down on the objective to evacuate the dead and wounded. Vincent and the remainder of his team returned to their forward operating base on another CH-47 Chinook. The flight took forty-five minutes, and not a word was spoken among the surviving team members. Four days later, the grim details of the mission were released to the public in the local newspaper back home at Fort Bragg, North Carolina.

3rd SFG Loses Three Soldiers in Afghanistan
Fayetteville Times-Press
October 17, 2006

Three members of the Third Special Forces Group died on October 13 in Khost, Afghanistan, during combat action.

Lieutenant General Bradley DuCheyne, head of the Army's Special Operations Command at Fort Bragg, called the men "…heroes who knew full well the dangerous nature of their task but went willingly into the heat of battle to confront and eliminate a Taliban bomb maker who was responsible for the deaths of scores of US service members." General DuCheyne went on to say the fallen Green Berets would be honored at a memorial service later this month.

The slain soldiers are expected to arrive at Dover Air Force Base in the coming days, where they will be received with full military honors. Individual funeral plans are not known at this time.

Special Operations Command identified the dead as Captain Thomas Alan Delaney, 32, of Pensacola, Florida, Sergeant First Class Victor Colon-Ruiz, 35, of San Bernardino, California, and Staff Sergeant Robert Charles Petty, 26, of Albuquerque, New Mexico.

CHAPTER 8

DONNIE'S PRESENCE was required in Atlanta, so Bryce made the trip to Fort Bragg alone. He met his contact, Army Criminal Investigative Division Special Agent Woody Barlowe, at the post's visitor center, where a fresh-faced young soldier filled out an entry pass for Bryce's car.

"Any weapons, sir?" the private asked.

What a stupid question. I'm an FBI agent. Of course I have a weapon.

Bryce decided against airing his thoughts and offered a more diplomatic response. "Yes. If you need me to lock it up in my trunk, that's no problem." He doubted his personal safety was at stake in the massive fortress, and if it was, a .40-caliber Glock wasn't going to save him.

"Sorry, sir, I can't let you do that. You'll need to stop at the provost marshal's office on your way to Third Group and check it there. Commanding general's orders."

So you don't trust me to lock it in my trunk, but you do trust me to stop at the MP station and let them have it? Nice logic.

Special Agent Barlowe broke in. "Thank you, Private. I'll see that he does just that. Let's go, Agent Chandler."

Once outside, Barlowe turned to Bryce. "Follow me to our office, then we can jump in my car. That pass will get you on post, but not to where we're going. Special Forces are very protective of their compound."

"Okay, so when do we stop at the MP station?" Bryce asked.

Barlowe laughed. "We don't. I just wanted to get you out of there. What that kid doesn't know won't hurt him." Bryce smiled as he hopped in his car and followed his CID escort across the mammoth military base. It took fifteen minutes to get to CID and another ten to make their way to the Third Special Forces Group. Barlowe talked as they drove.

"The guy we're meeting is the command sergeant major for Third Group, and he's been there forever. If your guy was in the unit, he'll know him. All I told him was I was bringing an FBI agent by to talk about a soldier who may have served here. I'll let you fill him in on the details."

They arrived at another guard shack, this one manned by a civilian sentry. Barlowe and Bryce produced their credentials, which the guard took inside his post to confirm their appointment with the unit's senior enlisted soldier. He issued directions as he handed them back.

"Straight ahead, left at the stop sign, building 355 two hundred yards at your twelve o'clock. Park in a visitor's spot and ring the buzzer at the front door. Have a nice day, gentlemen." There was something in his delivery that said, *And don't you dare deviate from what I just told you.*

They were met at the front door by a young soldier in workout gear, still sweating from whatever physical training he had been participating in before he was put on escort duty. As he led them through the building, Bryce noticed that none of the soldiers were dressed in full army uniforms. Some were in civilian clothes, others in their PT shorts and t-shirts, and still others in a mishmash of camouflage pants or blue jeans combined with flannel shirts and olive-drab sweaters. Most had beards and long hair, which was well outside regular army grooming standards. It was CrossFit meets Seattle grunge. Every one of them carried themselves with the deadly serious look of men who had been there, done that, and didn't care if you were impressed or not.

They walked past a bar that looked as if it served as the unit's museum. Color photos of soldiers in their dress greens lined the wall above the shelves of bottles, and Bryce rightly assumed these were the men who had given the ultimate sacrifice for their nation.

Barlowe noticed Bryce taking it all in. "Different world, right? Outside that fence is what we call 'Big Army'—starched uniforms, shined boots, and stupid rules. In here the whole culture changes. There's a reason they're called 'special.' These guys get the jobs other units don't have the skill set to handle."

Their escort led them to a closed door, where he knocked and announced himself. "Sergeant Major, two men to see you." He opened the door and ushered Bryce and Barlowe inside.

Their host stood and walked from behind his desk, greeting them with a smile and a handshake. "Tom Kraft, gentlemen. Welcome to Third Group." He was the first soldier Bryce had seen with a regulation haircut and uniform, and following the introductions, Tom motioned his guests toward a trio of easy chairs in the center of the ample office space.

"Agent Barlowe says you have questions about a former soldier in our unit," the sergeant major said. "I've been here almost twenty years. How can I help?"

Bryce smiled. "Thank you for having us. I'm in the middle of an investigation involving a professional hit man who managed to get himself shot, arrested, and locked up in Miami during one of his jobs. He's got an SF tattoo with a Third Group ribbon on it. He tried to laser it off, but some of the ink just wouldn't go away. And I'm sure the name he's using is an alias."

"And what name is that?" Tom asked.

"Robert Charles Petty."

Bryce watched the sergeant major's expression change in an instant. "Well, I'll be dipped in shit. I don't know what your guy's name is, but it ain't Robert Charles Petty."

"And how can you be sure of that?"

"Well, Agent Chandler, you walked past Staff Sergeant Petty on your way in here," he said in a measured tone. "On our wall of honor, over the bar. Bobby got blown up by an EFP in Afghanistan back in 2006. I was his team sergeant."

"Do you have any idea who might have taken on his identity?" Bryce asked.

"Given the tattoo, probably one of our people. Do you have a picture of your guy?"

Bryce pulled out his phone and scrolled to a Monroe County Sheriff's arrest photo, taken while Vincent was still recovering from surgery in Miami. He handed the phone to the sergeant major, who squinted, then cocked and nodded his head.

"I'm 90 percent sure I know who that is. Let me get a second opinion before I commit." He picked up his phone and dialed a four-digit extension. "Eddie, it's Tom. Can you swing by my office?"

A minute later a tall, thin soldier in his mid-forties, wearing Levi's and an Under Armour t-shirt, strode in.

"This is my first sergeant, Ed Schwartz. He's been here almost as long as me. Ed, these guys are with CID and FBI. Take a look at the photo they've got and tell me who you think it is."

Bryce showed him the picture. Ed's jaw dropped and his eyes lit up as he realized who he saw.

"Jesus Christ. Is that Vinnie?" he asked.

"Exactly who I was thinking," Tom added, turning toward Bryce. "Your man is Vincent Kamara. Former weapons guy on my team. He and Bobby were buddies from the Q Course. He tried saving Bobby the night he died, but there was nothing he could do. Nothing any of us could do."

"I mean, it's been a few years, but he looks like shit," Ed said. "What is he, in the hospital or something?"

"He got into a gunfight with a couple dopers and wound up getting shot," Bryce said. "They didn't do as well. He's in jail in Miami on a double murder charge. What else can you tell me about him?"

"Vinnie was divorced, if I recall," Tom said. Ed nodded in agreement. "Pretty common in this community. He had a kid, a daughter I think. He was from somewhere out west. He ETS'd about two years after Bobby was killed."

"ETS?" Bryce asked.

"End of time in service. His enlistment was up and he decided to do something else. And based on that picture and what you've told me, it sounds like whatever he decided to do wasn't such a good idea."

Bryce asked, "Can we get a copy of his personnel file?"

"Let me see what we still have here. If you go through the post personnel office, it'll take an act of God. I'll give you whatever I have, just don't tell the pencil pushers where you got it."

"Deal."

An hour later, Bryce was back in his Fayetteville hotel room, poring over the contents of the folder Tom Kraft had cobbled together. It was good information, and he knew he had the right man, but he wanted more before he confronted Vincent with what he knew. Kamara was in the Keys to do a job, after which he would return home to his real life and his real name. And wherever that home was, it could contain a treasure trove of information the FBI could use in its investigation into the Network.

He dialed the Key West RA and asked for Abbie Bishop. They had never met face-to-face, but each of their reputations preceded them. He was the agent with nine lives who had dodged firing after assaulting a supervisor in Atlanta, escaped a run-in with the notorious Chase Worthing drug trafficking organization, and outfoxed a professional hit man, all before being re-hired on orders of the director himself. She was a thirty-year veteran intelligence analyst with scores of major cases under her belt, including her career highlight, an analytical masterpiece that gave US prosecutors the ammunition they needed to extradite and convict Juan "El Pinto" Alessandro, the Sonora Cartel's most notorious drug kingpin. The case garnered her an Attorney General's Award and the option to pick any office in the bureau in which to retire. With only a couple years to go until that date, she chose paradise.

"Why, Agent Chandler," she said as she picked up the phone. "To what do I owe the pleasure?"

Bryce laughed. "Nice to meet you too, Miss Bishop. I'm almost embarrassed to ask this of an analyst with your credentials, but I need some basic 'who's who' information."

"Happy to help. What's our guy or gal's name?"

"Vincent Aaron Kamara. May 5, 1979. Last known address was outside Phoenix, Arizona, back in 2008. He'll also have addresses in the Fort Bragg, North Carolina, and Columbus, Georgia, areas."

"All right, let me get started. When do you need it?"

"Yesterday."

CHAPTER 9

GIL FLETCHER was nothing if not a creature of habit. He set aside Mondays for golf, Wednesdays for the beach, and Fridays for puttering around the house, fixing the odd leaky faucet or squeaky door. Saturdays were all about getting laid, and for a middle-aged fellow with a receding hairline, he did okay for himself. His strategy was simple: Find the right woman in the right place, then be the right guy at the right time. He shied away from high-dollar establishments and sleazy dives, having learned that women at the extreme ends of the socioeconomic spectrum were more complicated targets. The spaces in the middle—from shopping malls to bowling alleys to casual eateries—were proven territory and his regular go-to's. Tonight's hunting ground was TGI Fridays.

The bar was about three-quarters full, and he found a seat at one of the corners that would allow him to scan the talent in two directions. A television in front of him was tuned to a news station, and the top story—the only story, it appeared—was a Frank D'Angelo rally in progress in Boise, Idaho. The sound was muted, but between closed-captioning and the cameras panning the crowd, Gil could see the senator from New York was becoming a serious contender for the White House. He shook his head in disgust and got back to the business of tracking his prey.

Two candidates caught his eye: To his left, a forty-something brunette in jeans, cowboy boots, and a leather vest over a western shirt. Not your typical attire for Fort Walton Beach. She was probably from out of town, and that boded well for him. On the right, an older blonde with heavily applied makeup, Jersey-big hair, and a diamond the size of a golf ball on her right hand. Unless she was European, that meant she kept it after the divorce or the breakup with her fiancé. Again, opportunities abounded. He flipped a coin in his mind and decided to shoot (no pun intended) for the cowgirl.

"What can I get you?" the bartender asked as he slid a coaster and a menu in front of his newest customer.

"You can start by changing the channel," he said, motioning toward the screen where Frank D'Angelo was.

The bartender laughed. "Not a fan, I assume?"

"He's a pompous asshole. I can't believe anyone would even think of voting for him."

"Fair enough." The bartender reached behind him for a remote, pointed it at the television, and switched to the Orlando Magic game. "Now how about that drink?"

"Dos Equis and whatever she's having," Gil said, nodding to his left. It wasn't the bartender's first day on the job, so he understood the assignment. He even did it all in the right order: First give the guy his beer, then the freebie to the woman. That way the benefactor had something to raise in toast toward his recipient when she acknowledged his generosity.

"From the gentleman at the end of the bar," he said as he placed a Bacardi and Coke on a fresh napkin in front of her. And she did acknowledge his gift with a smile and nod in his direction, and he did raise his beer in response. It was all going according to plan.

She didn't seem occupied by anything, switching between watching the Florida/Tennessee football game on the TV in front of her, checking her phone, and nursing her drink. He waited ten minutes to make his next move, picking up his half-finished beer and sitting down on the barstool next to her.

"Hope you don't mind, but I can't see much of the game from where I was sitting," he said. "You a Gator fan?"

"Not really," she answered, not bothering to look away from the television.

Not much of a conversationalist either. Bad sign. Keep trying, though.

"Don't see many cowgirls in the panhandle. Especially ones as pretty as you. What brings you to town?"

She rolled her eyes and smiled. "Passing through on my way back to Houston. And you?"

"I'm a local. Been here going on ten years. Artie Campbell." He extended his right hand, and she shook it reluctantly.

"And what brings you to TGI Fridays on a Saturday, Artie Campbell?"

He smiled. "I'm all about a good time."

"And let me guess. I'm the guest of honor at your little good time party?"

His grin went from confident to sheepish. *Last chance.*

"Well, no reason we can't both have a good time, am I right?"

"And what did you have in mind, Artie? A quick blowjob in the parking lot, or the full monty back at your place?" Sarcasm oozed from her every word.

Game, set, match. Move on.

"Sorry. Didn't mean to bother you." He picked up his drink and stood.

"Sure you did, Artie. And a whole lot more. Sorry to burst your bubble. If it's any consolation, feel free to think about me while you're jerking off later."

"Goddamn, girl. Where did you learn to break balls like that?"

"I already told you. You just weren't listening. Texas. Thanks for the drink." She motioned to the bartender for her bill, and Gil slithered back to his original barstool as she paid her tab and left. There was still time to work on Jersey girl.

As he plotted his advance, another contender entered the bar, also in her early forties but a bit shorter than Cowgirl. Shoulder-length auburn hair and a body to die for, maybe one of those CrossFit junkies. No rings on either hand. Not too glamorous but no slouch, either. All Mary Ann and no Ginger. Just his type.

And there was something else—something vulnerable in the way she carried herself. Her face was disinterested, almost despairing, and she moved without purpose to the same barstool that Cowgirl had vacated just minutes earlier. She more plopped onto the stool than sat, letting out a visible sigh and a "what the hell am I doing here?" look as she did so. It appeared she wasn't meeting anyone, and she didn't ask for a food menu, just a mixed drink that looked like some sort of rum punch. In Gil's mind, there was only one reason a woman like this was drinking alone in a bar, and he figured tonight he could be her reason.

Ten minutes later he had a fresh Dos Equis, and the luckiest lady in Fort Walton Beach had another drink as well, courtesy of the gentleman at the end of the bar. Another smile, another bottle of beer lifted in a distant toast, and another "I can't see the game" excuse to sidle up to his new target. The bartender smiled through it all, but inside he was laughing.

The small talk went well, certainly better than with Cowgirl. A commercial for a slip-and-fall law firm appeared on the television during a time-out, and he made a lame lawyer joke ("What's the difference between a dead lawyer lying in the road and a dead possum lying in the road? There are skid marks in front of the possum.") She rolled her eyes and fidgeted with her hair. Always a good sign. Before long, they shifted their positions so they were facing more toward each other than the TV. Two drinks later he got the green light when he paid her a compliment and she touched his knee, letting her hand linger as she responded.

"You're sweet."

"Sweeter than you know. You wanna get out of here?"

She nodded. He pulled a credit card from his wallet, paid both their tabs, and led her away as the bartender watched, bemused, thinking to himself that even a blind squirrel finds a nut every now and then.

He offered her a ride to his place, but she didn't want to leave her car in the TGI Fridays parking lot overnight, so instead she followed him. Along the way he queued up his standard Saturday night playlist, which was dominated by Nickelback, Buckcherry, and Limp Bizkit. She rode in silence, and by the time they pulled into his driveway, they were both ready.

———

He wasted no time showing her to the bedroom. As she looked around, he put a hand on her shoulder, turned her to face him, and leaned in for the first kiss. She took his lips, his tongue, and his hands as they felt their way down her back before settling on her rear, where they stayed.

She broke the lip lock and moved her hands to his chest as she pulled her head away from his, nodding toward the bathroom.

"Do you mind if I freshen up first?" she asked.

"No need."

The slap caught her off guard and off balance. It was a swift, solid backhand to her cheek, knocking her backward onto the bed. It watered her eyes, loosened one of her teeth, and filled her mouth with the metallic taste of her own blood. His signet ring cut a deep gash under her eye.

"What the FUCK was that?" she screamed, as she abandoned her prone position and jumped to her feet, putting the bed between herself and him.

He licked his lips and smiled. "You know exactly what it was, you little cock tease. And you know you wanted it." He rounded the end of the bed and moved toward her as he unbuckled his belt.

She ducked and lowered her head, and he mistook it for cowering. As he lunged, she exploded upward with a perfectly placed palm strike that caught him flush underneath the chin, evening the bloody mouth score. He staggered backward, surprised but otherwise undaunted by the turn of events. He felt a rush of adrenaline and the beginnings of an erection.

"That'll cost you," he said, wiping a thin, bright-red rivulet from his jaw. "Don't worry, though, we'll still have us a good time. I like a little fight in my women."

She assumed a defensive stance and glared at him through murderous eyes. "Well then, you're going to love me."

He sneered as he took another step toward her, his right arm cocked. They were in front of the bed now, giving her the room she needed to defend herself with more than just her hands. As he swung wildly, she ducked the telegraphed punch, planted her left foot, and countered with her right, landing a lightning-fast roundhouse kick to the outside of his left knee. It buckled beneath him as the ACL snapped, and he fell to the floor with a yelp. He managed to stand on one good leg and lunged toward her again. She followed with another roundhouse, this time to his ribcage. The sounds of crunching bone were accompanied by the noise of the air rushing from his punctured lung and out his mouth, mimicking the noise of a deflating tire. He fell back to the floor, and she delivered an axe kick to his groin, shattering one of his testicles and ensuring his final moments on Earth would also be his most painful. For good measure, she added one more stomp to what had been his remaining healthy knee, separating bone, cartilage, and tendons in a devastating blow that left him crippled and helpless on the floor.

He was paralyzed, but only from the waist down, and she had no intention of taking another blow to the face. She moved alongside his torso, took aim at his left elbow with her heel, and destroyed it in another rage-filled axe kick. Once more to his right arm, and he was a quadriplegic.

His eyes filled with tears as his yelps gave way to good old-fashioned crying and he slipped into shock. She stood above him, then reached into the back pocket of her jeans for the stiletto he had come within inches of discovering earlier. She flicked it open with the touch of the blade's release button. It gleamed in the light from the bedside lamp. He looked up at her, agonized and puzzled.

"What do you want?" he asked. His words came out in broken bursts between pained, gasping breaths. He flopped and twisted as he spoke, in a futile attempt to get up, to run away, to be anywhere but here. "There's money in my wallet. And a Rolex in the nightstand. Take what you want and leave. Please."

But she was no longer his perky little conquest, rather the Devil incarnate, looming over him next to the bed on which he would have defiled her.

"I'm not here to rob you, Gilbert." She lowered her head and spit blood at his feet before once again meeting his eyes. "I'm here to kill you."

Agony and bewilderment were replaced by sheer terror at the reference to the life he had abandoned a decade ago. The last of his fight-or-flight reflexes kicked in, and though he could do neither, his face went ghostly pale as his vital organs sucked the blood away from the parts of his body that didn't need it.

She straddled him, kneeling until her hips met his, then lowering her full weight onto his battered body. She leaned forward until her mouth was close enough to his face to whisper in his ear. "Is this what you wanted, you dirty little piece of shit?" she taunted, grinding herself against him as she placed the tip of the stiletto at the base of his sternum. Blood dripped from her mouth and onto his face as she spoke. He tried to raise his arms in a last-ditch defensive effort, but only his shoulders budged. His hands remained on the floor, attached as they were to his dislocated elbows.

"It was just business," he pleaded, finally realizing who had sent her. "Nothing personal. Just business."

"So was this," she replied. "Until you made it personal." She drove the knife upward with all her strength, then pulled it back and repeated the motion a half dozen more times. It pierced his heart and ended his suffering, though if she had the time she would have extended it. When she was sure he was dead, she pulled the dagger from his chest, wiped it clean on his shirt, folded the blade, and put it back in her pocket. She stood, then gazed at her handiwork for a few moments before retreating to the bathroom to inspect the damage to her face.

Her cheek and jaw were starting to color, but it didn't look so bad that makeup wouldn't cover it. Her lip was puffy and bloodied. The tooth would need a dentist, and the gash under her eye would need stitches. Not her best day, but it could have gone much worse. She smiled at herself in the mirror. *You did good, M.K.*

She stepped over Gilbert Fletcher's lifeless body to retrieve her purse, double-checked that she wasn't leaving anything behind, and locked the door behind her as she left the house. On her way to the airport, she made the call.

CHAPTER 10

SAL WAITED until the following morning to notify Sonny. While murder and its attendant circumstances invoked a sense of immediacy in others, it was just another day at the office for men in their line of work. The phone call could wait at least until the boss had his morning coffee.

"Scratch the chief operating officer."

"Two down, two to go?" Sonny asked. It was a rhetorical question.

"Yep."

"What's the timing on the last two?"

"Like I said, Sonny, when the operators can find them and get to them. This guy was living as a commercial real estate appraiser in the Florida panhandle. The Marshals had him hidden well."

"How'd we find him?" Sonny asked.

"Same as usual. Contact with his previous life. In this case, a phone call to his mother on her birthday. The Marshals warn them ten ways from Sunday not to do stupid shit like that, but they never listen. Unacceptable risk with catastrophic consequences—we could learn something from that."

Sonny sighed. "Again with the hand-wringing? Why are you being such an old woman about this?"

"I told you, Sonny. We're repeating the same mistake we made when we took those jobs for Travis. Some cop or some fed somewhere is going to put this puzzle together, and when they do, we're finished."

"You going soft on me, or just getting old?" Sonny asked, only half-teasing.

"Neither. Just trying to be a good consigliere. You know I'll do what I'm told, and you know I'll always be grateful for what you did for me. But unless you tell me to shut up, I'm always going to give you the benefit of my counsel."

Sonny knew Sal was right. He was one of the few remaining old-school partners left in the Network, and if there was one thing Sonny could never question, it was his loyalty. Sal would never rat, would never so much as talk to the cops, and would take the secrets of his professional life to the grave. Part of it was rooted in his personal obligation to Sonny, who had killed the snitch poised to testify against Sal on a cocaine trafficking charge twenty-five years earlier. But part of it was just who Sal was, and the fact that he had grown up in the life. He, like Sonny, was a different breed, not just some military-trained killer looking to cash in on the lethal skills he had learned from Uncle Sam.

"You're a good counsel, Sal. I'm not going to get too specific about why we're doing this. Let's just say it has to do with our shared values. I know you'll respect that. Times like these, we need to remind ourselves who we are, and how we got here. Do you remember how you got started?"

Sal laughed. "It wasn't like I had a choice of this or going to Harvard. In my neighborhood, all the kids were doing some kind of knockaround bullshit. Me and my three best buddies were maybe twelve when we started running numbers at school for my old man. Two-dollar NFL strips. By the time I was fifteen I had my own little weed side hustle, making a couple hundred bucks a week. Back then, I thought that was all the money in the world. I whacked my first guy a week after my eighteenth birthday, and found out I was pretty good at it. Funny thing is, all the guys I've clipped, and the only thing I ever got locked up for was ag assault and that dope deal you and Travis got me out of. I guess you could say I've lived a charmed life."

"You and me both," Sonny replied.

"What about you? What got you into the business?" Sal asked his boss.

Sal could hear the sigh through the phone. "Same as you, Sal. It's all I've ever known."

CHAPTER 11

1974

The Godfather was credited with launching the American public's fascination with all things Mafia. And while it would be revered as a cinematic masterpiece for decades to come, the script writers' literary license gave rise to a number of historical inaccuracies in the way the mob and its membership were portrayed. Most real wise guys didn't dress in thousand-dollar suits, or live in mansions with round-the-clock security, or kiss the ring of the boss of the family as a sign of respect.

And not all of them lived and worked in New York City. As boss of the Philadelphia mob in the seventies and eighties, Nicky Scarfo ran an organization just as brutal, profitable, and notorious as any of those in the Big Apple. And unlike his colleagues to the north, Nicky didn't turn his nose up at criminal endeavors deemed to be beneath the dignity of La Cosa Nostra, which was to say drug trafficking. After loan-sharking and construction-based extortion rackets, illegal narcotics provided the lion's share of the revenue on which he built his empire.

But he did have a few restrictions; first and foremost was that only associates could get their hands dirty with the product. It didn't matter if it was cocaine, heroin, or marijuana—made guys who had sworn a blood oath to the family were forbidden from touching the stuff, and especially from using it. The reasoning was simple—penalties for drug trafficking were severe enough to tempt even the most loyal of Mafiosos to abandon their vows rather than dying as a guest of the government. Associates knew some of the mob's business, but not enough to bring down the entire organization in a wide-sweeping RICO case. They were trusted, but only to a point.

Tommy Costello was first-generation Irish American, and as there was no such thing as marrying into the Mafia, the fact that he wed a full-blooded Sicilian girl meant nothing when Nicky Scarfo opened the books for new members. He would never rise above the position of associate, but he was as valued an associate as there existed in Nicky's outfit. Tommy ran his crew like a military unit. He accounted for every gram of powder and every ounce of weed entrusted to his care. His dealers knew better than to short him, lest they short Nicky himself and not live long enough to regret it. In a business fraught with skimmers, scammers, and outright thieves, Tommy had never been put in the position of having to hand in a light bag. Until today.

And on this day, accounting issues weren't the only ones on his plate. Thomas Junior, or T.J., was the eldest and most aimless of his three children, and the "come to Jesus" meeting had been brewing for months. The final straw came as Tommy was walking downstairs to the kitchen for breakfast and saw the police cruiser parked at the curb in front of his North Philly row house. The officer rang the bell and waited, T.J. at his side with his head down. Tommy opened the door and ushered them both into the foyer and away from the prying eyes of his neighbors.

"Morning, Tommy," the officer said. "Sorry to bother you like this. Your boy got picked last night down by the Spectrum. He was in the holding cell this morning when I clocked in. Tony DiBartola was the booking sergeant, and he let me bring him home."

Tommy glared at his son with an expression that was equal parts anger, disappointment, and sadness. He jerked a thumb toward the kitchen. "Go sit with your mother. Eat your breakfast." T.J. shuffled away without so much as looking at his father.

"What did he do, Lenny?" Tommy asked.

"Stupid shit mostly. There was a show last night—Leonard Skinbird or something like that. Bunch of redneck bullshit. Anyway, your boy and his friends made like they owned a vacant lot a couple blocks away and were charging folks who didn't know any better five bucks to park. Trouble started when the guy who actually owns the lot tried to run them off, and one of the kids—not yours—pulled a gun. The owner called the cops. By the time patrol got there nobody knew anything about a gun, so it probably got tossed somewhere. But there were three underage girls with the boys, one of who was just thirteen. Long story short, she told the officers T.J. was her boyfriend, and they've been having sex for a couple months."

"Oh, fuck." Tommy rubbed his temples. "Where does it go from here?"

"The owner of the vacant lot is cool. He's got a juvenile record himself and a soft spot for kids who are as dumb as he once was, so he's willing to let it go as long as he never sees them on his property again. The gun is out of the picture, so no problem there. The problem is the thirteen-year-old's dad. He wants his pound of flesh from the kid who was banging his little girl."

"Any chance I could reason with him?"

"Tommy, it's Bill Cilente."

He hung his head and shook it slowly from side to side while staring at his shoes. "Jesus H. Christ. Kid really fucked up good, didn't he?"

And he had. As building and permits commissioner, Bill Cilente was one of, if not *the*, most powerful bureaucrats in the City of Philadelphia. On his say, commercial and residential real estate projects were given a thumbs up or down. Millions of dollars in revenues or losses hung in the balance, depending on which way he ruled. He'd been in Nicky Scarfo's pocket for years, green-lighting the projects that kept the mob and their trade unions fat and happy. Even if Tommy was able to leverage their shared relationship to get his son off the hook, it was going to cost him a small fortune.

"Sorry, Tommy. I gotta go. Juvie court is going to contact you in a week or so. As long as Bill is still worked up, that charge isn't going away. We did all we could."

"I know, Lenny, and thanks." Tommy reached into his pocket and pulled out a money clip. He peeled off a pair of hundred dollar bills and pressed them into Lenny's hand as he shook it. "Really, I appreciate your help. And thank Sergeant DiBartola for me as well."

Lenny pocketed the money and smiled as he turned for the door. "Any time, Tommy. You take care."

———————

They were seated at the kitchen table when he walked in, neither of them making eye contact or saying a word. Tension hung in the air. Tommy walked behind his son and delivered an attention-getting open palm slap to the back of his head that drove him forward in his chair.

"Thomas!" his wife screamed at him. In the Costello home, given names were for scolding purposes only. She got up and walked around the table, taking the seat next to her son and placing her arm around his shoulder.

Tommy moved to the stove, where the eggs and bacon were still warm in the skillet they had been cooking in minutes before. He addressed his wife over his shoulder as he fixed himself a plate.

"You want to know what your son did this time?" he asked. As with many marriages, when a child screwed up, they became the sole possession of the other spouse. He looked at Junior and asked, "You want to tell her or should I?"

T.J. wasn't in a talkative mood, so Tommy brought his wife up to speed on the charges pending against their eldest son while he ate. Before he was through, she was crying.

"What are we going to do?" she asked, all the while holding her son's hand and stroking his hair.

"We?" Tommy asked. "*We* aren't going to do anything. I'm going to go eat a giant shit sandwich with the people I work for, and hope I can persuade some other people not to throw my idiot son in jail for twenty years for statutory rape." The mention of the actual charge and its potential penalty made T.J.'s mother cry harder.

"What about you? Do you have anything to say for yourself? Look at me, goddammit!"

T.J. raised his head slowly and shook it from side to side.

"That's wonderful. You've been on a roll lately, haven't you? Straight D's and F's on your report card. You've been suspended from school now, what, three times this semester? You were an all-state safety, the only thing you've ever done right, and you blew that by smoking pot and getting booted off the football team. And now you're fucking children."

"Thomas! Language!" his wife protested.

He countered with a dismissive wave of his hand. "He's a loser, Marie. Never going to amount to anything. At least he'll be eighteen in a few months, then I can kick him out the door without child protective services climbing up my ass."

T.J. mumbled, "Maybe I can grow up to be a drug dealer for the mob like you."

Tommy's eyes lit red with rage as he stared at his son. "What did you just say to me?"

He raised his hand in a balled fist just as Marie jumped in front of her son with her arms spread wide.

"Don't you dare!" she shouted. Tommy unclenched his fist, but his glare never left his son's face. He downed a few more forkfuls of scrambled eggs and took a sip from his coffee cup as he pondered his next move.

"Go upstairs. Clean yourself up and put on some decent clothes. Not that street punk shit you wear. Man's clothes. And be back down here before your brother and sister wake up. Don't make me tell you twice."

For the first time in the last twenty-four hours, T.J.'s inner voice guided him toward a sound decision, and he followed his father's orders without saying a word. Worry turned to fear in his mother's eyes as she watched him walk away.

"Thomas, where are you taking him? He has school."

Tommy laughed. "Yeah, and a fat lot of good that's done him. He's clueless, Marie. He has no idea how food ends up on a table. We keep letting him go on like this, he'll end up in prison or dead."

"I don't want him around those people you work with," she protested.

"Oh, you mean the people who paid for this house and everything in it? For the car parked out front? For the clothes on our backs? You knew what I did for a living when you married me, Marie. Don't get a case of the conscience now."

Her tone went from pleading to defiant. "Yes, Thomas, I know what you do. That doesn't mean I want my son doing it."

"I'm not taking him for a job interview, Marie. He just needs to see how the world works, that's all."

They left home in Tommy's Lincoln Town Car. T.J. sat silently in the front passenger seat, waiting for his father to start the conversation, which he did in short order.

"So you think you know how I make my money, is that right?" he asked.

"I've heard you talking on the phone and with your friends," he said, head still down. "I'm not as dumb as you think."

"I don't think you're a dummy. I just think you need a lesson in how the real world works. And that starts today. You're gonna learn more in a couple hours with me than they'll teach you in a week at that school you go to. Just keep your ears open and your mouth shut, unless you're asked a question. Got me?"

T.J. nodded his understanding.

"Good. We're making a stop along the way, to pick up a friend of mine. When he gets in, you move to the back seat."

"Can I at least ask where we're going?"

"No."

They stopped at a corner bar about a mile from their house, and T.J. waited in the car while his father went inside. When he came out, he was accompanied by one of the biggest men T.J. had ever seen. He was six and a half feet tall and had to tip the scales at three hundred pounds. He was a huge, hulking specimen of a human being, and T.J. didn't need a life lesson to know why he was coming along for whatever business his father had planned. He slid into the back seat before they got to the car.

"Ralph, this is T.J. He's riding along today. T.J., this is Mr. McClaren."

"How ya doin', kid?" the giant asked as he turned in his seat and offered his hand. It swallowed T.J.'s.

"Good, sir. Nice to meet you."

They drove through the Fairmount and Franklintown neighborhoods, and T.J. watched the landscape disintegrate in front of him as they made their way into South Philly. Tidy row homes gave way to ramshackle tenements. Clean, orderly streets turned into pockmarked thoroughfares littered with abandoned vehicles. Some were on cinder blocks, with their wheels and tires removed; others were little more than burned-out shells. No children played in the streets, no parents tended to window boxes or front porch planters. There were no street vendors selling hot dogs. In a city where beat cops and police cruisers were fixtures on every corner, neither were to be found in this, the lawless adjunct of the City of Brotherly Love. It made T.J. think of a book he had read about the Wild West, and he gazed out the window in curious apprehension. Tommy and Ralph looked as if they didn't have a care in the world.

Tommy pulled to a stop in front of a dilapidated three-story red brick apartment building with plywood covering at least half the exterior windows. He motioned for his son to follow him as he and Ralph made their way up the cracked sidewalk and toward a pair of rusted metal security doors. Once upon a time the doors had been locked, and there was an intercom for residents to buzz their guests in. Now there was a hole where the lock cylinder used to be, and bare, frayed wires protruding from the wall gave away the former location of the call box. What windows remained were covered in years of accumulated grime. A pair of broken light fixtures flanked either side of the entrance, and cracked terra-cotta tiles shifted and crunched under the men's feet as they made their way through a vestibule and into the apartment's entryway. The walls were covered with spray-painted graffiti, cryptic symbols marking the sovereign territory of whatever street gang held power in this section of town.

They walked up a flight of stairs, turned right, and stopped in front of the door second from the end of the hallway, Tommy on one side and Ralph on the other. As they took up their positions, a rat the size of a small chihuahua scurried past them and into a hole in a nearby door marked *Incinerator*.

"Stay behind me and keep quiet," Tommy admonished his son. He knocked on the door with his fist, making a thumping sound that echoed down the empty corridor.

After a few moments with no reply, Tommy's knock was harder, longer, and angrier. A few seconds passed before they heard the sound of locks being thrown, then the creak of the hinges as the door opened a few inches. Only the brass chain kept it from opening all the way, and Tommy could have kicked the door in if he wanted to. Instead he spoke in a low, menacing tone to the young Black man with the bloodshot eyes on the other side.

"Open the fucking door, Blue. I ain't got time for this bullshit."

The door closed, the chain dropped, and it reopened. The trio made their way into the apartment. Another man lay on the couch, either asleep, drunk, high, or some combination of all three. Blue locked the door behind them and sat down at the kitchen table in front of a half-eaten plate of breakfast. His trembling hands betrayed him as he tried to nonchalantly finish his meal. He knew why his boss was here.

"Can I get you gentlemen something?" he asked without making eye contact.

"Yeah," Tommy replied. "You got a calculator?"

"A what?"

Ralph moved behind Blue, standing close enough for the dealer to smell the morning bourbon on his breath while Tommy continued.

"A calculator. Because I need to figure out how many grams are in a kilo. And what twenty thousand times five comes out to. I think I know, but I want to be sure."

Blue put his fork down, wiped his mouth, and looked at Tommy. "Listen, T, it's not like you think. Two of my boys got ripped. I know I was thirty short, but I'll make it up next week. I swear."

Tommy nodded toward Ralph, who reared back and brought a softball-sized fist crashing down on Blue's right shoulder, separating it from his collarbone and sending him to the floor, screaming in pain.

Tommy took a knee next to his dealer and put a hand on his unbroken shoulder. "The time to tell me about your problems is when they happen, Blue. Not when you're light, because then I have to go stand in front of my boss like a jerkoff and explain why *I'm* light. Do you want me to look like a jerkoff, Blue?"

"No, T," he whimpered.

"Good. Then you have until tomorrow to bring me my money, or I come back. And if I have to come back," he said, tapping Blue's shattered shoulder, "this is as good as it's gonna get, and it won't ever get this good again."

Tommy looked up at Ralph. "Toss the place."

He started in the kitchen, flinging open cabinet doors, knocking aside dishes and glasses as he went. The battered drug dealer looked on helplessly as Tommy's enforcer moved to the bedroom, where the sounds changed from breaking glass to drawers being ripped from their bureau and clothes being tossed to the floor. Blue heard the bed creak and the thud of a mattress hitting the wall, and a new level of fear washed over his face, one that hadn't been reached by the intrusion and the beating. Tommy saw it.

"Well, I'll be dipped in shit," Ralph shouted from the bedroom, moments before appearing in the doorway with a paper bag in one hand and two kilo-sized bricks of cocaine in the other. The cocaine was wrapped in pinkish-colored cellophane. "Looks like your boy's been holding out on us. There was a hollow spot in the bedspring where he was hiding this. And there's at least fifty large in the bag."

Tommy turned to Blue, his expression a mixture of rage and confusion. "Whose shit is that? Because it ain't mine."

Blue, normally a smooth talker, found his voice failing him. He mumbled a few intelligible words before Tommy pounced on him, pinning the doper on his back and delivering a knee strike to his groin that took his breath away and watered his eyes.

"You two-timing piece of shit!" Tommy screamed as Blue writhed under him. He glanced toward Ralph. "You believe this guy? Bag full of cash, and he was ready to send me away empty-handed. And to top it all off, he's humping for somebody else." He turned his attention back to Blue, and delivered an open palm slap across his face. "You weren't gonna short them, were you?" He reversed direction, backhanding his dealer on the opposite side of his face, his pinky ring opening a deep cut along the man's cheekbone. T.J. stared in amazement at the sight of his father in action, beholding the side of him he always suspected but never really knew existed. Ralph took it all in and laughed.

"I ought to kill you right here and now," Tommy hissed, grabbing Blue by the neck. T.J. heard the doomed man gurgle as he tried to speak. The next sound T.J. heard changed his life.

The roar of the large-caliber pistol came from the couch, and as T.J. turned toward it, he realized the man they thought was passed out was playing possum, lying in wait. He was sitting up now, and the smoking gun was pointed at Ralph, who was sporting a gaping hole in his skull where his right eye used to be. As Ralph fell to the floor, the shooter pivoted on his haunches and squeezed off another round, this time toward Tommy. It flew wide of its mark as T.J. landed a flying tackle that leveled the assailant and sent the gun clattering to the floor. They both moved for it at the same time, but T.J., younger and still blessed with the athletic prowess that had made him a high school football standout, got to it first. Rather than gripping it as if to shoot, though, he wrapped his hand around the barrel and bludgeoned his opponent with it, knocking him on the floor next to Ralph, who was breathing his last.

"Fuck!" he yelled in pain, dropping the gun as the adrenaline subsided and he began to feel the burn it had left on his palm. He picked it up, properly this time, and stood over his opponent, who had managed to sit up but was badly dazed.

Tommy stared wide-eyed at his son, his hands still planted on Blue's throat. The dealer struggled beneath him, but with each movement of his body, Tommy clamped down a little tighter. He froze, his eyes filled with horror as he realized the place to which his decisions had brought him.

"Son, we are in a trick bag here," Tommy said. "I need a minute to think."

"Dad, with all the shooting the cops are going to be here any minute. Shouldn't we leave?"

"It doesn't work like that here, Thomas. This is a war zone. These people hear gunfire all day long. And they never call the police. But we can't leave Ralph. And I have to do something with these two."

"I know."

"No, son, I don't think you do. It was one thing to rip me off, but—"

T.J. pointed the gun at the couch-possum's head and fired. The bullet tore through the upper part of his skull and sent bits of brain matter flying in a fine pink mist, some of which landed on Tommy and Blue. Blue began his struggle again in earnest, flailing with hands and feet against Tommy's chokehold, which he was now applying with deadly intent. Tommy bore down on him with all his weight, and finally Blue went still. His dead eyes stared at the ceiling. It had been less than ten minutes since Tommy Costello had knocked on the door, and now he and his son were the only two men left alive in the apartment.

"We need to get to our people so they can clean this up," he said, wiping the dead man's blood from around his eyes and mouth with a handkerchief. "Give me the gun."

T.J. turned the pistol over to his father, who used a dish towel from the kitchen to wipe it clean before dropping it on the floor at Ralph's feet.

"What about that stuff?" he asked, pointing to the haul Ralph had brought from the bedroom.

"Leave the coke. Take the cash."

"Isn't it worth a lot of money?" T.J. asked, gesturing toward the cellophane-wrapped bundles.

"It doesn't belong to us," he said. "Now let's get the hell out of here."

———————————

They drove, faster than before, so much so that T.J. worried his father would be pulled over for speeding or blowing through a stop sign. He knew the old man was in good with the cops, but he doubted their professional courtesy would extend to covering up a double murder.

They stopped at the same corner bar where they had picked up Ralph earlier in the day. Tommy gave his son explicit instructions before he went inside: Stay in the car and don't say a word to anyone. *Not a fucking word.* He took the bloodstained bag of cash inside with him.

Ten minutes passed, then twenty, then half an hour. When Tommy re-appeared at the bar's front door, he made a beckoning motion to T.J., who left the car and walked toward the bar.

"They want to talk to you," he said as his son approached.

"Who's 'they'?"

Tommy lowered his head and shook it before locking eyes with T.J. It was a look the young boy had never seen from his father before. Not angry. Desperate. Almost pleading.

"Son, if you never listen to another word I say, hear this. These are serious men you're about to meet. The slightest show of disrespect will get you killed. Speak only if spoken to, and when you do, pretend you are talking to God Himself. Do you hear me?"

T.J. nodded. Tommy led him through the bar and up a long flight of stairs to a closed door at the end of a hallway. He knocked, the door opened, and they walked inside.

There were four of them, all but one of whom looked old enough to be grandfathers. They were seated near the head of a long table, and T.J. could tell in an instant they were the shot-callers. Five or six younger men of lesser stature were either standing or sitting in chairs around the room's perimeter. The man seated at the very head of the table was perhaps sixty-five years old, with thinning gray hair, thick glasses, and the butt of a chewed but unlit cigar clenched between his teeth. He wore a gray cardigan over a white shirt buttoned to the collar, and T.J. couldn't help but think of Marlon Brando's character in the movie he'd now seen at least five times. The bloody paper bag lay on the table before him. The Don motioned toward the other end of the table and didn't need to explain himself. *Have a seat.*

Tommy and T.J. sat down opposite each other and angled their chairs toward the boss. T.J. folded his hands on the table in front of him in his best altar-boy pose and clamped his teeth down on the inside of his lips to remind himself of the need to remain silent.

It wasn't the Don himself who spoke first but the younger man to his right. He was the only one at the table wearing a suit.

"We need to get a few things straight before you leave here today."

If we let you leave here today.

T.J. remained quiet, partly because he had been told to and partly because he was frozen with fear. The consigliere continued.

"What you saw today was tragic. In our business, we have to deal with thieves harshly, or they won't respect us. Loyalty is everything in our business. When you steal from one of us, you steal from us all. So while your father made a mistake in taking you along with him today," he said, shooting Thomas Senior a disapproving glance, "maybe in the long run it was for the best."

Tommy spoke up. "I was—"

The consigliere raised his hand, and Tommy stopped mid-sentence, lowering his head at the silent rebuke.

"Young man, in this business your word is your bond. These men"—he swept his hand around the table—"are my family. If we welcome you into the fold, they become your family. If you get in trouble, we get you out. If you go to prison, we make sure there's food on your table. If you ever need anything, you come to us, just like you would with your mother or father. And most important of all, we handle our own business in our own way. We never, ever talk to the authorities. Capisce?"

T.J. nodded.

"No. I need an answer. Do you understand everything I just told you?"

T.J. looked into the man's eyes and nodded again, this time adding, "Yes, sir."

"Good. Then there's only one more piece of business." The consigliere turned to his Don, who spoke for the first time since Tommy and T.J. had entered the room.

"Sonny boy, you've angered a very important man. A man with whom I do a great deal of business. You insulted his family. You brought shame to his daughter, who is but a child. This man wants to avenge his family's honor, and unless I tell him otherwise, he will. What were you thinking, sticking your cazzo in that little girl?"

T.J. looked at the table and mumbled, "I don't know. I'm sorry."

The Don slapped his hand on the table. "Look at me when you speak, sonny boy! In the eyes! Like a man!"

T.J. glanced at his father, who was pleading with his own eyes for his son to understand the gravity of the moment. He turned toward the Don and locked eyes with him.

"I understand, sir. It will never happen again. You have my word."

The boss smiled. "See that it doesn't. You won't get off so easily next time. You did good today, sonny boy. We can use someone with your strength and courage, and your father says you need direction in your life. We can provide that."

He stood from his chair and motioned for T.J. to approach. When he did, the Don wrapped him in an embrace and kissed him on the cheek . "You're a good kid. Get your head screwed on straight." He nodded toward Tommy as an indication that it was time for them to leave.

As they drove home, T.J. noticed the change in his father's demeanor. There was a newfound respect in his voice as they discussed the events of the previous few hours.

"That was a lot for a seventeen-year-old to take in," he said. "You handled yourself like a man today, and I'm proud of you. But I don't want to gloss over the fact that you took another man's life. We need to talk about that. How did it make you feel?"

T.J. thought for a few moments. "Honestly?"

"Of course, honestly."

"I didn't feel anything. I still don't. It was us or them."

Tommy nodded. "You may feel different down the road. I've had to kill a few men. More than a few. Some haven't cost me a minute's sleep, but some I still think about. It's part of the life, a life I never wanted for you. But you're in it now."

"Can I ask you a question?"

"Sure."

"Those men we were just with—are they Mafia guys, like in *The Godfather?*"

Tommy winced. "First off, we don't use the term 'Mafia.' Not ever. But yes, they're part of an organization I work for. They pay me very well, and in return I respect their rules, just as you now will. I hope you were listening to the part about loyalty. There are no second chances."

T.J. nodded. "I understand. To tell you the truth, I kind of liked the older one. He reminded me of Grandpa. It was weird when he kissed me, though."

Tommy shrugged. "It's part of the culture. Get used to it."

"I guess. And I didn't like his nickname for me, either."

"What nickname?"

"Sonny boy."

"What's wrong with sonny boy? It's a term of endearment."

"I'm not a boy."

Tommy laughed. "We'll work on it."

CHAPTER 12

BRYCE BROUGHT DONNIE up to speed on the details of his trip to Fort Bragg, and they agreed the next step was a deep dive into the background of their newly identified hit man, Vincent Kamara. He had yet to set foot in his new office in Key West and decided he would make a sit-down with Abbie Bishop the centerpiece of his inaugural visit. He was anxious to see what information she had found on his no-longer-a-mystery man.

He introduced himself to Vic Martinez, the supervisory special resident agent, who under ordinary circumstances would have been his boss. Vic had been briefed by his SAC well in advance of Bryce's arrival, and he knew the "new old guy" was assigned to his turf for administrative purposes only. He welcomed Bryce into his office, shot the breeze over a cup of coffee, and sent him on about his business without prying into what that business entailed. Bryce liked him, much more so than most of his former supervisors. There were four other agents in the RA, two men and two women, and they were all too wrapped up in their own casework to care about why the legendary Bryce Chandler had been assigned to their corner of paradise. The support staff consisted of a squad secretary who looked old enough to be his mother and the award-winning intelligence analyst he hoped would live up to her hype.

Abbie met him at her desk, which was the most immaculately maintained workspace Bryce had seen in over twenty years in the bureau. Every stack of papers was fastened with a paper clip in the exact same spot and organized on the right side of the desk in a symmetrical pile. A stapler was centered at the top of the paper pile. Three ceramic coffee cups sat at the top center of the desk. One was filled with black ink pens, another with blue, and the last with red. There were no pencils. A small plastic mini-organizer held more paper clips, binder clips, Post-it tabs, colored thumbtacks, and an ancient bottle of Wite-Out correction fluid, all neatly stored in their own sections. An old-fashioned Rolodex anchored the upper left-hand corner of the space, and next to it sat the only frivolous item in the ensemble—a large glass Mason jar filled to the rim with miniature Reese's peanut butter cups. If first impressions counted for anything, Bryce's was that here sat an old-school, hyper-organized neat freak, and that usually made for an outstanding analyst.

"Nice to meet you in person," he said, extending his hand. "I've heard a lot about you. All good."

"Same here," she replied with a smile as she gestured toward the chair next to her desk. As he sat down, she turned in her chair, opened a file cabinet behind her, and retrieved a white three-ring binder, which she handed to him. "I have something for you."

An eight-by-ten color copy of an Arizona driver's license was affixed to the front of the binder. It wasn't the same one the DEA had shown him months earlier in Miami, nor should it have been. That one was from his fake license, the reason the State of Florida still knew him as Robert Charles Petty of St. Louis, Missouri. This one was from the real home of the real Vincent

Kamara, and it was just the gift wrap on the present. Inside the binder were pages of data including a copy of his birth certificate, passport, and DD-214 discharge paperwork from the army. And there was much more. Abbie had separated the information with tabs, and Bryce thumbed through them to find a complete credit report, an academic transcript from the University of Arizona, a divorce decree, and sales records for a condominium and a 2019 BMW X5. There were also three years' worth of paystubs from a Scottsdale-based company, AeroMed Life Flight.

"This is one of those air ambulance services, right?" Bryce asked. "What was he, a helicopter pilot?"

"Flight nurse," Abbie replied. "Looks like he started nursing school right after he got out of the army. I got the pay records from the Arizona Department of Labor. You'll notice the last one is seven months old."

Bryce was stunned by the sheer volume of documentation sitting before him. The last tab, labeled *Miscellaneous*, contained account statements from Marriott and American Airlines, his Arizona concealed-carry permit, and a copy of his fishing license.

She found the man's fishing license.

"You did all this in three days?"

"Honey, it was ready yesterday. But wait, there's more." She plucked a paper-clipped stack of documents from the pile to her right. "I finished this today. Everything I could find on the ex and the kid. Mostly the kid. The ex has gone off the grid. Anyway, there's the most recent addresses, phone numbers, employers, and some school records. Sorry I didn't have time to put it in the binder." From the look on her face, Bryce could tell she was actually sorry. The woman was a machine.

"I don't know what to say. This is amazing. Thank you."

Abbie smiled. "It's my job, you know. And it's not all I can do. I haven't been able to see your case in the system because it's restricted. Can you give me the five-minute highlight reel?"

Bryce did just that, although it took closer to twenty minutes. Abbie scribbled notes as he spoke.

"So has anyone done a comprehensive telephone analysis for you?" she asked when he finished.

"Analysis of what? There's nowhere to start. We don't know who any of the hit men are, except for Vincent Kamara and the one who got himself killed in Georgia. And even he's a John Doe. We did a dump on his phone, but nothing on it pinged against any numbers of interest in the system. It was probably a burner anyway."

Abbie shook her head. "You're looking at it the wrong way. You don't need to know what one phone did or didn't do. You need to know whether there is a commonality of connections between any two phones, nationwide, around the time and place your murders were committed."

"I'm not following."

"Where was your first murder?"

"I forget the name of the town, but it was just outside Terre Haute, Indiana."

"Okay. So for the date and time frame in question, we pull records for every cell tower within a set distance of the murder site. We can start at a mile, then work our way outward from there until we start to see results. Five miles, ten miles, whatever it takes. Once we have data from all the murder sites, we start looking for common denominators. Incoming or outgoing calls from the same number or to the same number. See what I mean?"

Bryce stared, dumfounded. "There have been two murders and a near miss that we know of. Plus the failed attempt at my house. So four scenes in three states, over a span of several months. We're talking about thousands of cell phone records."

She wagged a finger. "Tens of thousands. Hundreds of thousands. Maybe more. When we start expanding the area of interest, we could involve several hundred cell towers for each murder scene. And each of those towers might have handled thousands of calls over a period of just a few hours."

"And you can really pull that volume of data and do something with it?"

She smiled. "I can't. But the same friends who helped me track down El Pinto can. They specialize in metadata collection, and if you knew the details, it would freak you out."

"Are they bureau?"

"One of the three-letter agencies. And that, to quote Forrest Gump, is all I've got to say about that."

Bryce laughed. "I'm sold. What do you need from me?"

"Not much. Just have your supervisor, or ASAC, or whoever has the authority, grant me computer access to the case, and I'll take it from there."

"Done. How long will it take to get something back?"

"Before we go there, let's manage some expectations. Yes, I can gather a tremendous amount of information. Yes, I can use that information to generate some useful leads for you and your team. But none of this is a magic bullet, and much of it is a long shot. If this Network is as sophisticated as you think, no phone-record analysis is going to take you to their leader. That said, I should have some preliminary results by the time you return from Scottsdale. I presume that's where you're headed next?"

Bryce laughed. "Damn, you're good."

CHAPTER 13

EVERYONE HAS a dividing line in their lives, a moment or event that separates everything prior from all that comes after. In the same way world history is perceived to have occurred on either side of the birth of Christ, the human experience uses joyous or tragic episodes as mileposts to mark where we've been and where we are going. For some it is the birth of a child or the death of a loved one. For others it might be a momentous accomplishment, like graduating from medical school.

Bryce Chandler crossed his milepost on May 3, 2011, in a dilapidated single-wide trailer turned meth lab in Lamar County, Georgia. It was the worst day of his life, far worse than he could have imagined before it began. It was when he saw the very bottom of the well of human depravity, and the images of what the girl's mother and father did to her still haunted his dreams more than ten years on. It gave him little solace that they both sat on Georgia's death row, awaiting a sentence that would take far too long to carry out and could not be painful enough to repay what they had done to their child.

In the immediate aftermath, Bryce disappeared for three days on an alcohol-fueled bender he would never remember—just himself and four liters of Jack Daniel's in a cheap motel room on the south side of Atlanta. By the time he sobered up and returned home, his frantic wife and chain of command knew the secret he had hidden for years: He was a raging alcoholic, and he needed help.

The FBI's Employee Assistance Program had found a residential treatment facility in Minneapolis that his insurance would cover, and he spent six weeks drying out before coming home. When he returned, his supervisor and ASAC thought he should spend additional time decompressing, away from the stress, violence, and late-night hours of the gang squad. They suggested he take an eleven-week temporary assignment as a class counselor at the FBI National Academy in Quantico. The agents called it being "volun-told," and Bryce knew he had no say in the matter. He packed his bags and headed north.

The bureau meant well. The National Academy was a finishing school for upwardly mobile executives from state and local law enforcement agencies around the country and the globe. Its graduates went on to become chiefs of police and senior leaders in their departments and entered an elite fraternity who knew each other simply as "NA grads." Two hundred fifty attendees lived and worked on the academy's sprawling campus in northern Virginia, and each fifty-person section of the student body was assigned an active-duty FBI agent from the field to shepherd them through the course. It was a place for learning, for networking, and for fellowship.

It was also a place for drinking. The alcohol-related exploits of National Academy students were the stuff of legend at Quantico. From the late-night parties in the parking lot to the weekend trip to New York City sponsored by students from the NYPD, every off-duty hour of the students' time was an opportunity to imbibe.

And while Bryce had sobered up during rehab, the most important lesson he learned was how to be a less-noticeable drunk. He
slipped almost immediately back into his hard-drinking ways, but
with more cunning and discretion this time. A DUI and a night
in a Key West jail cell would bring him around seven years later,
but during his time at the National Academy, Bryce fit right in
with the crowd.

It wasn't all bad. Like his students, Bryce made countless contacts with police officers and sheriff's deputies who held positions
of power in their departments. These were friendships for life,
and it was never an imposition when a fellow graduate reached
out for help. It was more of an opportunity to help a brother
or sister who would no doubt return the favor when their turn
came. And so when Bryce called Lieutenant Jarvis Breckenridge
of the Scottsdale Police Department, his former drinking buddy
was happy to help.

"Bryce, great to hear from you. I heard you retired. Must
have been bad info."

"Actually, I did retire. Over five years ago. And now I'm back
on the job. It's a long story."

Jarvis laughed. "I'll bet it is. Can't wait to hear it. What can
I do for you?"

"I'm going to be in town in a few days with a search warrant.
I was hoping you could help me serve it."

"Of course. But why me? Why the local PD at all? Don't
you fed boys handle your own business with the field office when
you're in their territory?"

"This case is a little different. It's being run out of headquarters, so all the warrants are being issued by a magistrate in

the District of Columbia. Technically, we don't have to tell the Phoenix office anything at all, but it's common courtesy to at least let the SAC know an agent will be on his turf conducting an investigation. And I'm going to do that. But he doesn't need to know I'm executing a warrant. If he does, he'll want to see an operations order, assign an ASAC to oversee it, and maybe even make SWAT do the entry. SACs are scared of their own shadows these days, and they lose sleep over the thought of an agent kicking a door in without a small army behind them. I need this done discreetly."

"Well then, I'm your man," Jarvis answered. "Shoot me an address and I'll do some low-level checking around. Is your guy A&D?"

"Neither armed nor dangerous, at least not anymore. He's locked up in Miami."

"Alrighty then. When are you coming to town?"

"Day after tomorrow, if that works for you."

"I'll see you then. Safe travels."

———

"How long are you going to be gone?" Ashley asked from the bathroom, where she was finishing getting dressed for work.

"Couple of days, maybe three. This guy was leading a double life, so this is my chance to see what the actual Vincent Kamara is all about. And he has a daughter living out there I need to interview."

Ashley emerged from the bathroom with a look of concern on her face. "Promise me you'll be careful."

"You know I will."

Bryce looked up from his phone, where he was alternating between returning emails and solving the day's Wordle. He was still in bed, enjoying his first day off in over a week after returning from Fort Bragg and visiting his new office in Key West. His glance at Ashley became a stare when he saw she was only half-dressed in a tan knee-length skirt and a black bra, her hair still down around her shoulders. In another ten minutes she would be her professional alter ego, conservative business attire and all. But for now, she was a seductive vision of raw beauty, and he couldn't look away.

"You're leering at me," she said through a smile.

"Damn right," Bryce replied, smiling back. "Let me know if you want me to stop."

"You're terrible. And no, don't ever stop looking at me like that. I love it."

The human brain processes information at speeds faster than any computer, so fast, in fact, that it can get ahead of itself. In the split second after the words "I love" left Ashley's lips, Bryce anticipated "you" to finish the statement. And even as he heard what she actually said, his brain delivered a shot of dopamine at the notion she was finally broaching the subject. They had both been avoiding it, each wondering, even hoping the other would bring it up. He knew she, like him, was coming off a long-term relationship that had ended painfully, and neither could bring themselves to be vulnerable enough to risk the pain of rejection. So here they were. Stuck.

"Come sit with me," he said.

She sat down between his legs, leaned back, and rested her head on his chest. He put his hands on her shoulders and massaged them.

"I'm thinking about retiring again after this is all over."

She turned her head slightly toward him. "Really? Why?"

"I'm not getting any younger, Ashley. I don't want to spend what should be the best years of my life dealing with murderers, drug dealers, and other assorted scumbags."

"What do you want to do?"

"I want to be more than what I am right now. More than just a washed-up, alcoholic divorcé who ran away to the Florida Keys because nobody would know what a screw-up I was. I need a new start, but I don't know what it looks like or where it is."

Ashley put her hands over his. "First of all, you're none of those things. But whatever this new start looks like, does it include me?" She looked away as she asked the question.

Oh, for crying out loud, you coward. Tell her already.

It was on the tip of his tongue, but that was as far as it got. The best he could manage was a disastrously feeble response.

"If you want it to. You know I care about you." He regretted the words as soon as they left his lips, and he thought he felt her head slump forward in disappointment. It wasn't going to happen. At least not today. He changed the subject. "I'm sorry to be such a downer. I'm stressed out. This case has me running in so many different directions."

"Don't be afraid to ask for help," Ashley said. "You can't do it all yourself."

"Oh, I know. If it wasn't for Abbie Bishop, I'd be losing my mind right now."

"Who's Abbie Bishop?"

"She's an analyst down in Key West. And she's amazing. She's figured out a way to link telephone records together from our murder scenes to—"

Ashley reached down, grabbed Bryce's knees, and squeezed. "Stop, will you? No more shop talk. And I don't want to hear anything else about the man who tried to kill you. I hope he rots in jail where he belongs."

"Oh, he will. Even if he beats the Florida rap, I'm going to find a way to tie him to the Network."

She released her grip on his knees and turned to face him. "I'm serious. Stop. Talking."

"Make me." He pulled her lips to his, one hand caressing the back of her head while the other found its way under her skirt and onto her thigh. They kissed for a minute before she broke contact.

"You're going to make me late for work." The way she said it told Bryce it wasn't a problem. He reached behind Ashley, unhooked her bra, and pulled her down onto the bed with him.

"Yeah, that's the plan."

CHAPTER 14

OUR LADY of the Assumption was filled to the rafters. Again. It was the third Griffin funeral in six months, and as the departed was none other than the Air Force base's last commander, Brigadier General Oswald "Ozzie" McDaniel, it was standing room only in the century-old Catholic church in downtown Syracuse.

Father Antonio met the pallbearers at the doors of the church, where the honor guard removed the American flag from the casket, folded it into a neat triangle, and set it aside. The priest sprinkled the casket with holy water and covered it with a pall. The honor guard walked the casket up the aisle on the rolling catafalque, and positioned it at the altar. Then began the procession of dignitaries, led by the widow, Ruth McDaniel, and her grown children, Ozzie's ninety-year-old mother, and a smattering of brothers, sisters, nieces, and nephews. They occupied the first two rows of the church. Behind them sat the entire senior staff of Abbott and D'Angelo, three dozen strong, attired in their most somber dark suits, white shirts, and conservative ties. On this day there was extra starch in their shirts, and their shoes were polished to a higher gloss. Not because of the status of the deceased, but because the word had been passed through the office: The old man himself was going to be there.

Frank D'Angelo was traveling with security these days, as the Iowa caucuses approached and his presidential campaign developed enough steam to put him in the top five contenders for his party's nomination. It wasn't a full-on detail, just a couple of Secret Service agents who traveled with him and stayed close during public events, a minimal show of force to make the next Sirhan Sirhan wannabe think twice. They escorted the senator up the aisle after the family and the attorneys took their seats, and he slid into the end of the third pew next to his son, Max.

It was a closed-casket affair, and for good reason. A poster-sized photograph of the general as a lieutenant in flight training school sat on an easel next to the coffin. He was perched on the cockpit ladder of his T-38 jet, one hand on the rung at head height and the other cradling his helmet in what Air Force pilots called their "hero" pose. He was dashingly handsome, with dark brown skin that contrasted against a perfect white smile and the bright, shining eyes of a young aviator who knew he had the world by the balls.

There was little of that man left in the oak casket. Ozzie weighed 110 pounds when he died, less than half his playing weight as a standout tight end at the Air Force Academy. The cancer had ravaged his body like few others, taking its time with him, attacking first his liver, then his kidneys, then his lungs. He fought heroically, promising his bride with every new diagnosis he would never give up, but in the end the pain and suffering was too much to bear for both Ozzie and his family. He entered hospice care on a Thursday and was gone by the weekend.

Father Antonio led the liturgy, which included readings from Psalms 72 and 149, followed by extracts from the books of Isaiah and Revelation. The honor guard returned to their positions as the service came to an end and escorted General McDaniel's remains through the throng of mourners and out of the church. They were followed by Father Antonio and the family. As they passed the third pew, Ruth McDaniel stopped as she noticed Frank D'Angelo on the aisle. A smile came to her face for the first time that morning, and she halted the procession to greet the senator, who took both her hands in his as they spoke to one another.

"Ruth, I am so sorry for your loss. Ozzie was a great man, and our country is safer because of his service."

"Thank you, Senator. And God bless you and your firm for taking care of us." Her eyes were sad but dry, having been cried out over the last six months of Ozzie's life. She was fifty years old and looked seventy.

"We're all in this together, Ruth. Be well." He leaned forward and kissed her cheek, then turned to Max as she walked away.

"I need to talk to you outside."

The burial was a family-only affair, so the crowd dispersed quicky from the front of the church. As they made their way to their cars, Frank motioned Max toward the black Suburban parked in a spot with a portable VIP placard at its front bumper. The Secret Service agents were in their own identical Suburban in the next spot, sans VIP signage. Frank had told them they could leave after he went inside, as he doubted an assassin would make a move on him during a church funeral. As he approached his own vehicle, the driver got out, walked around to the rear passenger side door, and held it open. Frank's personal assistant, Stella, was in the rear seat on the driver's side.

"We need the car."

Stella and the driver nodded their understanding and took their coffee to the nearby church steps. Frank climbed into the Suburban on the passenger's side and Max slid in opposite him. As soon as they closed the doors, Frank got to the point.

"Who stopped the ads?"

"That was me. We were spending almost a million dollars a month."

"And what were our revenues last month?"

"Give or take, sixteen million."

"So six percent of revenue for advertising? Since when is that a bad business decision?"

"Dad, we've been over this. It's been fifteen years since the cancer cluster popped up, and ten since they closed the base. We're running out of victims. Anyone who is going to get sick is already sick, and we have 90 percent of them as clients. Death claims are falling off, too. We had twenty last year, and we're on pace for less than twelve this year."

Frank shook his head. "That's short-sighted thinking."

"How so?"

"We don't need to focus only on cases with a direct line of causation. We've never been required to prove that the groundwater at Griffin was 100-percent responsible for their cancer; all we've had to show was that the victim and the water were in the same place at the same time. Hell, for that matter we don't even need to show damage. If you were there, you drank the water. If you drank the water, you could get sick today, tomorrow, or ten years from now. You could pass it on to your kids. They could pass it to their kids. It's a victim list with no end in sight, and we've just scratched the surface."

"So what are you thinking?" Max asked.

"Start the ads back up again. Make it clear that they don't need to be sick in order to file a claim. And stress that they didn't need to be stationed at Griffin full time. If they even passed through on a temporary-duty assignment for a month or more, we need to talk to them. And run the campaign nationwide. Just because someone worked there twenty years ago doesn't mean they're still in upstate New York."

"That's going to double our advertising expenses."

"Then double it. Keep an eye on where we're getting the most bang for our buck in terms of new clients, then scale back from there if a regional market becomes an empty hole. Long term, son. I need you thinking long term." He put a hand on Max's shoulder to emphasize his point.

Max nodded. "I'll take care of it."

"Good. I need to get back to D.C. Keep me in the loop on any major decisions moving forward. You know I trust you, but this is still my firm, and I want it to be the richest and most powerful one in the Northeast when I leave it to you one day."

"Got it, Dad. I'll take care of it."

"I know you will." He hugged his son and watched him walk away, then beckoned through the open door to his assistant and driver to return.

Stella kept Frank's go bag, filled with everything he needed access to during the day but couldn't carry on his person. There were two laptop computers, a large leatherbound day planner, extra reading glasses, an assortment of ties in various patterns and shades of red and blue, and a Tide pen for the occasional food stain on his white shirt. And of course there were the phones. When it came to cell phones, he was especially old-school and refused to be seen using one in public, believing it made him look more like an employee than the boss. He kept four of them, one each for family, government business, and law firm matters, and another Stella called the Bat Phone. It was a prepaid, ancient-looking flip model Frank had her purchase at Best Buy a year earlier, and she suspected he used it to communicate with his mistress. Frank knew what she thought, and he let her think it.

"You're a wanted man," she quipped as she slid into her seat and closed the door behind her. "Your G-phone was blowing up during the funeral. I took messages." She read from a small yellow notepad as she spoke. "The speaker wants to have lunch tomorrow to discuss funding for the roads bill. You need to approve three new spots your campaign manager wants to run in Iowa and South Carolina, attacking the president for his soft stance on immigration. And Senator Crowley says it's a hard no on your resolution unless you add wording condemning the Qataris for their support of Hamas."

Frank placed his hand on Stella's knee and kept staring straight ahead. She cringed, but he either didn't notice or didn't care. The harassment had started a year ago in the form of sexually inappropriate remarks and jokes and had progressed to groping over the last few months. She had never stopped him, and to men like Frank, silence was consent. Besides, what was she going to do about it? He was one of the most powerful men in Washington, and she was a lowly civil servant living paycheck to paycheck. The deck was, and would always be, stacked in his favor.

"Senator Crowley needs to learn the old saying: The enemy of my enemy is my friend," he responded. As he spoke, he began massaging her knee and moving his hand up her leg. "The Qataris are in lockstep with the Saudis and Emiratis against Iran. They're a stabilizing force in the region. And just because they're not out hunting Hamas like Israel is, that doesn't mean they support them. I'll deal with the illiterate gentleman from West Virginia another day." He stopped well past the midpoint of her thigh, oblivious to the look of horror on her face.

Stella shifted in her seat to dislodge his hand, and as she did so she handed him the Bat Phone. "This one just started going off. It buzzed a couple times this morning. And before you ask, no, I didn't answer it, nor did I check the messages."

Frank flipped the phone open, knowing what he would find before he looked. Only one person had this number. And he only called for one reason.

"I'm going to need the car again," he said, without a hint of apology in his tone. Stella and the driver were used to being dismissed. They exited without comment and resumed their coffee break on the church steps.

Frank dialed, and the recipient answered on the second ring. There was not so much as a perfunctory greeting.

"We're halfway there."

Frank sighed. He knew he was alone, and he knew the phone wasn't registered in his name, but it still made him uneasy talking about it when there was even a remote possibility someone could be listening.

"That's good, I guess. How long before we're in the clear?"

"These things take time, Senator. And with each one we check off the list, the Marshals are going to ratchet down a little tighter on the remaining ones. The first VP, the accountant, he was easy. My guy tells me he was living as a fake war hero in the Midwest. Stupid son of a bitch was giving interviews to TV stations and newspapers—can you believe that? We got the COO yesterday in the Florida panhandle. He was more private, and a little tougher to track down, but we got it done."

"I don't need to know the details," Frank protested. "And stop calling me Senator. It's weird coming from you."

"Sure thing, Frank. And I'm sorry to trouble you with all the minutiae, but this is dirty work you've asked us to do. And mark my words, once the word gets out on the first two, the others are going to start running silent and deep, if the Marshals don't pull them off the street altogether."

"They can do that?"

"They can and they have. We've gotten to them even when they were under 24/7 security, but it takes more work and involves more risk."

"With what I'm paying you, pardon me if I'm not sympathetic to your risk issues," Frank said.

"Fair point. And speaking of that, there's the matter of payment for yesterday's job."

"It will be in your account by the end of the day."

"Much obliged. I know you're a busy man, but I'm happy to check in and keep you up to date as we track these fellows down."

"No thanks," Frank replied. "Just get it done, Tommy."

CHAPTER 15

JARVIS BRECKENRIDGE met Bryce at his hotel at 5:30 a.m. He offered to drive to Vincent's condo, and Bryce accepted. Along the way, Bryce brought his friend up to speed on the reasons for his interest in the flight nurse turned hit man.

"You gotta be kidding me. He was inside your house, waiting for you?" the lieutenant asked.

"We never figured out who got there first, him or the two goons from the cartel. All we know is they ended up dead, and he almost did. And by sheer luck I was spending the night at my girlfriend's house."

"Holy cow. You should buy a lottery ticket."

"You're not the first person to suggest that. How far to his place?"

"We're almost there. I have a ram in the trunk if you think we'll need it."

"I hope not. I'm trying to do this as quietly as possible. That's why you and I are doing this instead of me and half the Phoenix FBI office. I have my pick set with me, so hopefully he's got a standard keyed lockset on the door. If it's a smart lock, we'll have to find another way in. You did a drive-by, right?"

"Yep, yesterday morning. It's a luxury mid-rise in D.C. Ranch, which is one of the swankiest areas in town. His unit is on the fifth floor. The whole building is inside entrances. No on-site security, but you do need a keypad code to get into the lobby."

"And I assume the police department has the code?" Bryce asked.

"It's on a Post-it note in my wallet. There's also secured parking, which you access with an RFID sticker they give you for your car. There's a reserved spot for his unit, but it was empty, at least when I checked yesterday. What are you looking for once we get inside?"

"To be honest, I'm not sure. Anything that would tell me more about the organization he was working for. Or something I could use as leverage to get him to talk. He's a cool customer, but every man has his breaking point."

Jarvis hadn't oversold the swankiness factor of Vincent's condo building. It was a modern affair, a sleek combination of rough-hewn wood, polished stone, gleaming stainless steel, and mirrored glass. They parked in front of a café across the street, the kind of place where the cheapest cup of coffee was responsibly sourced from Guatemalan monks and cost six bucks. Jarvis punched in the code on the keypad, and they entered through a pair of massive oak doors into a lobby appointed with marble floors, leather sofas, and expensive-looking artwork adorning the walls. The murder business, it would seem, paid well.

They were alone in the early morning hours, save for a fit thirty-something woman dressed in yoga pants and a sports bra who exited the elevator as they were getting on. The fifth floor hallway was deserted, and Bryce stopped for a moment before they reached the door to Vincent's unit near the end of the corridor.

"Everything all right?" Jarvis asked.

"Yep, just getting my mind right, thinking about the last time I did something like this. It went a little haywire."

"How haywire?"

"I got shot."

"You serious?"

"As a heart attack. I'll share later. Let's have a look at his lock."

Both the handset and the deadbolt were straightforward four-pin setups, not the easiest to pick but not impossible either. Bryce made short work of it, and they were inside within minutes.

It was a small condo with a combination living/eating area and an adjacent kitchen. Other than a sofa, a coffee table, and a flat-screen TV, there was little in the way of furnishings and nothing hanging on the walls. There were a few dishes in the kitchen sink and a pile of unopened mail on the counter. A whirring noise was coming from behind a closed door next to the kitchen, and Bryce opened it to have a look. It was a stacking washer-dryer unit, and the washer was running.

He moved his right hand to the holster on his hip just as a shrill female voice blasted from behind the closed bedroom door.

"Get out!" she screamed. "I have a gun!"

Bryce and Jarvis pulled their pistols and trained them on the bedroom door as they moved to opposite ends of the living room and out of the potential line of fire. Jarvis spoke first.

"Scottsdale Police Department, we have a warrant!"

"Bullshit! Get out! I have a gun!"

Bryce chimed in. "So do we, ma'am. Don't make us use them. We have a search warrant."

"Let me see it." The voice was less angry, more of a request than a demand.

"Step out of the bedroom with your hands where we can see them, and we'll show it to you," Jarvis replied.

"No. Slide it underneath the door."

Bryce and Jarvis looked at each other from their positions of cover, more bemused than concerned for their safety. Jarvis held up the warrant, and Bryce shrugged as if to say, *Why not?*

"Okay, ma'am," Jarvis shouted toward the door. "Here it comes. But I'm warning you, if you shoot through that door, it'll be the last thing you ever do." He approached the door from the side, exposing only his arm as he reached around the jamb. He slid the warrant toward the other side, and when he got it halfway through, it disappeared as it was snatched away. A minute went by.

"All right. You can come in. I don't have a gun."

"No," Bryce responded. "You need to open the door and come out here. And like my partner said, keep your hands where we can see them."

There was a series of clunks and thumps from the bedroom before the door cracked open, then more as it opened a bit wider. Finally, the door swung open and Bryce was able to see why it was taking so long. She was in a wheelchair.

And she was telling the truth about being unarmed. Jarvis walked behind her into the bedroom, looked around, and emerged a few seconds later, flashing a thumbs-up sign to Bryce. They holstered their weapons.

"What's your name?" Bryce asked.

"Shayna."

"Shayna what?"

"Shayna Kamara."

"Are you Vincent Kamara's daughter?"

"Yes. Where is he?"

"We'll get to that in a bit," Bryce answered. "Is this his place or yours?"

"His. I've been staying here on and off for the last few months. Since he's been gone. I have an apartment across town, but I'm about to get evicted. He helps me pay my rent, and I haven't been able to work for a while. It's MS, in case you're wondering about the wheelchair. Stress makes it worse. And I've been seriously stressed out since he went missing."

Bryce nodded. "Did he tell you where he was going or what he was doing before he left?"

Shayna shook her head. "No. I assumed he was on another mission, like before."

"Mission?"

"He used to be a Green Beret. The government still calls on him every now and then. Usually he's gone for a few days, maybe a week. But never this long. I haven't seen him in almost a year. Is he dead? Is that why you're here? I thought the army sent guys in uniform to tell the family when a servicemember was killed in action."

Bryce and Jarvis exchanged a look of mutual sympathy for the naive young woman who, it appeared, had lost her only means of financial support. Bryce pulled a chair from the dinette and placed it opposite her. He sat down and leaned toward her.

"Shayna, your father isn't on a mission. He doesn't work for the government. He's in jail in Miami on a double murder charge. He killed two men in the Florida Keys."

Shayna's eyes went red and began to well with tears. "You're lying."

"I'm afraid not. Your father is mixed up with some very bad people, and he went to Florida to commit a murder for money. Only the two people he ended up killing weren't the ones he was supposed to." There was no point in bringing up the fact that she was speaking to the actual target.

She shook her head from side to side. "You're saying he was a...?" She couldn't bring herself to say the words.

"A hit man. Yes."

The tears gave way to a full-on sobbing attack as Shayna broke down in front of them. Bryce and Jarvis let her wail and pound her fists onto the armrests of her wheelchair as they sat quietly. When she appeared spent, Bryce resumed the questioning.

"Shayna, have you removed anything of your father's from the apartment?"

"Like what?"

"Like a computer, or a phone, or papers. Anything that could tell us more about who he was working for and how they communicated."

"If he had any of that stuff, it would have been in his safe. I never had the combination. And it doesn't matter now anyway."

"Why do you say that?" Jarvis asked.

"See for yourself. In the closet." She pointed toward the bedroom.

Bryce walked into the closet and surveyed the space. He began moving clothing out of the way, and behind a row of hanging shirts he saw it. A Mosler floor safe, about two feet tall and a little over a foot wide. It was empty, and the door wasn't just open;

it was removed from the box and laid on its side. Bryce looked closely at the hinges and saw where they had been severed with some sort of power tool, most likely a grinder.

He walked back into the living room and sat down. "Did you report the break-in to the police?"

Shayna shook her head. "It wasn't a break-in, at least not the regular kind. A couple of lowlifes came by here yesterday. When I opened the door they forced their way in and started going through the apartment, same as you. They asked me for the combination to the safe, and when I told them I didn't have it, they cut the door off."

"Do you know what they took?" Bryce asked.

"No idea. I'd never seen the inside of that safe. And obviously, I didn't call the cops."

"What do you mean, 'obviously'?"

"Dad said never call the police about him or anything having to do with him. Even if he went missing. He said his work was top secret, and the police wouldn't understand." She leaned forward and put her head in her hands. "I guess now I know why."

"Shayna, I'm sorry about your dad, and I'm sorry to be the one to have to tell you about it," Bryce said. "We still need to look around."

"Go ahead." She appeared catatonic.

Bryce and Jarvis made their way through the apartment, knowing their opportunity to find anything of value had come and gone. The Network had beat them to it. After half an hour, they abandoned the search.

"Shayna," Bryce asked, "is there anything else about your father we should know? Any friends or associates you saw him with? Did he ever tell you exactly where he was going when he left town?"

"No. He went to work and he came home. He had a girlfriend a few years ago, but not recently. You say he's in jail in Miami?"

"That's correct."

"Are the doctors taking good care of him?"

Bryce was puzzled; he hadn't mentioned Vincent getting shot. "Taking care of him how?"

"His condition. Please tell me they know about it."

"They might, but why don't you tell me about it so I can make sure he's getting the treatment he needs."

"He was having these headaches. They kept getting worse. The old fool's a nurse, but I still had to make him go see a doctor for it. They did an MRI and found spots on his brain. He was supposed to go in for more tests, but that was before he went missing. Are you telling me nobody knows about it in Miami? He needs to see a doctor." There was desperation in her voice.

"I'll check on that as soon as I get back," Bryce said.

Shayna nodded her understanding. "Don't take this personally, but I want you guys to leave. There's nothing here for you, and I've said all I'm going to say." They left a copy of the warrant on the kitchen table and returned to the car.

Jarvis spoke up first. "Somebody hit the place the day before us. That can't be a coincidence."

"Exactly what I was thinking," Bryce replied.

"You think she's telling us the truth?"

"I do. There's no way her father would have told her about his side hustle. She's just some poor kid who got dealt a shitty hand, from her parents to her health issues."

"I feel sorry for her," Jarvis said as he drove.

"Yeah, me too. It's not her fault her old man broke bad."

"I feel kind of bad for you, too, Bryce. You came all this way and we hit a dry hole."

Bryce smiled. "Oh, I don't know about that."

On the way to the airport, Jarvis's words rung in Bryce's ears.

This can't be a coincidence.

And he was right. Someone knew Bryce was going to Scottsdale and tipped off the Network. But who? The mole in West Virginia had no way of knowing what was going on in Bryce's case, so it wasn't him. He remembered the director's cautionary advice at FBI headquarters.

If there's one, there are probably more. Watch your back.

CHAPTER 16

BEAUFORT, SOUTH CAROLINA, sat just forty miles from Hilton Head Island, but the two locales may as well have been on different planets. Hilton Head was a ritzy beachfront destination for golf enthusiasts and well-heeled socialites with luxurious tastes and unlimited budgets. Beaufort was its laid-back southern cousin, as lush with history as it was with ancient live oaks dripping Spanish moss. The epitome of southern charm, it was home to Parris Island Marine Corps Recruit Depot and the legendary southern author Pat Conroy, of *Lords of Discipline* and *The Great Santini* fame. Most of the movie *Forrest Gump* was filmed there, and the iconic scene of Tom Hanks crossing the Mississippi River during his long-distance run was actually shot on the Beaufort River Bridge. From culture to climate to a modest cost of living, Beaufort had it all.

One thing Beaufort didn't have was murders, or at least not a lot of them. There were eight in the entire county over the past two years, and all but one of them were in the unincorporated outlying areas, not in the city itself. The Beaufort County Sheriff's Office had a criminal investigations section but not a dedicated homicide squad, and they often called upon the resources of the South Carolina Law Enforcement Division when a case exceeded their investigative capabilities.

Ellis Purcell was a cop at heart, but ten years of traffic enforcement and routine patrol work with the Columbia Police Department left him feeling underworked and uninspired. He joined SLED for the opportunity to become a full-time criminal investigator, and the move paid off. He spent the first five years of his career honing his skills in the public corruption arena, where he developed a well-earned reputation as an enemy of the local kleptocrats who ran South Carolina's rural counties. When an opportunity to attend the state's death investigation course presented itself, Ellis jumped, and the career move suited him well.

He pulled to the curb in front of the house on Beaufort's south side, shut off the engine, and flipped down the passenger-side visor to display the *SLED Official Business* placard. A Beaufort County Sheriff's Department crime scene van was parked in the driveway, and a pair of technicians in white Tyvek stood near the back door. A photographer was busy snapping closeups of the front door. A deputy in a sportscoat and tie met Ellis at the trunk of his car as he was retrieving the rolling duffle bag that contained his crime scene kit.

"Morning, Ellis," the deputy said as he extended his hand.

"Morning, Bill. What do we got?"

"Jack Barclay, sixty years old, lives alone. UPS driver found him. He had a package that needed signing for, and when nobody answered the doorbell he took a peek through the living room window. The body's lying in a recliner. Gunshot wound to the back of the head. Looks like he's been dead maybe six to eight hours."

"Anybody talk to the neighbors?"

"I didn't get that far before the feds showed up," he said, motioning with his thumb toward a black Ford Expedition parked two houses down the street. "That's when I called you."

"Feds? What do they want?" Ellis asked.

"Wouldn't say. He just asked if I was in charge, and I told him I was calling SLED. He said he'd wait."

"Alrighty then. Let me go introduce myself and then we'll have a look at your stiff."

Ellis made it about halfway to the Expedition before the driver stepped out, looking every bit the federal agent in his tan cargo pants, oversized North Face button-down shirt, and smoke-gray Oakleys. He pulled a set of credentials from his back pocket and had them at the ready as Ellis approached.

"Ryan Dougherty, US Marshals Service," he said, holding his creds in his left hand as he extended his right toward Ellis.

"Ellis Purcell, SLED. What brings the Marshals Service to a small town murder in the low country?"

A pained look came over the deputy marshal's face. "Man, I hate starting off this way, but I don't know what I can and can't say right now. What I can tell you is we have an interest in the victim. Do you mind if I go inside with you?"

Ellis shrugged. "I guess not. Just don't touch anything unless you ask first."

"Thanks. Are you ready to go in now?"

"Yep. Follow me."

The body was lying as the deputy had described, fully reclined in the leather La-Z-Boy, one hand at his side and the other over the armrest, pointed at the floor. Livor mortis was well underway, giving his face an ashen appearance. He was wearing a pair of blue

Nike workout pants, a light-gray t-shirt, and ankle-high white socks. A pair of reading glasses lay haphazardly in his lap, and a copy of John Grisham's *A Time to Kill* was on the floor next to the recliner. The smell of human feces hung in the air.

Ellis donned latex gloves and knelt behind the body. He picked up the head just enough to get a closer look at the entry wound. It was to the left of the center of the skull, three inches above the bottom of the occipital bone. He surmised it to have been caused by a nine-millimeter or smaller caliber round. The size and shape of the exit wound supported his theory. The bullet traveled through the left lacrimal bone, leaving his skull between the eye socket and the nose, both of which bore signs of trauma but were still identifiable and intact. A larger-caliber round like a .45 would have done far more soft-tissue damage.

The coffee table in front of the recliner caught most of the blood spatter, which had dried to a dark maroon, almost brown color. There was a small amount of blood on his pants and almost none on his shirt, at least none that looked as if they came from the spatter. There were a dozen or so small droplets of dried blood between the neckline of the shirt and the victim's navel, as well as several drops on his chin.

"Those aren't from the gunshot," Ellis said, pointing to the blood on the victim's t-shirt and chin.

"How can you tell?" Ryan asked.

"They're larger than everything in the spatter pattern. And he wasn't lying down when he was shot."

"What makes you say that?"

"The entry and exit wounds show a bullet path that would have been parallel to the floor if he was sitting up. That makes sense—he's sitting upright, head forward as he's reading his book, and the killer fires the gun from behind him in standing position. His head falls back against the back of the recliner. If he were shot in the position we found him, the shooter would have been underneath him, pointed toward the ceiling, which makes zero sense. And the spatter pattern would be mostly on the ceiling and his person as all the blood went straight up, then back down. Oh, and there would be a hole in the back of the recliner. So, yeah—somebody shot him and then laid him back."

"Why would someone change his position after they shot him?"

"Good question. It might have something to do with the blood spots on his chin and shirt." Ellis pulled a small flashlight from his kit and trained it on the blood trail. "The droplets are closer, almost touching one another here." He pointed toward the bloody chin. "Then as we get to here," he said as he moved the flashlight down the shirt, "they're further apart. Whatever it was, it was producing more blood near his mouth and less as it was pulled away."

"Could he have wounded his attacker? Maybe bitten him or something?"

"Doubtful. If there had been a fight, maybe. But this was an execution. He never saw it coming. And there's some bruising around his lips. But not like someone punched him in the mouth. Like they did something to his mouth after they shot him."

Ellis moved alongside the body and changed his gloves. He inserted two fingers into the victim's mouth, felt for a gap between the upper and lower teeth, then inserted two fingers from his other hand and began pulling the jaw in opposite directions. "The medical examiner will have my ass for this," he remarked. Rigor had set in, and the jaw made a sickening, crunching sound as he pried it open and shined his light inside.

"Bingo."

"What is it?" Ryan asked, his eyes fixed on the floor. He had moved to the other side of the room, and between the smells, sights, and sounds of Ellis's postmortem exam, he looked like he was about to puke.

"He's missing a tooth. Somebody pulled it out of his mouth after they killed him. That explains the blood on his face and shirt. They pulled it, held it over his chin for a moment, maybe admiring it. Then they pulled it away in the direction of the blood spots."

"You can tell all that from looking in his mouth?"

"The hole the tooth came out of is fresh. There's blood pooled in it. And I've seen this kind of trophy-taking behavior before. Killers take something belonging to the victim, or in some cases, a piece of the victim themselves. Come here, have a look."

"No, thanks. I need to call my boss."

Ryan's supervisor was Rick Rosecroft, the chief deputy marshal for the District of South Carolina in Columbia. As soon as Ryan finished briefing him on the situation in Beaufort, Rick called his counterpart, Albert "Butch" Langham, who held the same position in Atlanta. After a brief introduction, Rick got to the point.

"Butch, I was on the shooting review board for your deputy who was killed last year. If I recall, the subject he was protecting was also murdered, and didn't the killer remove one of his teeth after he shot him?"

"James Todd," Butch replied. "Scumbag defense attorney. I still can't believe we were protecting him. A few weeks earlier they got his secretary. One of her teeth was missing as well."

"Yeah, well, we had a replay of all that up here in Beaufort County last night. We weren't sitting on the guy, but he was in the program."

"No shit? What else can you tell me about him?"

"His name was Jack Barclay, and he was one of the Griffin four. You remember that Air Force base in New York where everyone got sick ten years ago?"

"Sure do. Matter of fact, they just started running commercials down here, looking for more victims. I guess there's no expiration date on that stuff once the lawyers get involved."

"You got that right," Rick replied. "Anyway, the whole thing was laid on some sham environmental company that was responsible for hazardous waste disposal and didn't do their job. Billions of dollars' worth of fraud and a trail of sickness and disease that could last for generations. Four of the company's top executives cut a deal with the government and threw their middle managers and worker bees under the bus. The sacrificial lambs went to jail, and these guys went into the program. And now three of them are dead."

"Where's the fourth one?"

"I'm not sure. Headquarters is handling all that. But when the first two got knocked off, we recommended to Mr. Barclay that he let us put him in the high-threat program and give him a 24/7 detail. The arrogant prick wouldn't listen."

"Can I assume you're treating this as a professional job?" Butch asked.

"Most definitely."

Butch sighed and rubbed his temple with his free hand. "Well then, I've got to make a call I don't want to make."

"To who?"

"To the people who got my deputy killed. The FBI."

CHAPTER 17

JUST AS BRYCE was boarding his flight to Key West, Donnie called and told him to come to Atlanta instead for a meeting with the Marshals Service. He didn't give any details, other than to say there was a potential break in the case. They met in the parking lot at the Richard B. Russell federal building, and Donnie brought Bryce up to speed on what he knew.

"The guy we're meeting with is Butch Langham, the chief deputy. He's got a real hard-on for the bureau over the James Todd situation."

"He should," Bryce replied. "We got one of his deputies killed."

"That wasn't our fault. Peoples was the idiot who held the press conference."

"Doesn't matter. It was a bureau fuck-up, and to him, you and I are the bureau. We might as well own it."

"I know. Still, it sticks in my craw."

They took the elevator to the twenty-third floor, then walked down the hallway to a pair of glass doors with the Marshals Service seal etched across them. The receptionist buzzed them into the lobby and announced their arrival to Butch Langham, who kept them waiting ten minutes beyond their appointment time. Finally, she told them they could go in, and pointed the way to the chief deputy's office.

"Good morning, gentlemen," Butch said as he stood and shook hands across his desk. He motioned for them to have a seat in a pair of chairs on the other side. "Glad you could make it." All of it—the initial greeting, the handshake, and the salutation that followed—was cold and obligatory. He made no attempt to disguise his scorn for the FBI.

"Thank you for having us," Donnie said as he settled into the upholstered leather wing chair.

"It wasn't my choice. The only reason you two are here is because headquarters told me how it was going to be. Your people and my people had a talk way above my pay grade, so here we are. How much do you know about this so-called Griffin four?"

"Just what you told me on the phone," Donnie replied. "They were the heads of a company that got caught dumping chemicals on an Air Force base, worked themselves a plea deal, and went in the program. Now three of them are dead, and there's a tie-in to the murder of one of your deputies?"

"He had a name. It was Sam Degenova, and whoever killed him did it to get to James Todd. After they killed Todd, they pulled one of his teeth, probably as a trophy or memento. Todd's secretary was murdered two weeks before him, and same thing—missing a tooth. So it appears this Network of yours is at it again, only this time they're targeting a new set of victims."

Bryce fumed as his mind spun. The FBI hadn't let up in their search for Sonny and his band of hired assassins, but it seemed as though the killings had stopped or at least slowed while James Todd was in custody. Bryce had hoped, naively, the Network would be spooked over the long term by their former associate turning government witness, but apparently Todd's murder was all they needed to begin again in earnest. The FBI was back to square one.

"We need to talk to the sole surviving member of this Griffin four," Bryce said. "Where is he?"

"It's she, not he. We pulled her off the street and have her under 24/7 security."

"Where?" Bryce repeated.

"Slow your roll. I'm going to follow orders, but there are still some conditions. And they come from the top."

"Such as?" Donnie asked.

"Such as that idiot Greg Peoples isn't allowed within a hundred miles of our operation."

"Not a problem. He's been exiled to North Dakota."

"Good. Next, you two will be the only FBI employees who know the protectee's location. Your bosses, your secretaries, your buddies—breathe a word of it to any of them and the deal's off. You'll also be the only two allowed to talk to her. And any report you generate that references her identity or location has to be approved by the Marshals Service, which is to say me. You'll meet her when we say, where we say, for as long as we say. We will pick you up at a staging location, and you won't know where we're keeping her until we take you there. Again, break the rules and it's over. If you have a problem with any of this, now's the time to let me know."

It was a power play, an old-school dressing down, and there was nothing they could do about it. Bryce sat quietly and let his supervisor do the talking. There was an uncomfortable silence while Donnie mulled it over.

"We're in. What's next?"

"Pack a bag. You'll hear from me within twenty-four hours." Butch motioned toward the door. "Good day, gentlemen."

Two days later, Bryce and Donnie departed Atlanta Hartsfield airport on a direct flight to Biloxi, Mississippi. When they landed, they headed northwest on State Route 67 in their rental car, strategizing as they drove.

"I checked out the Earth Tech case yesterday," Donnie said. "Opened in 2010, closed in 2015. It was worked out of the Albany division, jointly with EPA and DoD. All told there were forty-seven plea deals and two jury trials. Most of the sentences ranged from five years' probation to ten years in jail. One poor schmuck got fifteen years. He was the one in charge of picking out the dump sites. He turned down the government's deal and went to trial. Told the jury he was just following orders. It worked about as well for him as it did for the Nazis at Nuremberg."

"And the top brass took their deal, went into WITSEC, and walked away."

"Pretty much. One thing I'd like to figure out tomorrow is why now? The case has been over and done for eight years. Why did somebody just now decide to start whacking these guys?"

Bryce asked, "So who's the last man—excuse me—woman standing?"

"I couldn't tell. All the cooperating witnesses were identified in the case file by their CW number, and their individual source files are locked down tight. Probably purged altogether since they went into the program."

"So do you think our mystery woman can shed any light on who's behind the killings?"

"I hope so," Donnie replied. "For now, she's all we have."

They continued on State Route 67 until it met US Route 49 northbound. "Where the hell are we headed again?" Bryce asked.

"Wiggins."

"Boy, they aren't taking any chances this time, are they? Talk about the middle of nowhere."

"We don't even know that's where she is. It's just where we're spending the night."

They pulled into the Comfort Inn an hour later and went inside to check in. As the clerk handed them back their credit cards and driver's licenses, he reached under the desk and retrieved a sealed bulky manila envelope with *Mr. Morris* written on it. "This was left for you," he said, handing the package to Donnie.

They made their way toward the elevator. "Come by my room when you get settled, and we'll see what this is about," Donnie told Bryce.

When Bryce got to Donnie's room, the envelope was open and the contents were on the coffee table. It was a pre-paid off-brand burner phone with a charger, and Donnie had just powered it on when the incoming text notification beeped.

Let me know when you get this message.

Donnie typed in his reply. *Got it.*

The response was immediate. *8 am out front. Leave your phones. Bring this one. Dress casual. Acknowledge.*

Donnie did as he was instructed. "I guess they're taking this secret squirrel stuff to the next level," he said.

Bryce shrugged. "Can you blame them? We're on their turf now. Their house, their rules. Want to get some dinner?"

Donnie shook his head. "I'm going to have something delivered. I have a call with you-know-who in an hour."

"The AD?"

"Yep. It's a daily thing now. He's becoming quite the pain in the ass."

CHAPTER 18

A LONE DEPUTY marshal picked them up at 8:00. He was polite and professional but not chatty. After some brief introductions, the entire drive to the safe house was made in silence. Bryce watched as the familiar landmarks of his southern upbringing rolled by, waxing nostalgic as they passed a Piggly Wiggly supermarket, a Dollar General store, and a Tastee-Freez (they were well past the line of societal demarcation where Dairy Queen reigned supreme). There were no Shell or Exxon stations, just the odd mom-and-pop convenience store with decades-old pumps, the kind that displayed the fuel quantity and cost on spinning dials instead of digital readouts. A weathered billboard proclaimed Stone County, Mississippi, to be Jack Daniel's country. Bryce wondered if he had lingered on the sign too long when he noticed Donnie watching him from the corner of his eye.

The icons thinned and then disappeared as they drove, giving way to endless acres of cotton, soybeans, and little else. By the time they turned off the county two-lane onto an unmarked dirt road, the only buildings in sight were a two-story farmhouse and an adjacent barn a mile or so in the distance. The driver pulled around to the barn, and as he approached, one of the sliding doors opened to allow them inside. There were four other vehicles parked among the hay bales, all government issued—two low-slung full-sized sedans and a pair of dark-colored Tahoes, all with tinted windows.

The driver led Bryce and Donnie through a rear door into the house, where another half dozen Marshals were hard at work doing nothing in particular. One was fixing breakfast at the stove, two were watching the morning news, and two more were tending to their laundry in the room next to the kitchen. The eldest of the group was on the front porch, smoking a cigarette. When he saw Bryce and Donnie, he crushed out his butt, flipped it into the front yard, and came inside.

"You must be Morris and Chandler," he said, extending his hand. "Ed Haworth, detail supervisor."

Bryce and Donnie shook his hand, and Donnie led off. "Quite the setup you have here. Nobody's sneaking up on this place, are they?"

"Not if we can help it. My boss tells me this network of yours is for real. We're not taking chances."

"Good idea. So where's our girl?"

"Upstairs. She'll be down in a minute. I take it you've never met Norma. You're in for a treat." He rolled his eyes as he spoke.

A door slammed upstairs, and there was the sound of footsteps in the hall, then on the stairs as she made her way down. She shuffled into the kitchen, stared at Bryce and Donnie, and snorted. "I guess this is the FBI, am I right, Eddie? Norma Whitehurst. I wish I could say it was a pleasure." She poured herself a cup of coffee and plopped down in a seat at the table.

Norma had once been attractive, a knockout even, but those days were long gone. Her eyes were sunken in dark hollows, deep creases assaulted the skin on her forehead and around her mouth, and her hair was an undressed mangle of gray that looked as if it hadn't been tended to in years. She wore a pair of baggy blue sweatpants and an even baggier flannel shirt buttoned to the neckline. She pulled a cigarette from a pack in the shirt pocket and a lighter from her sweatpants.

"Norma, I thought we talked about this," Ed said from across the room. "No smoking in the house."

"You're right, Ed," she replied as she lit the cigarette. "We did talk about this." She took a long drag as she stared at him.

Ed shook his head and walked into the living room. The deputies who had been fixing their breakfast finished in a hurry and joined him, leaving Norma alone in the kitchen with Bryce and Donnie.

Bryce started the conversation. "Good morning, Miss Whitehurst, and thank you for seeing us. I'm Agent Chandler, and this is Agent Morris."

She smiled. "It's not like I had a choice. These marshals have me locked up here like a dog in a cage."

"That's because there are some very bad people after you," Bryce replied. "And the reason we're here today is to see if you can shed some light on who they are and why they want to hurt you."

"Hurt me? Or kill me?"

"Fair enough. It appears they want to kill you. And we want to know why. So let's start with what you did during your time at Earth Tech."

She took a long drag from her cigarette and exhaled toward the ceiling. "Is it true they're all gone? Alvin, Gil, and Jack?"

Bryce nodded.

"So they saved me for last. I don't know whether to be flattered or insulted."

"I'd say you're lucky," Bryce replied. "Now about Earth Tech."

"What about it?"

"It was your company, wasn't it?"

"Yeah, so?"

Bryce was getting annoyed. "So how about you knock off this coy little act of yours and help us figure out who wants to put a bullet in your head?"

"You really don't know?" she snorted. "I thought the FBI was better than that."

Donnie stepped in. "Ms. Whitehurst, we're not the enemy. That would be the person who ordered the murder of all your former colleagues. So in the interest of helping everyone, including yourself, could you please just answer our questions?"

Norma crushed out her cigarette, lit another, and shrugged. "Sure. What was the question again?"

"Earth Tech," Bryce snapped.

"What is there to tell? It was my company. We started as a residential cleaning service, you know, one of those places that comes in after a fire or a flood and makes it look like nothing ever happened. Back then it was called Service Tech. I had about twenty employees, and we did okay for ourselves. In the early nineties we branched out into asbestos mitigation." She took a sip of her coffee and smiled broadly, as if reliving a fond memory. "And then we hit the lottery."

"How so?" Donnie asked.

"Griffin Air Force Base started renovating their family housing. Most of it was built in the fifties, and that meant asbestos everywhere. In the ceilings, the roofs, the insulation around the heating ducts. Everywhere. I got the contract. Big surprise." She rolled her eyes.

"Sounds like there's a story behind that," Bryce said.

"Well, we were a woman-owned business, so that gave us some leverage. But the bidding process was all for show. The Griffin contracting office had their marching orders."

"From who?"

"From the man who wrote the checks. Frank D'Angelo."

"The senator from New York?"

"Back then he was a congressman. But a powerful one. If he wanted something to happen, it happened. And he wanted Service Tech to run the asbestos mitigation project for Griffin."

"Any reason he was throwing the business your way?" Bryce asked.

"Sure. He had bigger plans. And we were in a—shall I say—relationship."

"A romantic relationship? Were you his mistress?"

"No need to be so formal. We were fucking. For about ten years. Frank knew he could trust me." She looked down at the table and muttered, "And I thought I could trust him."

Bryce and Donnie were scribbling notes as fast as their hands could move. "So you said Frank D'Angelo could trust you. To do what?" Donnie asked.

Norma sighed. "The asbestos removal project was just the starter. The main dish was a biohazard management contract that was a hundred times larger. Frank wanted my company to run it. So over the next couple years, we branched out even further. Frank had contacts everywhere. He hired on a few former EPA administrators to give us street cred, and the next thing you know, asbestos gave way to benzene, arsenic, mercury, lead, PFAS, you name it. We were one-stop shopping for all your biohazard disposal problems. And when Griffin dodged the BRACC cuts and they decided to make it a DoD superbase, we got the contract. Déjà vu all over again, to quote Yogi Berra."

"So what was in it for Frank D'Angelo?" Bryce asked. "Was he taking a cut of the contract money?"

"Oh," she said, shaking her head. "If it was only that bad. Frank never took a dime from me."

"Then what? What was his angle?"

She stared back at Bryce in amazement. "You really don't know, do you? Ten thousand people got sick at Griffin. A couple thousand have died. And the lawyers got rich. You're the professional investigator, figure it out. Frank owns the largest personal injury law firm in the entire Northeast. Do you have any idea how much money he's made off that disaster?" She made air quotes with her fingers as she said the word *disaster*.

"I'm sure it's a lot," Bryce answered. "But at the end of the day, it was your company's negligence that spawned the cancer cluster. Sure, it doesn't look good for Frank D'Angelo to be profiting from it, but bad optics isn't a crime."

She shook her head again. "You're still not getting it. Frank D'Angelo is a monster."

"Why? Are you telling me he helped you build your company, then got you the contract, knowing you'd screw it up and he could step in and represent the victims?"

"Worse."

"Oh, come on. How much worse could it be than that?"

"Honey, there never should have been any chemicals in the drinking water. We could have run that contract with our eyes closed. Without spilling a drop."

"Then why didn't you?"

She crushed out her second cigarette and lit a third. "Because Frank D'Angelo didn't want that. Like I said, he's a monster. He wanted dirty water so he could make his dirty money. He poisoned Griffin Air Force Base. We just carried out his orders."

It took a few seconds for Bryce and Donnie to process the magnitude of what they were hearing. They stared at each other, then back at Norma. Bryce put aside his notebook, inched his chair closer to Norma's, and stared at her.

"Let me get this straight. You're saying Frank D'Angelo orchestrated the drinking water crisis at Griffin Air Force Base, knowing he would benefit financially from representing the victims?"

"That's exactly what I'm saying. Earth Tech was more than capable of meeting our contractual and environmental obligations. Instead, on Frank's orders, we drew up a plan to make sure anything toxic was fed into the groundwater. Not accidentally. Sometimes we would dump benzyne and firefighting foam right into the treatment tanks. We had to back off a little when residents started complaining that they could smell chemicals in the water coming out of their taps. But by then the damage was done."

"If you knew it was going to do this much damage, why'd you go along with it? Were you in love with him?"

"Oh, please. Let's not make me out to be some doe-eyed romantic pawn. I did it for the money. Same as Frank."

"Who else knows about Frank D'Angelo's involvement?" Bryce asked.

"All my dead colleagues. Which, I'm guessing, is the reason they're dead."

"Why didn't this come up with the prosecutors when you made your plea deal?"

"Because what we did was so fucked up, it never crossed their minds that it could have been done on purpose, much less the brainchild of a United States congressman. To the Department of Justice, we were just an inept bunch of contractors who got in over our heads and cooked the books to cover it up. The lawyers wanted scalps, the more the better, and the four of us were the only ones who could give them what they wanted. So we sacrificed our employees and left Frank out of it. I'm not proud of what we did, but it is what it is."

"So safe to say, you think Frank D'Angelo is the one behind the murders?"

Norma shrugged. "If not him, who?"

"Something still doesn't make sense," Donnie said. "Why now? If Frank D'Angelo knew you turned into government witnesses almost ten years ago, why didn't he have you taken care of back then?"

"Like I said, he trusted me," Norma said. "He figured his name would stay out of it. And it might have, until he decided to run for president. When you enter that arena, the next-level snooping begins. They find the girl you felt up at the senior prom and the roommate you smoked weed with in college, and turn it all into front page news. In Frank's case, a reporter for the *Utica Herald* found an old picture of Frank and me looking a little too chummy at a campaign fundraiser back in 1992. Kind of like the photos of Monica Lewinski and Bill Clinton that started that whole mess. Anyway, the reporter ran the photo in a story about Griffin, sort of a "Remember when?" piece to remind the readers that I was the head of Earth Tech, Frank owned the firm that was profiting off it, yada, yada, yada."

"But the reporter never made the link to Frank being responsible for it all?"

"How could he? How could anyone? This is some Darth Vader-level evil shit. I still can't believe it myself." She shook her head. "And that dirty son of a bitch got away with it, too." She shook her head. "If I could go back—"

Bryce noticed tears beginning to form in the corners of Norma's eyes.

"What else do we need to know about Frank D'Angelo?" Donnie asked.

"Just that he's as fake as any politician, more so than most." She pulled a tissue from her shirt pocket and wiped her eyes. "D'Angelo's not even his real last name. He took his mother's maiden name after law school when his grandfather told him he wouldn't hire a mick lawyer."

"Do you remember what his name was before he changed it?"

"No. Obviously something Irish, based on what his grandfather said."

The interview continued for another hour. The ashtray filled to overflowing as Norma shared everything she could remember about Frank D'Angelo, Griffin Air Force Base, and the part that she and her colleagues played in laying waste to its populace. Part of her original plea deal included a stipulation that there would be no future prosecutions, even if new information came to light. She bared all.

Donnie and Bryce thanked her for her time, had a brief conversation with Ed Haworth, and gathered their things for the ride back to the hotel. As they walked toward the door, they heard Norma yell toward them.

"Wait!"

They returned to the kitchen, where she was now standing next to her chair, lighting a fresh cigarette. Her face bore the expression of someone who was trying their best to recall a distant memory.

"Frank and I used to joke about it. About him changing his name. Because if he hadn't, and his grandfather hired him anyway, the name of the law firm would have been something funny. Something famous. We used to laugh about it." Her expression grew more pained as she tried to recall.

"Well, if you remember, Ed can get ahold of us," Donnie assured her. He motioned with his head toward the door, telling Bryce that it was time to leave. As they walked away a second time, she shouted loud enough to startle them both.

"Abbott and Costello!"

They turned and saw her smiling from ear to ear.

"Frank's last name was Costello."

CHAPTER 19

DONNIE WAS BACK in the FBI director's conference room, only this time there was no crowd. The FBI attendees included just the director, Assistant Director Caine, Donnie, and Bryce. They were joined by the director of the Marshals Service and his deputy, neither of whom looked as if they wanted to be there. Given the history between the two agencies with regard to the Network, their standoffishness was to be expected.

The FBI director got things started. "Thank you all for being here. This is a peculiar meeting, but I think we'd all agree we find ourselves in a peculiar situation. Agents Morrison and Chandler have briefed me on their interview with Norma Whitehurst, and if what she says is true, this case is about to take us deep into 'special circumstances' territory. Not only has she accused Frank D'Angelo of creating the cancer cluster at Griffin Air Force Base, but her theory that he's hired the Network to get rid of the witnesses makes sense. So we're talking about capital charges against a sitting United States senator and presidential candidate. And as Miss Whitehurst is the only living witness, we have a vested interest in keeping her alive. Thoughts?"

The Marshals Service director spoke next. "Mark, you know WITSEC's track record. We've never lost a protectee until Atlanta, and that was because one of your agents led the Network to him.

And yes, the three that got taken out in this case were in the program, but they had all declined protective details. Since we got ahold of Norma, she's been safe and will continue to be safe. But there's the problem of her being your witness, and the access you're going to need to her in order to run your case. Frankly, we're not comfortable with continuing to protect her and allowing the FBI to come and go every time they need to talk to her. And I'd guess you're not happy sharing the details of your case with us. So we need to make a decision. Either she stays with us or she goes with you. And to be honest, we don't have a problem giving her up. My guys tell me she's been nothing but a colossal pain in the ass from day one."

Director Angiulino looked to Donnie. "What do you think?" he asked.

"If there's a trial, she's our star witness," Donnie replied. "And we've only begun to scratch the surface of what she knows. Norma Whitehurst is the only person who can diagram the entire Griffin case from start to finish. She may be able to identify additional witnesses and evidence to tie Frank D'Angelo to it all. Her testimony also ties him to the Network murders. We need her, and we need to be able to talk with her, face to face, whenever the need arises."

The director nodded. "Looks like we've made a decision." He turned to his assistant director. "Sully, come up with a protection plan for our star witness. It needs to be robust." He lowered his head and strummed his fingers on the conference table before raising it again. "Strike that. It needs to be infallible. Am I clear?" The assistant director nodded his understanding.

Bryce, as the junior-ranking person in the room, had been

silent until that point. He raised his hand, a single finger pointed upward as he spoke.

"I have an idea."

The pair of Blackhawks touched down in unison, and the landing party disembarked before the rotors stopped spinning. There were eight of them, all dressed in olive-drab tactical uniforms and ballistic protective vests. They carried Springfield model 1911 .45-caliber pistols on their hips and had M4 rifles slung across their chests. They retrieved their charge from the second helicopter and escorted her to a waiting Suburban for a thirty-second ride to the huge brown brick building some four hundred meters away. A short ride up a service elevator brought them to the eleventh floor, which was deserted except for an improvised security checkpoint consisting of a desk with another heavily armed man seated behind it. He waved them past, and they proceeded to the last room at the end of the hallway. Inside was a bed, a dresser drawer, and a desk, all of which looked to have been plucked from a seventies-era Motel 6, along with a small black-and-white television. The large window looked out on a vast expanse of forest to one side and a long line of shooting ranges on the other.

"What the hell is this place?" Norma asked as two of the men deposited her bags near the foot of the bed.

"The FBI Academy," one of them answered. "You're on the top floor. They cleared it out just for you."

"Where do I eat?" she asked.

"Your meals will be brought to you. Your laundry will be picked up every other day and done for you. Everything you need is in this building. But you are confined to this floor. If you want to go outside, get some fresh air and exercise, we'll go with you. From this point forward you will go nowhere without armed escorts. And you're not leaving until we're given the word."

"And who exactly are you?"

"I'm Supervisory Special Agent Tom Billingsley. FBI Hostage Rescue Team. And before you start asking for details, let me tell you I know almost nothing about this case, other than we are to keep you alive until you're needed for trial. Beyond that..." He shrugged his shoulders and raised his palms toward the ceiling in his best "I don't know nuthin'" pose.

"Great," she replied. "I might as well be a prisoner."

"Well, for what it's worth, lady, we ain't too shot in the ass about this detail ourselves," the agent replied. "This isn't what we do, but the marching orders came straight from the director himself, so it's what we do now. You might as well settle in. Somebody will be here to take your dinner order around six. Welcome to Quantico." He left her alone, pulling the door behind him.

She unpacked the bags she had thrown together when the Marshals Service scooped her up in Des Moines, before spiriting her away to the redneck hellhole she had called home for the past four weeks. They had taken her cellphone in Iowa, and to the best of their knowledge it was her only tether to the outside world. But contingency planning was a necessary part of life on the run, and for years she had maintained a second, secret phone in anticipation of the day when she might have to leave everything behind. In Mississippi she broke it out behind her locked bedroom door, and only to check the news and do enough web browsing to maintain her sanity. She dared not use it to reach back to anyone from her current or former life, fearful of both the government that was holding her and the hit men who were trying to find her.

Self-pity turned to rage as she pondered her circumstances. Sure, she had done some shitty things, but did they even compare to the atrocities committed by her former lover turned boss and now stalker? He was living in the lap of luxury, traveling in private jets and raking in donor dollars at black tie fundraisers, while she languished in America's flyover country. And now she was confined to a virtual jail cell in Northern Virginia, waiting for his hired assassins to do his bidding. And the irony of it all? She never had any intention of ratting him out. Not at first, anyway. Not until he sicced the dogs on her.

Fuck Frank D'Angelo. Norma fished her secret phone from its hiding place, tucked in her suitcase amid the oversized granny panties no federal agent had the stomach to rummage through. She powered it on, and to her joy and surprise, got four bars and an LTE signal. Not 5G, but good enough. A quick Google search uncovered a reference to a *Washington Post* reporter who in the previous year had broken what industry watchers called the story of the decade. It involved the secretary of commerce, his ties to a Shanghai multibillionaire, and the millions of dollars in bribes he had taken to keep Chinese goods flowing into the United States in the face of anti-China trade sentiment. The commerce secretary was led out of his office in handcuffs, the US government suffered a huge black eye, and the reporter, one Kevin Rosen, won the Pulitzer Prize for Investigative Reporting. Two short Google searches later, Norma found an email address and phone number for the aspiring Bob Woodward.

She spent the next two hours composing the email. After she sent it, she left a voice message on Kevin Rosen's phone for good measure.

CHAPTER 20

VINCENT LAID ASIDE his book, Stephen King's latest, and tried for a second time to down a few bites of his lunch. Prison food was shit, to be sure, but what they called jambalaya was usually pretty decent. Not today. It looked like dog food and tasted worse, even though it was the same version of the Cajun staple they'd been serving the entire time he had been a guest of Miami-Dade County, almost a year. His appetite was waning by the day, and the diagnosis from the Department of Corrections doctor a week prior had sent it into a tailspin.

Glioblastoma. Six months, maybe nine at the outside, the last few of which would be spent with tubes and needles running into his body, as the State of Florida employed every available medical measure to keep him alive long enough for the attorney general to send him to the death chamber. Life was funny that way.

He thought about ending it in his cell, on his own terms, but surprised himself with his reluctance to commit the act, which he would have seen as quitting. And he had never in his life quit anything—not a sport, not an academic course of study, not the grueling Special Forces assessment and selection process. It wasn't in his nature. Neither was being an invalid, but that changed when he got shot. He figured if hanging on to the bitter end meant the

State had to wipe his ass for the last months of his life, there was a certain poetic justice to it all.

The guards came after the orderlies collected his uneaten meal. They handcuffed him to his wheelchair and pushed him along a familiar set of corridors to an even more familiar interview room where his visitor was waiting. It was him. The retired fed he was supposed to kill, but somehow missed twice, the second occasion coming on his last day on Earth as a free man. Bryce Chandler.

He was alone this time, and got right to it. "Hello, Vincent."

It was the first time anyone in the system had referred to him by his true name, and it caught him by surprise. The jail staff was still calling him Robert Petty, which meant that, whatever Chandler knew, he wasn't sharing it with his law enforcement colleagues. And that meant he wanted something. Vincent was tired of the game, and in that moment he decided to engage with his adversary, unlike their previous encounter during which he hadn't uttered a word.

"Congratulations. You must have been at the top of your class at the FBI Academy," he replied.

An expression of mild surprise registered on Bryce's face. "No more silent treatment?" he asked.

Vincent shrugged. "If you know my name, you know everything else about me, including the fact that I'm a walking dead man."

"Yeah, sorry to hear about that," Bryce replied, feigning compassion as best he could. "Feel like talking today?"

"Not really. I may be dying, but I'm not a rat."

"What if I could make it worth your while?"

Vincent scoffed. "With what? Commissary money? You think I'm going to sell out for some peanut butter crackers and instant soup?"

"Of course not, Vincent. I'd be disappointed if you did. I know you're a man who values loyalty. But I also know there's one thing in this world that matters more to you than anything, and that's your daughter."

The smugness disappeared from Vincent's face at the mention of the only person on Earth who still mattered to him. Curiosity and anger took its place. "What do you know about Shayna?" he asked, then chastised himself for letting her name slip. Maybe Chandler didn't know.

"I went to visit her in Scottsdale. Found her at your place. She's doing okay. A little better now that she at least knows what happened to you. Still, it was a lot for her to take in."

"You told her about me? Everything?"

"Only what I know. What was I supposed to do? Let her keep believing the army was sending you on secret government missions? One way or another, you're never walking out of here. She deserved the truth."

"So what are you offering?"

"Simple. You tell me everything you know about the Network. How the business operates, who's who, and where they lay their heads at night. All the jobs you've done, and any others you're aware of. In the simplest terms, I ask a question, you answer it. I catch you lying even once, the deal's off."

"I wasn't aware we had a deal."

"Right. My bad, as the kids say these days. Here's the deal: You do what I tell you, and we move you out of here to a federal facility. Better surroundings, better food, better medical care, none of which I think you give a shit about. But there's one more thing: Unlimited visitation with Shayna."

"She could just come see me here."

"Not if we talk to the sheriff and have you put on 'no visitors' status. It's easy to do, and I promise we'll do it. You'll die without ever laying eyes on her again."

Vincent smiled. "You're a heartless prick, you know that?"

Bryce shrugged. "I've been called worse. Like I said before, Vincent, this is business. We both have something the other wants, so let's put aside our personal feelings and make this work. Shayna wants to see her dad, and I'm sure the feeling is mutual. The clock's ticking."

The room fell silent as Vincent pondered his options. The look on his face was easy to read: resignation. Bryce waited for the answer he knew would come.

"When can I see Shayna?" he asked.

"She's here in the building. Let's you and me have a brief chat, then I'll give you two an hour together. If we're simpatico after that, we'll move forward with the plan."

Vincent was a different man after his visit with Shayna, relaxed and forthcoming, in some cases answering Bryce's questions more thoroughly than was necessary. For their first debriefing, Bryce only wanted a thumbnail sketch of the Network's operating strategy, an overview he could use to develop more detailed questions down the road. They talked of Sonny, the purported head of the organization.

"From what I know, he was a hit man for the mob," Vincent began. "He started out somewhere back east and then moved to Vegas. About ten years ago one of his partners got popped on a gun charge, and Sonny got all hinky about how maybe the guy was going to rat him out. So he moved, but stayed out west. Colorado, Wyoming, something like that. And he's old school. 'Never go against the family' and all that bullshit."

"Do you know Sonny's real name?"

Vincent shook his head. "I don't think anyone does."

"Did you ever meet him face to face?"

"I was too far down the ladder for that. There are only a few people in the organization who even know what he looks like. One of them is this guy named Sal, who's sort of the chief operating officer for the Network. Or a consigliere, to use the mob term. He's another one of those OG mafia types. He puts out the contracts, takes the calls from the operators whenever they finish a job, and reports to Sonny."

"Where does Sal live?"

Vincent shook his head. "Not sure. Someone said they heard him talking once about how cheap real estate was in Texas."

"How do you know all this? I thought the Network's strength was that everyone was anonymous."

Vincent laughed. "What's that old saying? 'Two can keep a secret if one of them is dead?' This is a small community. Most of us have a special operations backgrounds and know each other from our former life. And the partners are all former operators, so there's that. I mean, there's supposed to be all these firewalls between us, but in reality we gossip like a bunch of schoolgirls. Our OPSEC is shit."

"Do the lawyers know who all the players are?" Bryce asked.

"Lawyers?"

"The ones who come see you when you're locked up. Not your actual lawyer, but the one they send to make sure you behave. Aren't they also supposed to be your communications line to the Network while you're locked up?"

"Oh, those guys. No, they don't know much of anything. They're messengers, mostly. Mine brought me a note reminding me to keep my mouth shut. Asked if I had any issues that needed taking care of, anything I wanted to pass to the Network, et cetera. It was a waste of time."

"Do you remember his name?"

"It wasn't a him, it was a her. A real looker, too. Tall, blonde hair. Pretty sure it was a wig, though, or maybe a bad dye job. Her eyes and her eyebrows were dark brown. She had this buttoned up look about her, but you could tell she was smoking hot and trying to keep it under wraps. Can't say as I blame her, in a place like this."

"Did she give you a name?"

"Yeah, wait a minute." Vincent's face scrunched and he gazed toward the ceiling as he tried to remember. When it came to him, he looked back at Bryce.

"Ashley something."

Bryce's poker face held fast even as his other involuntary reflexes kicked in. A knot formed in his stomach, his heart raced, and he had to rest his hands on his legs to keep them from shaking. He tried not to get lost in the moment, to refocus on Vincent so as not to give his emotions away. Still, in those few fleeting seconds, his brain had time to process a single, horrible thought.

She knew I was going to Scottsdale.

Bryce gathered himself. "Do you remember her last name?"

Vincent scrunched his lips and shook his head slowly, the classic "I'm not really sure" response.

"It's not coming to me. Sorry."

Bryce nodded. "Was it Smith?"

"No, I don't think so."

"How about Williams? Was it Ashley Williams?"

Another head shake.

Bryce knew he had to ask, and he set his gut for the response.

"Was her last name Oliver?"

Vincent's face lit up. "Yep, that's it. Ashley Oliver. Why, do you know her?"

CHAPTER 21

BRYCE'S HEAD SPUN as he drove in silence from Miami to Marathon. Had he been played? How long had his girlfriend been working for the same organization of hired goons that sent a former Green Beret to his house to kill him? Was it before they met? Before they became intimate? Was she doing it for the money? He tuned the radio to a hard rock satellite station and tried to drown out the questions swirling around his head, but to no avail. He flipped it off and continued driving, running what-if scenarios through his mind.

It was 7:00 when he got to her condo, and her car was parked in front. He let himself in with the key she'd given him. Ashley had changed into a pair of sweatpants and a t-shirt and was sitting on the couch drinking a glass of Chardonnay when he walked in. She looked up at him and smiled.

"How was your day, babe?" she asked.

Bryce didn't respond. He walked past her to an overstuffed chair opposite the couch, sat down, and stared at the floor, waiting for the right words to start the conversation he still couldn't believe was about to occur.

Ashley's expression turned quizzical. "Bryce, what's wrong?"

He shifted his stare from the floor to her eyes. "How long?"

"What do you mean?" she asked.

"How long have you been working for them?"

"Working for who?"

He slammed his hand down on the armrest and shouted "*Them*, goddammit! You know exactly who I'm talking about!"

It was the first time he had ever raised his voice to her, and she matched his volume in her reply.

"Don't you dare swear at me! You have no idea what I've gone through for you. This isn't what you think."

Bryce took a deep breath, reined in his temper, and adjusted his tone. "Really? Tell me what I think and what it is, then."

"Listen to me. I had no choice. Some gargoyle-looking mobster came to my office and threatened me. Threatened you. He said he was with the people who sent the hit man to your house, and they'd come back and finish the job if I didn't do what he said."

"And when did you plan on telling me?"

"Never. I hoped it would all just go away. I did what they wanted, at least the part about visiting their man in jail. I had no intention of doing any of the rest of it."

"What else did they ask you to do?"

She told him about the Network's orders to report on him, his investigation, and whether he was able to flip Vincent Kamara.

"Oh, God," he moaned, with his head in his hands. He looked up at her. "How could you do this? How could you not tell me? I trusted you, Ashley, and you betrayed me."

"Whatever I did, Bryce, it wasn't betrayal. Not even close. How could you *think* that?

"Did you tell them about Scottsdale?"

She shook her head vigorously from side to side. "No."

"And I'm supposed to believe you? Two days before I left, I told you where I was going and why. When I got there, the Network had beaten me to the punch and cleaned out Vincent Kamara's safe. You're telling me you didn't tip them off?"

"That's exactly what I'm telling you."

His voice began to rise again. "If you told them, Ashley, that's obstructing justice. And if you think the fact that you're my girlfriend will keep you out of jail—"

It was her turn to be angry, and she interrupted him and screamed her retort. "How *dare* you? Did I ever, even once, press you for a piece of information? Did I ever ask you about your investigation? Everything I know, I know because you told me! I never snooped, I never pried, and I gave that goombah mother-fucker just enough information to keep him from coming back here and killing us both!"

She stormed into the bedroom and emerged a minute later with a manila envelope in her hand. She threw it into Bryce's lap, stood over him, and lowered her voice.

"There's twenty-five thousand dollars in there. That's what they paid me. And it's been sitting in my closet since the day that goon came to my office. I haven't spent a dime. So spare me the whole victim narrative, Bryce. I made the best decision I could make at the time, and I did it for your safety and mine."

He stood and dropped the envelope on Ashley's coffee table. "I'll send somebody by for that. It's evidence. Whatever your reasoning, you had plenty of time to tell me. And you should have." He walked toward the door.

"Are you leaving?" she asked. There was an incredulous tone to her question, as if she couldn't believe he was still taking a hard line.

He paused at the door and turned toward her. "Yeah." She walked toward him, and he held one hand toward her. The universal stop sign. Then he shifted his fingers so his thumb and forefinger were half an inch apart.

"I was this close," he said. His eyes were red and moist.

"To what?" she asked.

"To finally getting up the courage."

"The courage for what?"

"To move forward. To have a life with someone again. To be more than just me."

"That doesn't have to change, Bryce. We can work this out. I feel the same way." Her arms were folded across her chest, but her eyes were pleading.

In that moment, he wanted to walk across the room, wrap his arms around her, and tell her everything would be all right. Whatever she had done, they could get past it. Instead he opened the door and stepped outside. He turned back toward her and added a final comment, one he would come to regret.

"Leave me alone."

———————

Lower Keys Liquor shared space with a gas station in an RV park on the gulf side of Route 1, three miles east of the only stoplight on Big Pine Key. Bryce passed it every day, ignoring it more often than acknowledging its presence. It had been his go-to spot back in the day, when he was still reeling from the fresh scars of his divorce and forced retirement from the FBI. They knew him by name there, knew his favorites, and knew when he'd be back in for a resupply. He hadn't been inside in years, since the DUI that almost derailed his second chance at a productive life.

Sometimes the store tempted him as he passed, with its convenient drive-thru lane and ever-changing marquee out front hawking weekly specials. Today it beckoned him like a lighthouse in the fog. The special of the week was two-liter bottles of Captain Morgan for forty dollars, but as he parked in a familiar spot, he knew what he wanted. He walked inside to the surprised stare of George, the sixty-something clerk who had served him back in the day and knew his story. Bryce offered a nod as he walked past George to the whiskey aisle, where the black-label square bottles of Jack Daniel's sat, just as he remembered. He snatched a liter bottle from the shelf and walked it to the register, where George, who knew better than to ask, took his money without comment.

He almost opened it on the way home, but thought better of making himself such an obvious target for a passing sheriff's deputy. Instead he waited until the car was in the garage and he behind closed doors, away from the prying eyes of his neighbors who also knew about his hard drinking past. He plopped down in a recliner, placed the bottle opposite him on the coffee table, and stared at it.

When alcoholics are tempted, they fill their heads with competing narratives, the proverbial angel on one shoulder and the devil on another, arguing back and forth, telling the addict why he shouldn't take a drink and why he should.

Four years of sobriety, down the tubes.

It's one drink. Not the whole bottle.

Call your sponsor.

I can handle it. I just need to take the edge off.

Get to a meeting.

This will prove I can have an occasional drink and it's no big deal.

As he reached for the bottle, his phone began buzzing where he had laid it on the table. He glanced and saw the Key West number and knew it was someone in the office. Better to deal with the call before the Jack.

"Hello?"

"Bryce, it's Abbie Bishop. We just got the first round of phone dumps back on your case. I think we have something."

"Define 'something.'"

"Remember I told you we were looking for commonalities in calls made from the vicinity of your murders? Well, we found some. Actually, we found a lot. I can explain it much better in person. Can you come by in the morning? I'm at my desk by seven."

"I'll be there. Thanks." He hung up and put the phone back on the table next to the bottle. Never a believer in phenomena like divine intervention, he was still struck by the fact that Abbie's perfectly timed phone call came when it did. Of course, he knew he would have polished off the entire bottle, and morning would have found him blacked out, reeking of booze, and unable to drive to Key West, let alone spend any amount of time poring over a monotonous pile of telephone records. He picked up the bottle and walked into the kitchen with it, pausing at the sink.

Pour it out. You just dodged a major bullet.

You're not a child. You can handle adult situations. It's just a bottle of Jack, for crying out loud.

He stowed the bottle high in an unused cupboard, out of sight.

CHAPTER 22

ABBIE WAS at her desk as promised. When she saw Bryce, her eyes lit up like a mother about to watch her child unwrap a Christmas present.

"Follow me," she said, motioning for him to walk with her down a hallway and into the resident agency's conference room.

The long conference table, which could seat sixteen, was covered with folders, each with a yellow sticky note on the cover denoting the contents. There must have been forty folders in all. But what captured Bryce's attention wasn't the table, rather the windowless wall behind it. Oversized framed photographs of the president, the attorney general, and the FBI director had been removed and laid aside on the floor. In their place a massive chart, easily ten feet long by four feet high, had been duct-taped to the wall, and at first glance it resembled a map of star-filled constellations. There was a central hub with spokes poking out in all directions, and where they ended still more spokes pointing toward still more data points. There were probably three hundred points in total. It was all superimposed over a map of the United States, and after taking a moment to digest what he was seeing, Bryce realized it was a telephone link analysis chart, and an impressive one at that.

"Someone's been burning the midnight oil," he quipped as he shot Abbie an approving glance and smile.

"Team effort with the folks in Miami," she replied. "Three analysts helped me put all the data together. The printer they used is a custom-made unit that cost the Bureau a quarter million dollars."

"Amazing. I hope you can turn all this into something a non-analyst like me can understand."

"I think so. Let's start at the beginning." Abbie walked to the end of the conference table and picked up a folder. Bryce recognized the name on the sticky note: Andrew Pittman.

"Mr. Pittman was killed at his home in Fairview Park, Indiana, around five thirty in the morning. Remember, we were looking for commonalities in phone traffic in the hours before and after each of the murders, so in this case, I pulled all the cell traffic in a twenty-mile radius from five thirty a.m. the day before until five thirty the day after. Lucky for me, it's not a major metropolitan area, so I ended up with just under a hundred thousand calls processed through a hundred and thirty-five towers."

Bryce stared, incredulous. "*Just* a hundred thousand calls?"

"Oh, that's nothing. When we get to Atlanta we're in the millions. But I'm getting ahead of myself. Stay with me, this is going to take a while." She repositioned herself at the center of the chart and pointed in the direction of Indiana. "So since this was our first point of interest, there's nothing we can discern from a massive pile of cell-phone calls. We need something to compare it all against, so do me a favor and pick up the folder next to where Mr. Pittman was lying."

The name on the sticky note was even more familiar to Bryce; it was his old friend Julia Martinez. When he looked up, Abbie had repositioned herself in front of Georgia on the map.

"Like I said," she began. "Major metropolitan area, so now we're dealing with huge numbers. Ms. Martinez was also killed in the early morning hours, but not wanting to start with an unmanageable amount of data, I trimmed down both the search radius and the time frame. Still, within ten miles and six hours on either side of the murder, we got almost two million cell-tower transactions. We fed everything into the system, and within an hour we had our first hit. There was a call placed three miles from Mr. Pittman's house and another about a mile away from where Ms. Martinez was shot, both to the same number." She pointed toward south Texas. "Here. San Antonio."

"That's great!" Bryce exclaimed. "What do we know about that number? Landline? Cell phone? Exact location?"

Abbie laughed. "Slow your roll, Agent Chandler. Like I said, this is going to take some time. There's much more to it, so bear with me."

Patience wasn't Bryce's strong suit, but he knew it would serve him well to let Abbie explain it all at her own pace, so he smiled and nodded his assent.

"Moving on." She pointed toward another folder, another name Bryce knew well. Judge Wendell Branch.

"If memory serves me, the attempt on Judge Branch's life was unsuccessful?" Abbie asked.

"Correct. The judge had a pistol in his waistband and used it to kill his attacker."

"Well, that makes perfect sense, because this was one of two points of interest in your case where I couldn't find any cell traffic to our target number. My guess is these hit men were on orders to let their bosses know when a job was done, and this one never got done."

"What was the other location?" Bryce asked.

"Your house. I canvassed the cell towers from Miami to Key West, and nothing. Again, it was an aborted mission. You weren't home, and didn't the hit man end up shooting someone else and getting shot himself?"

"Right again. Vincent Kamara, a.k.a. Robert Petty, currently locked up in Miami-Dade Pre-Trial Detention Center."

Abbie nodded. "Then we move to the latest round of murders. The so-called 'Griffin Four.' Well, three of them, anyway. Alvin Donaldson, Gil Fletcher, and Jack Barclay." There were, of course, folders with each of their names on the table, and Abbie pointed toward them as she called their names and pointed toward the map, this time in the Midwest.

"Donaldson was killed here, in Adairsville, Iowa, which before a few days ago I didn't even know existed," she said. "We're not sure of the exact time of his murder, but around eleven in the morning, we have a phone call that pinged off a tower five miles from the murder site and went to our target number in San Antonio." She moved her finger down the map to the hub where all the spokes reached their termination point.

"Fletcher was killed at home in Fort Walton Beach, Florida." She gestured toward the panhandle. "Again, not sure of the exact time of death, but around nine thirty the night he died, there was a call to the target number from a tower two miles from his house.

And last but not least, Mr. Barclay, murdered in Beaufort, South Carolina. His body was discovered in the morning by a delivery driver, and the autopsy put his death around ten o'clock the previous night. Well, at a quarter to eleven, we have another call to the target in San Antonio, and this one was initiated a mile from the scene of the crime."

"So that's seven crime scenes, five of which you can link to the same number in San Antonio?" Bryce asked.

"That's only part of it," Abbie replied. "Like I said, this thing has lots of tentacles. Once I found the numbers that were calling San Antonio from our known crime scenes, I queried subscriber information for each phone. No surprises there. Every one of them was a burner phone from a low-rent, pay-as-you-go company. The kind of throwaways you buy for thirty bucks at a Walmart or a truck stop."

"So a dead end?"

"For the burner phones, probably. We could run the IMSI numbers and find out where they were sold, then send agents to the point of sale to go through hundreds of hours of video to see if a camera captured the actual purchase of the phone. Of course, that's *if* there is any video footage, and *if* it hasn't been erased or recorded over. Most retail places keep their systems on a loop that records over itself every week or so. It's not even a needle in a haystack; it's a near impossibility."

"Agreed. But what about the target number in San Antonio? Another burner?"

Abbie shook her head. "No, that's where the good news starts. Believe it or not, it's a landline. Registered to a business, McNair Industries. Service was established four years ago. The billing address is all that's listed in the publicly accessible records, and it's a PO box. So we sent an emergency subpoena to the phone company for the physical service address, and they complied. It's all in there, along with everything I could find on the company." She pointed to the thickest of the folders on the table. Bryce picked it up and thumbed through the contents.

There were two reports on McNair Industries. The first was from a commercial operation that gathered data on corporations and sold it to their clients. The second was from the Texas Secretary of State's office. Both contained the same information. The company had been established and incorporated in San Antonio in 2014. Under "Business Type" was the vague and somewhat confusing description, "International Shipping and Third-Party Fulfillment Services." The most recent available revenue statement showed annual earnings of $10.6 million, and the principal was listed as one Salvatore Pinti.

Bryce looked up from the folder in Abbie's direction. "It makes sense, right? The landline? I mean, the hit men could use burners, but they needed a constant, reliable number to call when they needed to contact the Network. One that wouldn't change week to week, or day to day."

Abbie nodded. "Unless somebody did a comprehensive analysis like we just did, they'd never see anything suspicious about McNair Industries. It was a perfect cover. One of a million boring, nondescript companies engaged in a business nobody cares about."

"Speaking of that, what do you make of the business description? What exactly does a third-party fulfillment company do?"

"Let's say you're a toy manufacturer in Hong Kong and you want to sell your stuff here in the States. So there are a few dozen retailers who want your merchandise on their shelves, but you only make the toys; you don't have a logistics and shipping operation to get them to the retailers. A third-party fulfillment operation does that for you. They arrange warehousing, overseas shipping, customs clearance, and transportation through the US supply chain to the end customer. Some of these fulfillment companies do it with their own infrastructure, meaning they own the ships, the trucks, and the supply hub warehouses. But most do it as brokers, arranging all the services with existing shipping companies. They own nothing other than the business contacts between the manufacturer and the customer. They're just a paper enterprise. And my guess is McNair Industries is structured to operate as the latter rather than the former."

"Because it's the perfect setup for a shell company to launder money, right?" Bryce asked. "Generate a bunch of dummy invoices, bills of lading, et cetera, and pay yourself with the ill-gotten gains, which in this case are the fees they're charging their clients to carry out their hit jobs. Then you're free to use the cleaned-up money to pay your contractors. Simple yet brilliant. And like you said, boring as hell."

Abbie nodded. "To the casual observer, there's no way to know McNair Industries is anything but legitimate. Even though we're pretty sure they're the front for the Network, we don't have enough to prove anything in court, at least not at the moment."

"Vincent Kamara mentioned this Pinti guy during our interview. Do you have anything on him?" Bryce asked. He knew in an instant it was a foolish question. Abbie pointed toward a folder with his name on it. Bryce picked it up, opened it, and commented aloud as he read.

"Interesting record. Agg assault and a dope charge. That's it?" There was a copy of Sal's Texas driver's license in the file. "Looks like a character straight out of *Goodfellas*. Do we have a location on him?"

"The address on his driver's license and the business address for McNair Industries are one and the same. It's a two-story house in an upper-middle-class neighborhood just outside Loop 410. That's the interstate that circles San Antonio, sort of like the Capital Beltway. He bought it for seven hundred thousand dollars in 2014, the same year McNair Industries was incorporated, and paid it off in 2019." She handed him yet another folder as she spoke. Bryce opened it and was greeted by a Google Maps street view photo of the front of the house. Flipping through the contents, he saw the most recent tax assessment, utility bills, and an aerial shot from an unknown source. He reminded himself to never question Abbie Bishop's thoroughness.

Bryce closed the folder and put it down, then made a gesture toward the remaining ones taking up most of the space on the table. "What's all this?" he asked.

"I was wondering when you were going to ask. Once I had the target number in San Antonio, I reversed the process and ran sixty days' worth of call records for that phone. To say the results were interesting would be an understatement."

"How so?"

"Well, for starters, there wasn't a single outgoing call placed from the target phone."

"So that all but confirms our theory that it's not a legitimate business phone. More like a check-in line for the hit men once they finished a job, so Salvatore Pinti could keep track of the Network's activity."

"My thoughts exactly," Abbie said. "And if my next guess is correct, we've only scratched the surface of the murders these people have committed. Over that sixty-day span, there were thirty more calls, all from burners, to the target number. No two calls were from the same number. And so far I've found news stories about murders on the same day and in the general vicinity of three of those calls. I'm still looking, but I ran out of time before our meeting today."

"What you've done is amazing, Abbie. I can't thank you enough."

"My pleasure. Bryce, do you think Salvatore Pinti could be Sonny?"

Bryce thought for a moment. "My gut says no. From what we know about Sonny, he's very secretive. I can't imagine him using his actual name to buy a house and set up a business. Also, Vincent Kamara heard Sonny was living somewhere in either Colorado or Wyoming, and he mentioned something about Pinti living in Texas. If Sonny is really the head of the Network, it's more likely Pinti works for him."

"So what's next?" she asked.

"We have enough for a search warrant of McNair Industries, or Salvatore Pinti's house, whatever we're going to call it. I'll bring Donnie into the loop on everything, and he can have the affidavit drawn up. And I'm going to pack a bag for San Antonio."

CHAPTER 23

SAL'S WIFE KNOCKED on the door to his office, where he was taking a nap in his recliner. There had been a welcome respite in Network business, and with Norma Whitehurst under FBI lock and key, he didn't have to worry about eliminating the last of the Griffin Four. Even Sonny had acquiesced to reason and seen the foolhardiness of trying to take out such a hard target.

"There's a call for you on the main line," she said as she cracked the door open. "Ashley Oliver. Says it's important."

"I'll take it in here. Close the door behind you." He moved from the recliner to his desk and picked up the receiver.

"Ms. Oliver, how can I help you?" he began.

"He knows."

"Who knows what?"

"You know who. Bryce. He confronted me in my apartment. I don't know how he found out, but he did."

"And what did you tell him?"

"I admitted to it. I told him I visited your guy in jail, took him the envelope, and told him I was his communications link to you and your people if he needed one."

"I thought I was clear, Ms. Oliver. You weren't to tell Mr. Chandler anything about our conversation."

"Are you listening to me? He already *knew*! Your guy must have told him. He walked in here and lost his mind over it."

"So what's the point of this call, then?"

"To tell you we're through. Don't call me. Don't come back here. Don't come anywhere near me or Bryce ever again, or you're going to regret it."

"Are you threatening me, Ms. Oliver?"

"You're goddamned right I am. I told you, I used to deal with scumbags like you when I first started practicing law. So I took precautions. I have your fat fucking Guido face on video, and the license plate of the car you drove to my office. Mess with me and it gets released to the authorities and the media. I'll tell them everything I know about you, and what you made me do. I'm serious. Leave me alone."

"Ms. Oliver, I strongly recommend you reconsider your present line of thinking. This isn't good for anyone."

"Go to hell." The line went dead.

Sal returned to his recliner, leaned back, and closed his eyes. He could feel the headache coming on. A worry-free day had turned anything but, and now he had to call the boss with the latest development from South Florida.

Sonny sounded annoyed when he answered the phone, and his terse greeting confirmed his mood.

"What is it?"

Sal filled him in on the details of Ashley Oliver's call.

"Dammit, Sal, I told you not to handle that one yourself. You think she's bluffing?"

"I don't know. And I didn't see any video cameras, but the way they make them these days it could have been hidden anywhere. Sonny, if she's got a clear picture of my face—"

There was a long silence while Sonny pondered his con-sigliere's dilemma. Finally, the boss replied.

"If she's not bullshitting, you're cooked. But taking her out opens up a whole other can of worms. You said the boyfriend knows. And he's back on active duty with the FBI. So even if they're splitsville, he's still going to know who did it and why. And that picture of you will be in every FBI office from New York to Los Angeles. Is that what you want?"

"Of course not. I'm just trying to weigh my options here. I was hoping for some guidance."

"You want my opinion? It sounds like if you leave her alone, she'll return the favor. But if you do take action, there can't be a body. She has to disappear. At the end of the day, Sal, it's your call. But whatever you decide, you make sure it doesn't come back to me or any of the partners. China shop rules here: You break it, you own it. Capisce?"

"Understood."

"One final thing. Does the girl know anything about me?"

"I can't see how she would. And even if she follows through on her threat, you know I'd never turn on you."

"Of course, Sal. But just to be safe, whatever you decide to do, I don't want to know about it. And we never had this conversation."

"Got it, Sonny."

After they hung up, Sal pondered his options. He thought about the assurances he gave Sonny, and in a moment of self-re-flection he wondered if he really meant it. Would he go back to prison for the rest of his life to protect his boss, or anyone else in the Network for that matter? It sounded noble when he said it, but he was getting on in years, and the thought of dying in a concrete cell wasn't as romantic as the wise guys made it sound when they took their vows of silence.

There was no way to know if Ashley would carry through on her threat, and only one way to make sure she didn't. She had left him no choice.

CHAPTER 24

SAL PINTI WASN'T the only issue on Sonny's plate. Frank had been blowing up his phone, and he knew why. They had been over and over the Norma Whitehurst matter, and the senator didn't want to take no for answer. They were at an impasse. Sonny dialed the number, let it go to voicemail, and waited for the return call. He knew Frank needed to separate himself from whoever was nearby before he could talk on this phone.

The call came ten minutes later. "Where have you been?" Frank asked. "I've called you five times this week."

"Yeah," Sonny replied. "And I know what for, and we've been over it, and it's not happening. End of story."

"We had an agreement. Every step along the way, I've honored my end. And you're backing out on me with one left to go?"

"That last one is inaccessible. It would be a suicide mission. Not one of my men would take this job. And I don't blame them."

"Goddammit, Tommy. I have 17 percent heading into Iowa next week. In a seven-man field. Do you understand what that means? You could be talking to the next president of the United States, and that miserable old bitch can ruin it all for me. I need this done."

"Then find someone dumb enough to do it, or at least to try. You and I are done doing business, little brother."

"You sanctimonious little shit. Do you have any idea who you're talking to? I can expose you and everyone you work with. And I can do it without implicating myself. I write the checks for Justice, Homeland Security—all of it. You'd better rethink that attitude of yours."

"What did you just say to me?"

"You heard every word."

"Yeah, I did. And I'm wondering if you remember anything our father taught us about blood. About family. About loyalty. Do those words mean anything to you anymore?"

"Piss off, Tommy. That was always your thing, not mine. You grew up to be a thug just like Dad, and look where it got him. I got out of that house as soon as I could and never went back."

"You sure did. And you cleaned up nicely. Changed your name, even. And now you think you're better than me. Do you remember Billy Francis from down the block? He was a couple years ahead of you in school."

"I don't have time for a trip down memory lane, Tommy."

"Too bad. Anyway, Billy's parents were poor as church mice, and one day he asks me to steal a candy bar for him from the corner store. So I did. The next day, he asks me again, and I do it again. This goes on for a couple weeks."

"What's your point?" Frank asked.

"I'm getting there. Anyway, after a while, he's asking for a candy bar every day, and finally I says to him, 'Why don't you go in there and steal one yourself?' And do you know what that slimy little piece of shit tells me?"

"No, what?"

"He looks me right in the eye, and says, 'Because I'm not a

thief.' Just like that. Except he says it all snooty like, with this air of superiority. Like the way you've made yourself out to be. And would you like to know what I did then?"

"Not really."

"I busted him square in the nose. And when he went down, I hit him a few more times. In the face, in the stomach. Then I stood up, kicked him in the nuts, and told him, 'If you ever ask me for another candy bar, I'll kill you.'"

"And the moral of your story?" Frank asked.

"I know what I am, Frank. I own it. And I make no apologies for it, unlike you. You abandoned your family, your name, your entire identity and traded it for three-thousand-dollar suits and a fancy title. And then you sit there, all high and mighty, and pretend you don't have blood on your hands because you got someone else to do your dirty work. You may have the rest of the world snowed, but not me."

"Watch your back, talking like that. I'm not fucking around," Frank hissed. "If I go down, you go with me."

"Yeah, I heard you. Impressive resume. And for what it's worth, you should know I would never give up what I know about you. That's not how I operate. But you've forgotten what I do for a living. And if you think our blood relationship gives you the right to talk to me like that, you're dumber than I thought. You just threatened the wrong man."

———————

Fifteen miles away from Frank D'Angelo's office, the wire room of the FBI's Washington field office came to life. There were four agents in the darkened, windowless space at a time, each assigned to monitor one of the senator's telephones. Most of the traffic was routine and boring, everything from legislative wrangling to Mrs. D'Angelo reminding her husband of their upcoming social engagements.

They had been up on the wire for almost a week, ever since the FBI had managed to flip Frank's assistant, Stella, who had finally had enough of the harassment. She gave up everything, from his government and personal cell-phone numbers to his daily planner. She kept track of who came and went from his office and when he excused himself to take private calls or otherwise distance himself from the reporting requirements of the official calendar every senator's staff was required to keep. She even offered to wear a body recorder around him, though Donnie nixed that idea, figuring the senator would be reluctant to discuss illegal matters in front of his assistant.

The agents had adopted Stella's use of the term Bat Phone, and a picture of the iconic prop from the sixties television show was taped to the wall above the computer that recorded its activity. When a call came in, agents had thirty seconds to listen in and determine if the conversation they were eavesdropping on was related to illegal activity. Having read the affidavit for the wiretap and knowing full well the particulars surrounding the Griffin Four, they knew the threat-filled dialogue between Frank and Sonny was a pertinent call, and they had to notify the supervising case agent.

Donnie was in his Atlanta office, tending to the day's administrative chores, when the call came from Washington. He glanced at the screen on his desk phone, saw the 202 area code, and knew it was either Sullivan Caine or the DC field office calling. He hoped for the latter, and his hope was rewarded.

"Donnie Morris."

"Good afternoon, Mr. Morris," the voice on the other end answered. Donnie figured it must have been a new agent, as it was overly formal among agents to address a first-level supervisor by anything other than his first name.

"Donnie. To whom do I owe the pleasure?"

"Special Agent Thad Dekker in WFO, sir. We just had a pertinent call on one of the personal cell phones. The one they call the Bat Phone."

"Incoming or outgoing?"

"There was an outgoing call that went to voicemail on the receiving end. Then, about ten minutes later, that number called the senator back and they spoke for about three minutes."

"What did they talk about?"

"If you'll hold on, I'll play it for you." Agent Dekker queued up the call, transferred it to the hardline he was sharing with Donnie, and pushed Play. A minute later, Donnie was scribbling notes on a legal pad in a tortured handwriting only he would be able to decipher:

Sonny???
they know where Norma is
FD wants Sonny to finish the job
Sonny won't do it
little brother/blood relationship
FD/Sonny=brothers?
threats/FD will expose Sonny
Sonny's going to kill FD

"Mr. Morris? You still there?"

"I am, just writing down a few things. How soon can you get me a copy of that call?"

"As soon as I download it from the computer, burn the case copy of the CD, and log it into evidence," Agent Dekker replied.

"Perfect. And what do we know about the other telephone number?"

"It's from a 703 area code, which is Northern Virginia. But it looks like a voice over internet protocol, or VOIP line. If it is, the caller could have taken several different steps to spoof his number and make it look like it's coming from somewhere other than his actual location. The tech guys will have to work on this one with the phone company and internet service providers to see if we can locate him. That can take a while."

"I understand. As soon as you're done logging the call into evidence, get me a copy over my bureau email, please."

"Will do, sir."

CHAPTER 25

IT TOOK THREE DAYS to write the affidavit for the search warrant, then another twenty-four hours to amend it with the information from Sonny's call to Frank D'Angelo. Everyone, including Bryce, Donnie, and the entire command structure at FBI headquarters, was convinced of several facts: First, that they had located the Network's nerve center in an affluent swim/tennis neighborhood in San Antonio, and that a former mob leg-breaker named Salvatore Pinti was running the show, at least at that location. A dispute broke out among several supervisors and senior executives as to whether Sonny and Sal were one and the same, and after a few contentious meetings and teleconferences, Donnie was able to make everyone see it his way. It would have been an even harder sell if Assistant Director Sullivan Caine had been involved, but fate had intervened disguised as death, and he was instead using several personal days to tend to the final arrangements for his mother in Orlando.

One thing everyone agreed with was the fact that Frank D'Angelo was dirty. They had him dead to rights for interstate solicitation of murder, but the Griffin disaster was the big prize, the one that would send him away for life and grant closure to the families he had destroyed and from whom he had so richly profited. It was imperative they get Norma Whitehurst in front of a grand jury and gather whatever evidence they could to support her testimony before indicting and issuing an arrest warrant for the senator. The sticky point was the presidential race, where he was now a bona fide contender. They needed to move carefully, but with a sense of urgency. Nobody wanted to arrest a candidate on the cusp of becoming his party's nominee, or even worse, the president-elect.

It wasn't well known to the general public that Frank D'Angelo was born Frank Costello, but neither was it hard to research, and the team of analysts at the Washington field office had built a Costello family tree and added it to the investigative file. Frank was born the second of two sons in 1961 to Thomas Costello Sr. and his wife Marie. Their eldest, Thomas Costello Jr., was four years senior to Frank and six years older than the baby of the family, Theresa Costello, now Theresa Moore. Frank legally changed his name to match his mother's maiden name, D'Angelo, after graduating from the Syracuse University College of Law in 1985.

Thomas Jr. had a string of arrests in and around Philadelphia from 1974 to 1981, mostly for low-level mob-related activities including misdemeanor assault and running a gambling operation. Then something odd happened—he disappeared. The arrest record screeched to a halt, and his last known address was the house he shared with his parents when he graduated from high school. Nationwide, there were no employment records, no rental or mortgage transactions, no phone numbers listed in his name. It was as if Thomas Costello Jr. ceased to exist.

The dead end of T.J. Costello's existence coincided with one of the most notorious and brazen mob hits in Philadelphia's history. According to sources close to the investigation, a ski-masked gunman entered Giovanni's Pizzeria in broad daylight, walked straight to the table of Michael "Mikey Suits" Castricone, started shooting, and didn't stop until Mikey, his wife, and one of his soldiers were dead. Castricone was an up-and-coming capo in Nicky Scarfo's outfit, and had earned the ire of several of the larger and more powerful New York families by pushing heroin on their territory. The word was that New York hired out-of-town muscle to pull off the hit, which meant nobody associated with the Big Apple. Word also was that they contracted a Philly associate to do the job, and suspicion fell quickly to T.J., who was already making a name for himself in the murder trade at the ripe old age of twenty-four. When he went off the grid, the suspicions were confirmed, at least among the upper echelons of the Scarfo family. Unable to exact revenge on Mikey Suits's killer, they took the next logical step, and Thomas Costello Sr. was found floating face down in the Delaware River a week after the bloodbath at Giovanni's.

While nobody knew what name he was currently using, another agreed upon fact was that Sonny was the man formerly known as Thomas Costello Jr. Finally, everyone agreed the best chance of finding Sonny was to search the house of the only member of the Network (other than Vincent Kamara) the FBI had been able to identify to date.

United States Magistrate Court Judge Dennis Hagy saw it all the same way, and signed the search warrant without so much as a question for the prosecutor who presented it to him in chambers. An hour later, a PDF copy was in the waiting hands of Bryce Chandler in San Antonio.

CHAPTER 26

THAT THE FBI San Antonio SWAT team was unavailable was of little concern for Bryce. Ironically, the team had been tasked to support the Secret Service with a security detail for a presidential candidate stumping in nearby Austin (the candidate was not Frank D'Angelo, which would have elevated the irony to epic levels.) It meant executing the search warrant on Sal Pinti's house without the benefit of the FBI's most imposing and lethal tactical force, but as Bryce and the team assigned to support him had decades of experience confronting armed and dangerous subjects, he was confident as he briefed the plan to his team one last time.

There were a dozen of them, all dressed in street clothes and olive-drab ballistic protective vests emblazoned with bright yellow FBI patches. Glock .40-caliber pistols rode low on their hips in black nylon tactical rigs. Three carried M4 rifles and would be the first to enter the home. They were required to knock and announce their presence, but assuming Pinti didn't meet them at the door in ten seconds or less, their entry would be facilitated by the team's largest member. He was a muscular, twenty-five-year-old newbie who five years earlier had played defensive tackle for the University of Alabama. In his massive hands he held a thirty-five-pound battering ram that, if properly wielded, would make short work of most residential entry doors.

The warrant also required they wait until daytime hours to begin, which was recognized by the courts as 6:00 a.m. At 5:45 they conducted one last equipment check, mounted their vehicles, and prepared to depart the staging area, a Whataburger parking lot about two miles from the target location.

At 5:57, they rolled through the ritzy subdivision's security gate, having pre-arranged access with the private security company the day before. The sun had not yet broken the horizon, and they switched their lights off on Bryce's command as they came within a block of Pinti's house. The six-car caravan came to a stop two houses shy of the target, and the agents dismounted and moved toward their predetermined locations in the "stack" outside the front door.

At 5:59, Bryce knocked gently on the door, a massive double-hung unit made of stained oak, black wrought iron, and windows of intricate leaded glass. As he knocked, he issued the required announcement—"FBI, search warrant"—at a decibel level barely louder than that of an ordinary conversation. The rules said he had to knock and announce. They did not say how loud or vociferous his warnings needed to be, and he had no intention of giving advance notice of his presence to a hardened killer. For a fleeting moment, the thought of destroying such a beautiful and expensive piece of art gave him a twinge of remorse. But it was gone as quickly as it came, and he motioned for the breacher to move forward and do his job. It took three strikes to the commercial grade lockset and deadbolt, but on the third, one of the doors gave way and swung inward on its hinges, creating the hole Bryce's team needed.

The first of the riflemen plucked a flash-bang grenade from his vest, pulled the pin, and held it high for the rest of the team to see. The message was clear: Don't go inside until this goes off. He tossed it into the foyer, and three seconds later a blinding light and thunderous explosion ripped through the home and shattered windows on either side of the broken entry door. They piled through the opening—the riflemen first, followed by Bryce and the remainder of the team—and split into two-man teams to clear the first and second floors. Per the plan, Bryce joined with the three M4 carriers to search the upstairs, where the master bedroom was located.

The announcements were purposeful and loud now, and the agents screamed "FBI! Search warrant!" at the top of their lungs as they made their way through the home. At the second floor landing, Bryce and his three teammates split left and right, two in each direction. There were two doors on each side of the hallway, and he heard the team behind him kick the first of theirs in and call out "Clear!" three seconds later. Bryce and his partner moved forward, breaching the first door in their path, clearing the room, and making their declaration for the others to hear. The two teams hit their final doors at the same time, and as soon as Bryce kicked theirs in, he found himself face to face with Sal Pinti, who was sitting up in bed and pointing a pistol straight at him.

The time for warnings had passed. Bryce already had his pistol at chest level, and in a single motion he raised it, acquired Sal in his sights, and pulled the trigger. As he fired, both Sal and Bryce's partner followed suit. Sal's nine-millimeter round struck Bryce in the center of his chest, where it did no damage other than to the fabric of his ballistic vest. His second shot went wide, and he would fire no more. Bryce and his partner each fired two rounds center-mass into Sal's chest, and another for good measure into his head; the oft-trained "failure to stop" drill every agent knew well.

In the adrenaline-filled moment, the pair almost didn't see the movement under the covers in the bed, next to where Sal now lay dead. There was the muffled sound of whimpering, and Bryce gave the command: "FBI! Show me your hands!" as they trained their weapons on the mystery mass under the blanket, lest there be another shooter lying in wait. A pair of small shaking hands emerged, and Bryce moved forward, grabbing one of them by the wrist and pulling Sal's nightgown-clad widow to the floor, where he handcuffed her.

The other upstairs team was in the room with them by now, and they searched and cleared the master bathroom and closet. The dazed wife was taken downstairs, and Bryce called the San Antonio ASAC to let him know the scene was secure, all the FBI employees were safe, and the subject was dead. Within hours, the house would be swarming with an evidence response team and the San Antonio office brass, and by the next day there would be an FBI headquarters shooting review team on site. Bryce didn't feel like dealing with any of them, so he knew he needed to move with a purpose. He gathered the team in the home's kitchen, leaving one member behind with Mrs. Pinti in the living room.

"Good job, everyone," he began. "I can't go into details about what happened upstairs, because the first thing OPR is going to ask us all is if we discussed the shooting with each other. So let's just leave that alone."

He continued, "The reason we're here is to dismantle the Network. We also want to find the leader of the organization, this so-called 'Sonny' character. I think Salvatore Pinti knew him well, but unfortunately we can't talk to him anymore. So while we're searching for evidence related to how the Network conducts its business, be alert for anything that mentions Sonny, or a boss, or anything like that. Split up into two-man teams and get going."

He walked into the living room, where Mrs. Pinti was seated on the sofa and wrapped in a blanket, her hands still cuffed behind her. She appeared catatonic. Bryce pulled a chair opposite her and drew his face close to hers.

"Mrs. Pinti, can you hear me?"

She stared past him and said nothing.

"I'm Bryce Chandler, with the FBI. Do you know why I'm here?"

Her eyes darted around and settled on his. "No. Is Sal dead?"

"I'm sorry, ma'am, but he is. We have a warrant to search your home, and when we entered your bedroom he shot at us. We had no choice."

"Why are you here?"

"Your husband worked for an organization that committed a number of crimes, including interstate murder for hire. Are you telling me you didn't know about that?"

She shook her head. "All I know about is McNair Industries."

"Tell me what you know about that."

"There's a phone in his office. If it rings and he's not there, I'm supposed to answer it. McNair Industries. If they ask for Mr. Jackson, I put the phone on hold and go get him. If he's not here I take a message. If they ask for anyone or anything else, I tell them they have the wrong number and hang up." She rattled off the instructions as if they had been drilled into her head.

"And where is his office?"

"The door past the powder room, on the right," she said, still in a daze. "Am I under arrest?"

"Not right now, ma'am. Could you stand up for me, please?"

She did as she was asked, and Bryce moved her a few steps away from the couch. He turned toward the agent who had been assigned to watch her.

"Did you check the couch before you sat her down?" he asked. The agent nodded.

"Turn around, Mrs. Pinti. I'm going to take those cuffs off, and they'll stay off as long as you behave. Do you understand?"

"Yes."

"Can we get you something from the kitchen?"

"A cup of coffee. There's a Keurig on the counter."

Bryce nodded toward the junior agent, who shot him a disapproving glance. Bryce walked toward him and lowered his voice to a near whisper.

"She's cooperating. Now go get the woman a cup of coffee." His glare and tone told the rookie this was no time to quibble. He turned back toward Mrs. Pinti.

"How do you take it?"

"Black is fine."

Bryce jerked his head toward the kitchen and the agent slunk away. He guided Mrs. Pinti back to the couch and took his seat again.

"What's going to happen to me?" she asked. As she spoke, she reached up with one hand and massaged the right side of her face. Bryce hadn't seen it before but now took notice: It was a bruise, almost healed, stretching from just underneath her eye socket to her cheekbone.

"Did Mr. Pinti do that to you?"

She nodded. It was at this point Bryce realized something else: She had yet to shed a tear. She was dazed. She was in shock. But she wasn't in mourning for her deceased husband. Most importantly, she was talking.

"Mrs. Pinti…"

"Claire."

"Claire, did you have any idea that McNair Industries was a front for something else, something illegal?"

"I had my suspicions. I'm not stupid." She paused and stared at the floor. "On second thought, I let Sal abuse me for twenty years, so maybe I am."

Bryce resisted the urge to console her. "Did you ever meet anyone named Sonny?"

"No, but Sal talked about him all the time. Like Sonny was his boss. I do know Sal got into some legal trouble years back, and Sonny got him out of it."

"Do you know what kind of trouble it was?"

She shook her head. "No."

"Did Sal ever travel without you?"

"Some. He went to Las Vegas a lot in the early years of our marriage, back in the 2000s. Then he stopped. There was one trip about six months ago that was strange."

"Strange how?"

"Sal just kept saying he'd been summoned. He said he had to go kiss the ring. But he never said what it meant."

"Did you ask him?"

"You saw this, right?" she said, pointing to the bruise on her face. "I stopped asking Sal about his business years ago."

"Do you remember where he went?" Bryce asked.

"If memory serves, Denver. I took him to the airport and picked him up when he came back. He was only gone overnight."

"Did he say anything about where he was staying in Denver?"

"No. I don't even know if that's where he stayed. I only know that's where he flew to."

"Do you know if Sal had a favorite hotel chain or rental car company?"

"He was a Marriott guy. As for rental cars, he hated them. Said you never knew what some lowlife had been using them for. Sal always took taxis, and in the last couple years he fell in love with those rideshare apps."

"You mean like Uber?"

"That's right. Sal used to say it was the greatest invention of the twenty-first century."

"Where is Sal's phone?" Bryce asked.

"It should be on the nightstand charging. Right next to where you shot him."

CHAPTER 27

SINCE THE ADVENT of the smart phone in 2007, courts had been forced to adapt to a changing legal landscape. More and more people used phones to store their most important and private data. As a result, the phone began to be viewed as more sacrosanct than the original subject of the Fourth Amendment, the home itself. It wasn't long before judges required separate warrants for cell phones found during the search of a subject's house.

But if the owner of the cell phone was dead, that simplified matters. Dead men couldn't claim constitutional protection from warrantless searches, and neither could third parties, who lacked legal standing to mount a court challenge. With nobody to question the manner in which it was seized and searched, Sal Pinti's cell phone was fair game for Bryce Chandler and the FBI.

He chose George Clancy, one of the senior agents on his team, to accompany him back upstairs to the bedroom where Sal Pinti lay dead. While some things may have changed regarding search warrants during Bryce's tenure in the FBI, one thing did not—it was always best to have a second person with you if you felt you might find something a prosecutor would have to present to a jury one day. To nobody's surprise, Sal was where they'd left him, with four well-placed holes in his chest and two more in his face and forehead. The back of his head had come to rest against the headboard, but judging from the blood spatter on the wall behind him, the exit wound from the M4 rifle headshot was significant. He had only been dead a half hour, but already his face had begun to take on a grayish hue as blood drained to the lower parts of his body.

The cell phone was on the nightstand as Claire had said. It was an iPhone, and as there was no fingerprint sensor, Bryce knew it was a model ten or newer, meaning it would rely on facial recognition or a PIN code to unlock the device. He donned a pair of gloves, picked it up, touched the screen, and swiped upward to wake the phone. As expected, the face-ID command flashed for a second or two, then the passcode screen appeared with a blank six-digit display above the keypad.

"You think this will work?" Bryce asked.

"I don't know, man. His face is pretty screwed up. And his eyes are closed," George replied.

"Well, we can fix the eyes." Bryce reached forward with a gloved hand and used his forefinger and thumb to open the dead man's eyes. He woke the phone up again, placed it in front of Sal's face, then turned it toward himself to view the results. The phone reported back: *Swipe up for face ID or enter password*. No dice.

"His right cheekbone is obliterated, and his jaw is all out of whack," George observed, pointing as he spoke. "I don't think we can fix the upper part of his face, but maybe if we get his mouth back in line it would help." Bryce took hold of Sal's lower jaw and manipulated it into position so that his mouth was no longer agape. In doing so, he forced a macabre smile onto the corpse's face, and it was enough to make George laugh out loud.

"Oh my god, this is some of the most messed-up shit I've ever seen," he chortled as Bryce read the same message on the iPhone for a second time.

Bryce never looked away from Sal Pinti's corpse as he delivered his terse reply. "Well, you haven't seen much then. I think the head shot is playing with the facial recognition feature," Bryce said. "Look in his closet and see if he's got a hat, like a baseball cap."

"I don't think it's a good idea to move him around, Bryce."

"We're not going to move him. I just want to place the hat on his head so it hides the entry wound. Go see what you can find."

George emerged from the closet a minute later with a hat emblazoned with the logo of the San Antonio Missions, the double-A minor-league affiliate of the San Diego Padres. Bryce undid the Velcro adjustment strap at the back to make the cap as loose as possible and used it to cover the bullet wound on Sal's forehead. George began laughing again.

"What is it this time?" Bryce asked. He was getting annoyed.

"Seriously, dude, this is like a scene out of *Weekend at Bernie's*. I mean, look at him in that hat, with that goofy smile. If the left side of his face wasn't caved in, he could be just another drunk on the Riverwalk."

The iPhone still wasn't having any of it, and displayed the failure message a third time.

Bryce relented. "We're not going to beat the facial recognition feature. Put the hat back where you found it and let's go talk to the wife. Is anyone on the team a tech agent?" Technically trained agents, or TTAs, were FBI agents who, as their title implied, specialized in all things electronic, including placing and monitoring bugs and wiretaps, rigging tracking devices into vehicles, and breaking into telephones.

"Rudy Robles is on the tech squad," George answered.

"Good. Have him come talk to me and the wife."

Bryce took the phone with him as he rejoined Claire in the living room. Rudy swapped places with George and became Bryce's new partner.

"Claire, did Sal ever share his passwords with you? Specifically for his cell phone. Do you know his six-digit PIN?" Bryce asked.

She didn't answer, just shook her head with a look that said, *You're kidding, right?*

Bryce pulled Rudy to the side. "Do you have anything back at the office that can get us into this phone?"

Rudy shook his head. "We used to have something called the forensic retrieval device, or FRED for short. Every field office had one. But then some idiot stole one from the Columbia division a couple years ago, and headquarters decided we weren't responsible enough to have such a sensitive piece of equipment in the field. So they're all at Quantico now, and that's where we would have to send this phone."

"How long does that take?"

"Depending on the urgency and what's in line ahead of you, a couple days to a week. Plus the time to get it up there."

Bryce shook his head. "We don't have that long. Sal Pinti was Sonny's right-hand man, and if he can't get ahold of him, it might spook him enough to run. We need to do what we can right here and right now. In your experience, what are the most likely sets of numbers that people use for passwords?"

"Birthdays and anniversaries. But not always their own. Could be a family member's special day. And before you start plugging numbers into that phone all willy-nilly, remember that Apple gives you ten tries to unlock one of their phones, and then it really locks up, even if you're the owner."

"So can they still unlock it at Quantico if we exceed the limit?"

"Oh, sure. FRED operates on a whole other level than the user-level security functions Apple built into their phones. They'll get in."

"So really, there's no harm in us trying here and now."

Rudy shrugged. "I guess that's true."

They returned to Claire Pinti in the living room, where Bryce began the interrogation.

"What was Sal's birthday?" he asked, only at the end of his question realizing the significance of phrasing it in the past tense.

"December 12, 1956," Claire answered.

Bryce tried 1-2-1-2-5-6 to no avail.

"And your birthday?"

"March 9, 1960."

0-3-0-9-6-0 met with an identical result.

"Do either of you have children?"

"No."

"Anniversary?"

"February 20, 2002."

There was still no progress, nor with either of Sal's parents' birthdays. With five attempts down, the phone was now displaying the warning of how many attempts were remaining before lockdown.

"I don't suppose Sal would have been this obvious, but what do we have to lose?" Bryce mused as he typed 1-2-3-4-5-6 into the keypad. Another failure. Four attempts remaining.

"It's not always a number per se," Rudy offered. "Sometimes it's a word, and the corresponding numbers from the word on the phone keypad."

Bryce's eyes lit up. "There are six letters in 'Claire.' How about we start there?"

"I'd be surprised," Claire said. "Sal wasn't sentimental that way."

"Still, let's give it a try." Bryce typed 2-5-2-4-7-3. Three attempts remaining.

"Sorry, but I told you so. That son of a bitch loved his dog more than me," Claire said, motioning toward an urn on the fireplace mantel. "I guarantee you if I had gone first, I wouldn't have rated a place of honor like that."

"What was the dog's name?" Bryce asked.

"Travis. Sal named him after some lowlife he was locked up with back in the nineties. He said this Travis guy saved his life. How, I don't know. But for some reason Sal held him in high regard."

It took everything Bryce had not to react to the mention of Travis Conway, and he hoped the involuntary shock making his head spin wasn't reflected on his face. He took a moment to gather himself, then typed 8-7-2-8-4-7.

The phone came to life, and Bryce shook his head. A strange day indeed.

"You said you took your husband to the airport six months ago? And he flew to Denver?"

Claire nodded.

"Do you remember what airline he flew?"

"No."

Bryce thumbed through Sal's phone, where he found the apps for all the major airlines and a few minor ones.

"The most likely candidate is United," Rudy said. "Denver's their hub and they have a bunch of direct flights out of San Antonio daily."

Bryce opened the phone's email application and entered "Denver flight" in the search bar. There was a confirmation from United Airlines from six months prior for a round-trip flight from San Antonio to Denver, with a return the following day. There were also two emailed receipts from Uber for the day of the outbound and return flights, but there was no information on the destination.

"If you go to the app, the ride info should be in there," Rudy offered.

The Uber app, of course, required a login and password.

"I don't suppose you know your husband's email address?" Bryce asked.

"Actually, there I can help you. It's Salvatore1956@aol.com," Claire replied.

Bryce stifled a laugh. "You're kidding, right? Wasn't AOL the company that used to send out the CDs in the mail to get you to sign up for their internet service in the nineties? Is that still even a thing?"

Claire shrugged. "What can I say? Sal was a creature of habit."

Bryce typed the archaic email address into the login space, and was prompted to enter a six-digit PIN. He said a silent prayer and typed in the numerical version of "Travis" once more. His prayer was answered when Sal's Uber home page popped up on the screen.

A string of rides appeared in the activity log. He scrolled through the list until he reached the dates that matched Sal's flight to Denver. There were two, one on the day of the outbound flight and other on the morning of the return. They were to and from the same address: 1565 Samford Road, Fort Collins, Colorado.

CHAPTER 28

BRYCE SEARCHED the address in Google Maps, and the overhead satellite view showed a single family residence in a densely populated area of grid-like streets on the north side of Fort Collins. He called Abbie, gave her the address, and asked for everything she could find as quickly as she could find it. He had no sooner hung up with her and walked out on the front porch of the house than his phone rang. It was Donnie.

"Hey, partner," Bryce answered.

"Hi, Bryce. Are you okay? We just got word there was a shooting during the warrant execution."

"You heard right. Pinti's dead. Everyone else is fine. I'm waiting for the San Antonio suits to get here."

"Did you find anything worthwhile?"

"I think so." Bryce recounted the last thirty minutes of his day for Donnie, up to and including the most important part, the address in Fort Collins believed to be home to one Thomas Costello Jr., a.k.a. Sonny.

"How sure are you about this?" Donnie asked.

"I won't know anything until I get there, but this is the best lead we've had to date on Sonny's location. Which is to say the only lead, other than Vincent telling me he may have settled somewhere in Colorado. I'd say better than fifty-fifty we've found him."

"Okay, hang on. I have Assistant Director Caine on the other line."

"He's back?"

"Yeah, this morning."

Bryce's phone went silent for a few minutes while Donnie switched calls. When he came back, there was urgency and excitement in his voice.

"Bryce, can you get to Randolph Air Force Base in about four hours?" he asked.

"I'm sure I can. Are there commercial flights out of there?"

"We're not going to need one. AD Caine and I are coming to get you on the director's jet. A few of his horse holders too. Everyone's going to want to say they were there when we hooked Sonny up."

"Sounds good. What about OPR? They're going to be here tomorrow to start the shooting review board, and since I was one of the shooters—"

Donnie cut him off. "This is coming straight from the director himself. You don't need to worry about OPR. Wrap up what you need to with the search team, call the Agent's Association attorneys, and get to Randolph Air Force Base."

"Way ahead of you. See you in a few hours."

"Yeah, one more thing," Donnie added. "Caine is on the warpath. He didn't know anything about the search warrant in San Antonio. Since he was on leave burying his mother, he got left out of the message traffic. I messed up, and I'll handle him. But when we get there, you might want to avoid engaging him in conversation. Or making eye contact."

"Oof. Sorry to hear that, but thanks for the heads-up."

The special agent in charge, two of his assistants, and the chief division counsel arrived at the Pinti residence in a single black Tahoe. Behind them, a pair of converted ambulances emblazoned with the FBI seal and the words *Evidence Response Team* pulled to the curb.

The SAC was straight out of central casting. Early forties, tall and handsome, with chiseled features and an air about him that said, *I'm in charge here.* He was dressed in a tailored navy suit with contrasting red tie and a pair of Ferragamo cap-toe oxfords, and he approached Bryce with his hand out.

"Stan Galloway. Glad everyone is okay."

Bryce took his hand and shook it. "Bryce Chandler. Thank you for coming out."

"Of course. I already had a call from the deputy director, so I know you're heading out shortly. I won't keep you. But I do need you to leave your gun for OPR. Sorry about that."

"No problem." Bryce pulled his gun from its holster, removed the magazine, and racked the slide to the rear to clear the weapon, in the process securing the chambered round in his left hand. He laid everything on a small table in the home's entryway.

"Here. Trade you." The SAC pulled his gun, paddle holster and all, from his hip and handed it to Bryce, who had never seen such a humbling gesture from an FBI executive.

"Sir, that's not necessary."

"Sure it is. You're still in the fight. And I can get another one as soon as I return to the office. Whoever this guy is you're after, I hope you get him." He extended his hand another time, and

Bryce shook it with a newfound level of respect for the man who was almost fifteen years his junior.

The evidence response team had begun dragging their impressive array of black tactical equipment cases past Bryce and into the house, where they would continue the search and preserve the shooting scene for the headquarters investigators. Their leader sought Bryce out and introduced herself as Special Agent Hannah Drummond, and they spoke briefly in the kitchen.

"Of course, we'll follow the parameters in the search warrant," she began. "But before you go, tell me if there's anything of particular interest."

"We're just starting to figure how the Network is configured and how it operates. And this might be their nerve center," Bryce began. "Sal Pinti was close to Sonny, who we believe is the organization's leader. Pinti had their hit men checking in with him whenever a job was completed, so at the very least he was in some sort of a management role. We understand the Network has a roster of partners who make all the big decisions, and he may have known the names of those partners, the hit men, and how the money moved back and forth. If he did, it's all somewhere in his computer or computers."

Hannah nodded. "Everything on the computers will have to be imaged and downloaded by the CART guys," she said, referring to the computer analysis and response team, the FBI's very own Geek Squad. "As soon as it's ready I'll get you a copy. And if we see anything we think is a red flag before then, I'll call you."

"Great, thanks. Any chance someone could give me a ride to Randolph Air Force Base?"

"I'm sure we can make that happen."

CHAPTER 29

THE JET WAS referred to as the director's plane, but it was shared between the FBI's top man and his boss, the attorney general of the United States. It was a Gulfstream G650 with a cruise speed near six hundred miles per hour and a range of seven thousand nautical miles, meaning it could take the nation's two top lawmen nearly anywhere in the world without a refueling stop. On the director's orders, it departed Manassas, Virginia, with Sullivan Caine and three of his deputies, stopped in Atlanta to pick up Donnie Morris, and then raced toward San Antonio. Bryce was waiting at the base operations center at Randolph when it taxied to a stop, its passenger door aligned with the red carpet painted on the concrete tarmac.

He climbed the steps and looked around the impressive space. At six feet four inches, he could stand straight up without his head touching the ceiling. There was seating for fourteen. A forward cabin held two of the leather seats. They were the largest and most opulent on the aircraft, and Bryce surmised they were reserved for the director or the AG when they were aboard. A bulkhead separated the forward and mid cabins, and the latter space was where Sullivan, Donnie, and the rest were gathered around a conference table. A large television monitor affixed to the bulkhead was tuned to a cable news network, and a story about soaring oil prices dominated the headlines. Bryce greeted his friend and the assistant director and introduced himself to the others. Donnie wasn't kidding; the AD was still fuming and the tension in the air was palpable.

Abbie Bishop had already emailed her findings to Bryce. He had forwarded them two hours ago to Donnie, who printed copies for everyone in the Gulfstream's office suite. They pored over the results as the aircraft taxied and took off.

Donnie led the conversation. "The homeowner is Stephen Davenport, sixty-five years old. He bought the place in 2011, so that jibes with what Vincent Kamara told Bryce about Sonny's move from Las Vegas. Paid cash. There's a driver's license photo on page two." Everyone turned the page as Donnie continued.

"There are no employment records with the Colorado Department of Labor, but that could be due to his age. Abbie Bishop is working on copies of his tax returns, but that's a whole separate process through the IRS, and they can be a pain. Denver has SOG headed to the house now; they should have ground and air units on it when we arrive. SWAT is on standby. The squad at WFO is working on the affidavit for a warrant."

"Nice work, gentlemen," Sullivan said, nodding toward Donnie and Bryce. "That said," he added, "The next time either one of you cowboys run an operation, or serve a search warrant, or put a piece of paper in the file without letting me know first, it will be the last thing you do as an FBI agent." Bryce glanced toward Donnie, who shook his head as a warning to his friend to remain silent. Instead, Bryce gave the assistant director a half-hearted smile and a deferential nod, but the look in his eyes said what he was thinking: *Asshole.*

Satisfied that the dressing down had put his subordinates in their place, Caine continued. "The director is meeting with the attorney general tomorrow to discuss indicting Senator D'Angelo on charges of interstate solicitation to commit murder, based on the call you intercepted between him and Sonny. We're still not sure if Norma Whitehurst's testimony alone will be enough to charge him with the crimes involving the Griffin Air Force Base matter. This is the mother of all sensitive circumstances, what with him being a United States senator and presidential candidate, so…" He noticed Donnie staring over his shoulder, toward the television that moments before was broadcasting a story about the nation's energy woes. "Agent Morris, am I boring you?"

Donnie didn't say a word, just pointed. The AD turned and read the headline along the bottom of the screen: "WAPO Source: Griffin Disaster Was No Accident." It was superimposed over B-roll of a recent Frank D'Angelo campaign rally, showing the senator delivering one of his trademark firebrand speeches, a clenched fist pumping the air.

"Turn it up!" Sullivan ordered. One of his deputies searched for the remote and did as he was told, just in time to tune into the discussion between the anchor and the network reporter, who was standing outside the north wing of the United States Capitol.

"There has been neither an appearance nor a statement from Senator D'Angelo, which comes as no surprise given the seriousness of the charges and the fact that these revelations are not even an hour old," the reporter gushed. "We've been told the senator will make a statement when he and his staff have had an opportunity to gather their facts, and when they do, they will deny the allegations in the strongest possible terms."

"And what do we know about the source responsible for the story?" the anchor asked.

"Other than that it was someone close to the matter, nothing," the reporter answered. "Kevin Rosen, our viewers will recall, is a Pulitzer Prize-winning investigative reporter, and you don't reach that level in this business without knowing how to protect your sources. But whoever it is, you can be certain Mr. Rosen and the *Washington Post* have done their due diligence before releasing this story, which is sure to rock Washington to its core."

"For those of you just joining us," the anchor continued, "the *Washington Post* is reporting that a confidential source has tied United States Senator and presidential candidate Frank D'Angelo to the Griffin Air Force Base tainted-water scandal, going so far as to allege that he orchestrated the disaster in order to benefit financially through his law firm. The firm of Abbott and D'Angelo has represented the vast majority of Griffin victims, recovering over fifteen billion dollars in damages for the families of those who were sickened or killed by the drinking water at the now-closed military base. Our reporters will stay at the Senate office building until there is a statement from Senator D'Angelo or his staff, and of course we will keep you up to date with the latest developments as they occur."

The screen faded briefly to black, then cut to a commercial. Sullivan, Donnie, and Bryce stared at each other in dumfounded silence. Sullivan spoke up first.

"Obvious question, but the source has to be Norma Whitehurst, right? Unless there's a leak? There were four people who could testify against Frank D'Angelo, and she's the only one still alive."

"It has to be her," Bryce agreed. "We have her under protective custody, but we haven't cut her off from the outside world, at least not as far as I know. She wasn't happy about Frank D'Angelo throwing her under the bus—hell hath no fury, right? She must have gotten ahold of this Rosen guy somehow and spilled the beans."

"Okay, no more mister nice guys," Sullivan said. "We were keeping her under a mutual agreement, right? She came with us voluntarily?"

Donnie nodded, and Sullivan turned to his deputy.

"Well, all that changes now. Have WFO draft up a warrant to take her as a material witness. Throw her ass in a proper lockup and take away her phone, her computer, everything."

"Sir, if I may?" Bryce asked.

"Yes?"

"If the Network is still after Norma Whitehurst, they can get to her in a local jail, or a federal prison. I agree we need to shut her down with regards to phone and email, but for her safety and for our case, she's best off where she is, at the FBI Academy under HRT's watch."

"Fine. Just shut her up," he said, turning his attention back to his deputy. "And get her in front of a grand jury to lock down her testimony before she has the chance to do something stupid. Again."

The rest of the short flight was spent planning the approach to Sonny's house and checking on the status of the search warrant. As the plane began its descent into Northern Colorado Regional Airport in Loveland, Donnie's phone buzzed, and he saw an incoming email from his counterpart in Washington with an attachment named *Costello_Warrant.pdf*. He flashed the phone toward Bryce and gave him a thumbs-up as the airfield came into sight.

CHAPTER 30

FRANK D'ANGELO bent over the sink in his office bathroom, spitting out the remains of his lunch and rinsing his mouth with cold water. He was sweating profusely, and his shaking hands gripped the sides of the porcelain pedestal fixture, lest his buckling knees betray him.

He was in a planning session with his staff when the story broke, and Stella came into the conference room to tell him. He excused himself and locked the door to his office, then sat on the couch and watched in horror as the nation's biggest cable news network all but labeled him a mass murderer.

It was Norma. It had to be. The only other person who wanted to hurt him this badly was his own brother, and Tommy didn't operate that way. No, this was the work of the sole remaining member of the Griffin Four, his little piece of unfinished business.

He barely had time to throw off his jacket and loosen his tie before the panic attack began. His vision narrowed to a tunnel, his breaths came quick and shallow, and the unmistakable feeling of bile rising in his throat let him know he needed to hurry to the nearest facility. The bathroom was steps from the sofa, and he dropped to his knees in front of the toilet just as the first spasm hit and his stomach gave way. He retched three more times, each one more violent than the last, until he was certain there was nothing left in him.

As he stared into the mirror above the sink, he started regaining his sense. *You can do this,* he told himself. Whether in a court of law or the halls of Congress, acting had been his professional stock-in-trade for his entire adult life. Acting as though a client was innocent. Acting like he cared about constituents. Acting as if he had the best interests of his country at heart. And if there was ever going to be a test of his acting skills, it was right here, right now, and it began with his staff. He wiped his face clean, straightened his tie, donned his jacket, and called them all back together in the conference room.

"All right, team," he began. "It appears someone, most likely a political opponent, has decided there is no level to which they won't stoop in order to derail our campaign."

Their faces were almost expressionless, as if they either weren't sure what to think or were too afraid to show what was on their mind. In either case, they had seen the story. Of that much he was certain.

"Let's address the elephant in the room, shall we?" he continued, flashing his signature smile. "You all know me. Some of you have worked for me from the early days in the House of Representatives. You've had dinner at my house and fished with me and my family on Seneca Lake. I've been to some of your weddings and your children's first communions. Again: You know me. And you know I can't be the same horrible person some deranged lunatic is describing to the *Washington Post*. I will be cooperating with the authorities from this instant, in order to put to rest these insane accusations and bring to justice the person who is slandering my good name. In the meantime, I expect every one of you to keep on doing the good work of this campaign. There are to be no statements of any kind to anyone about this. Not the media, not your friends or family. Of course I expect you to cooperate with law enforcement officials should you be asked to do so. Any questions?"

Not a hand went up. Frank's speech had done little to change the mood in the room, which was equal parts shock, confusion, and fear. Livelihoods hung in the balance of what happened next.

"Mark and Jim, come with me, please." Frank nodded toward his chief of staff and campaign manager as he walked toward the door that connected the conference room to his office. Once inside, he got straight to the point.

"How badly does this hurt us?" he asked.

It was a question for the campaign manager, so he spoke first. "It doesn't help. The story is just hours old, and there are no polls that account for that short of a time period. The next round of polling is due out in three days, and I'd say you'll be crucified."

"But it's a lie! All of it! Made up by some psychopath who wants me out of the race!" Frank screamed.

The chief of staff nodded his concurrence. "I'm sure that's true, boss. But the damage will have been done. It won't even matter if people believe it's true or not. What will matter is that it damages you in their eyes, at a time when there are still six other candidates to choose from. If you were the nominee it might be different. But that's not where we are. Voters can just pivot to whichever of your opponents they feel closest to, ideology-wise."

Frank's demeanor turned from panicked to resolute. "All right. Well, we're not going down without a fight. I'm not going to hide from this. And I'm damned sure not going to go the 'no comment' route as I shuffle past reporters asking questions. We're facing this head on. Book the call-in shows. Get me on ANN and Guardian. Where are our next three rallies?"

The campaign manager scrolled to the calendar in his phone. "We're in Wheeling, West Virginia, tomorrow, then Dayton, Ohio, and the big finish in Des Moines the night before the Iowa caucuses begin."

"Perfect. We'll open every speech with an acknowledgment and denial of this bullshit story. And I want to work the crowds. Plenty of hand-shaking and baby-kissing. Guilty people don't do that." His two senior staffers nodded their assent, while their faces looked anything but convinced.

"One last thing. Anybody, and I mean anybody on this staff breathes a word about this, answers a reporter's question, speaks out of turn—they're gone on the spot. No questions asked. I'm doing the talking, nobody else. Clear?"

"Clear," they answered in unison.

"Good. Now get back to work. And send Stella in here."

———

It was the story of the day, perhaps of the year, and it blanketed the airwaves around the country within hours of the *Washington Post* morning edition hitting the newsstands. The left-leaning American News Network was first to the air. Its conservative competitor, Guardian News, was minutes behind them. Guardian usually downplayed or ignored stories they deemed harmful to the right, but this one was a beast, and to disregard it would have been shameless even by their own marginal journalistic standards.

Utica, New York, was Guardian country, as was most of the upstate. It was also Frank D'Angelo territory, and its denizens watched in stunned silence as the networks laid bare the accusations against their senator. It was almost too horrible to believe, and had it aired only on ANN, Frank's constituents would have dismissed it out of hand as just another dirty trick by the loony left. But here it was, on Guardian, and the usually perky blonde anchor looked physically ill as she read the words on the teleprompter. So the people watched, and they listened.

Destito's Bar and Grill was a Utica institution, catering to the local blue-collar crowd at the corner of 4th Avenue and Genesee Street for six generations. The story broke around noon, so only the hardest of the hardcore day drinkers were on hand for the spectacle. Like the rest of the city they stared in shock, and none more so than Joe Newberry, who by that early hour was already on his third Jack and Coke. The bartender, who was familiar with Joe's story, made a move to change the channel, but Joe himself stopped him.

"Joe, you don't need to see this," the well-meaning bartender implored.

His response was cold and monotone, and his eyes never left the screen. "Let it play."

Joe watched as the anchor and reporters ran out of things to say, at which point the story looped back on itself and began anew. Another compassionate attempt by the bartender to switch channels was met with the same pushback from Joe, and over the next several hours he watched the piece another eight times, along with an equal number of Jack and Cokes.

Joe didn't think his soul could be crushed more completely than the day he buried Dani, but he was wrong. As he watched, the hatred billowed inside of him, and not just for Frank D'Angelo. He hated himself for outliving his wife and children. He hated himself for not having the guts to join them after Dani's funeral. Most of all, he hated himself for being powerless. His entire life had been ripped from him by the ones who wielded real power, and he knew there was nothing he could do about it.

CHAPTER 31

THE CLOSEST AIRPORT to Fort Collins was in Loveland, just fifteen miles south, and the Gulfstream landed two and a half hours after leaving San Antonio. The Denver FBI office had been mobilized and met the landing party on the tarmac with all the vehicles, personnel, and equipment they would need to execute the search warrant on Sonny's presumed home. As was expected, the Denver senior staff turned out in force as well. It was a rare day when an FBI assistant director's visit didn't attract upwardly mobile special agents seeking face time with the shot callers who could make or break their careers.

The entourage left the airport in Loveland and headed north on US Route 287, entering the hometown of Colorado State University fifteen minutes later. The staging location was a parking lot behind a shuttered elementary school about a mile from the house. Once everyone arrived, the operations plan was briefed by a Denver ASAC, with the SWAT team leader detailing the tactical portion. The supervisor of the division's special operations group was responsible for ground and air surveillance, and she brought everyone up to speed on the units watching Sonny's house from near and far, including a fixed-wing aircraft turning circles over the neighborhood at five thousand feet above ground level. Unlike San Antonio, this was not Bryce's show. He, Donnie, and Sullivan would sit back and allow the Denver squads to do their thing, and hope that all the decisions that had led them to this point were the right ones.

On the signal from the ASAC, the small army of SWAT operators, evidence technicians, and agents who would provide perimeter security started moving. It took two minutes to reach the house, where cars pulled to the curb and doors flew open. Agents jumped out and surrounded the three-bedroom brick ranch. SWAT pulled their armored vehicles onto the front lawn, where they dismounted, eight strong, and stacked on the front door. Bryce and the others watched from a government sedan three houses down the block.

Just as in San Antonio, the breacher made short work of the entry door. A loud explosion was followed by the rapid ingress of the SWAT team through the mangled door, and then three more detonations as the team used flash-bang grenades to clear the bedrooms. Bryce listened for the sound of gunfire, but heard none. He got out of the car and began walking toward the house. When he got within fifty feet of the front porch, his heart sank as the SWAT team leader emerged and gave a thumbs-down signal. It was an empty hole.

By now Donnie and Sullivan were walking up behind him, and the security perimeter of non-SWAT agents was beginning to disperse and move back toward their cars. The neighbors had taken notice and were gawking from a respectable distance, none wanting to wander too closely to whatever was going on in their otherwise quiet neighborhood.

"Sorry, man," the SWAT team leader said as Bryce approached. "Nobody home, except for a scared-shitless little

French bulldog in the laundry room. But there was someone here pretty recently."

"What makes you say that?" Bryce asked.

"Follow me." Bryce walked with the team leader to the kitchen, where there was a collection of dishes in the sink and a few more in a drying rack on the counter.

"The clean ones still have a few little drops of water on them," the team leader said. "And the ones in the sink don't look like they've been there too long. The food isn't dried on. I think your guy left in a hurry."

Bryce nodded. "Okay to look around?"

"The place is all yours."

As the SWAT team left, their places were taken by the evidence response team, whose job it was to inventory and photograph the house, then document and seize any evidence of Sonny's involvement with the Network. The team trouped into the home wearing navy-blue windbreakers with *ERT* emblazoned across the back and carrying four large black plastic Pelican cases. Inside the heavy-duty boxes were everything from fingerprint brushes and powder to professional-grade cameras and evidence swabs and containers. It was their scene, and Bryce knew not to touch anything without first asking. He introduced himself to the team leader and asked if it was all right to look around, getting a thumbs-up in response.

Donnie joined him, and they started in the master bedroom, where it became apparent the SWAT team leader's assessment was on point. Someone had been here very recently. There were clothes strewn across the neatly made bed. A pair of drawers in the bureau were open, and it looked as though Sonny had grabbed all but a couple pair of underwear and socks from them. In the bathroom there was a toothbrush holder but no toothbrush, and in the closet a number of clothes hangers lay on the floor in an otherwise immaculate space. Assistant Director Caine followed them from a distance as they worked their way through the house, and Bryce did his best to ignore him. Donnie was right. The guy was a micromanaging pain in the ass.

They walked back into the bedroom and paused near the nightstand. There was an unopened utility bill addressed to Stephen Davenport lying on top.

"Looks like we got the right house," Donnie remarked.

"Yeah. And he didn't just pop out for groceries, either," Bryce added. "He's gone, and he left within the last few hours. You think there was any way for him to know we were hitting Sal Pinti's house?"

"Your guess is as good as mine. Did Pinti have time to get to a phone?"

"No way. From breaching the door to entering his bedroom was ten, maybe fifteen seconds."

"Well then, either Sonny has ESP or somebody let him know we were coming," Donnie said.

Sullivan Caine broke in, his tone verging on taunting. "Looks like you have another mole, gentlemen. One thing for sure, he's long gone by now. Maybe he's headed back to Vegas. Fugitives run to places they know, where they feel comfortable."

Bryce ignored the gibe, other than to nod his head in faux agreement. "Speaking of ESP," he said, pointing to a purple business card in an open jewelry box on the nightstand. The word *Psychic* was printed in bold cursive gold leaf and took up the center of the card. There were details in smaller print along the bottom.

Donnie leaned forward and squinted, not wanting to touch the card. "It says Madame Marie, spiritual advisor. Readings by appointment. And there's a number."

Bryce pulled his phone from his pocket and snapped a picture.

"What are you doing?" Donnie asked. "I thought you didn't believe in that mumbo-jumbo stuff."

"I don't. But if Sonny did, it might be worth a trip to this psychic to see what they talked about, assuming he was a client."

"Suit yourself. Let's keep looking around." Bryce followed Donnie into another bedroom, which was empty, and a third, which looked like it was used as an office. A telephone line was plugged into the wall at one end and into nothing at the other. Two ethernet cables lay on the floor beside the desk. There was no computer, no telephone, no cell-phone charger. A small Mosler industrial safe, perhaps two cubic feet in capacity, sat in a corner, open and empty. More signs of a hasty and permanent departure.

Sonny was in the wind.

The evidence response team took three hours to dissect the house, finding almost nothing of evidentiary value. Agents from the Denver office canvassed the street and spoke with the neighbors, all of whom identified Stephen Davenport from his Colorado driver's license photo. Beyond that they were of no help, offering little more than the ubiquitous "He was a quiet guy, kept to himself" description that was the bane of every criminal investigator's existence. A worker from the local animal rescue came to collect the French bulldog and assured all the dog lovers, including Bryce, that theirs was a no-kill shelter and the little fellow would be in a foster home by the end of the week.

As everyone was preparing to leave, Sullivan got a call from the Gulfstream's pilots. An airspeed indicator was on the blink, and the replacement part was being flown in from Savannah, Georgia, overnight. They weren't going anywhere. He had his assistant book rooms for everyone in Loveland.

Bryce finagled a car for himself and told the others he would meet them in Loveland, perhaps in time for dinner. Donnie knew why his friend was sticking around, and didn't offer to stay with him. If Bryce wanted him tagging along, he would have asked. Besides, that psychic stuff was just a waste of time.

CHAPTER 32

THE DRIVE FROM Sonny's place took ten minutes. It was a tiny cottage-style house, no more than a thousand square feet, painted the same garish purple as the business card. It had a screened front porch and colorful Christmas lights ringing a pair of windows on each side of the door. The house sat two blocks from the enclave of fraternity and sorority homes known to the Colorado State student body as Greek Row. *All the better to separate naïve college kids from their beer and pizza money,* Bryce thought as he rang the bell.

The door cracked open and an ancient wrinkled face peered around it.

"Can I help you?" she asked.

"Are you Marie?"

"It's Madame Marie, and I only do readings by appointment."

Bryce had his badge and credentials at the ready and held them up for her to see. "I'm not here for a reading."

"Do you have a warrant?"

"No, ma'am, I do not. But I'm not here to search your place or to cause any trouble. I just want to talk to you."

"About what?"

"Is there any chance we could do this inside? I really don't want your neighbors to hear you talking with the FBI."

It was one of Bryce's oldest tricks, and it usually worked. *Let's not air your dirty laundry to the neighborhood, shall we? Because, you know, this is about my concern for your best interests.* It was, of course, pure bullshit, but it worked, as the door opened and the old woman waved him in with a skeletal hand.

Bryce entered into a living room of sorts, with an ancient leather button-tufted sofa to his left and a wood-burning fireplace to his right. Dark wood paneling covered the walls. A weathered round oak table, six feet across, dominated the center of the room and was ringed by eight Victorian high-backed chairs with red velvet seat cushions. A pair of floor lamps with fringed shades created more shadows than light, and mystic-themed tchotchkes and candles were crammed into every square inch of space atop the room's abundant collection of antique furnishings. It was a purposefully designed space, and Bryce knew the purpose—to sell the aura of clairvoyant authority to the curious and desperate souls who wanted to believe.

She shuffled toward one of the chairs and pointed toward another. "Have a seat."

Bryce opted to stand and pulled a copy of Stephen Davenport's driver's license photo from his pocket. He unfolded the picture and showed it to her. "Do you know this man?"

She donned a pair of glasses hanging from a chain around her neck and still needed to squint in the dimness of the room. "Perhaps. What's his name?"

"Stephen Davenport. I found your business card in his house."

"And what's this Mr. Davenport done to get the attention of the FBI?" she asked.

"That's not important. I was hoping you could tell me what he discussed with you, assuming he was a client."

"A few things, dear. First, I don't have clients. I have sitters. And when someone sits for a reading, it's in confidence. I don't discuss what they tell me with their family members, and I certainly don't discuss it with the police. I have a legal obligation."

Bryce shook his head. "Sorry, but there's no such thing as psychic confidentiality. Between a client and their doctor, perhaps. Between them and their lawyer, absolutely. But a psychic has no such privilege. Don't try and bullshit me, lady. It's not my first day on the job."

She cast a long, disapproving stare at the intruder who dared to come into her home and question her professional standing. "Call it a moral obligation then. I'm still not going to share a sitter's personal information with the FBI."

Bryce smiled. "Maybe I can change your mind."

"I doubt it."

"Have you ever been to our nation's capital?" Bryce asked.

"No, why?"

"Because the case I'm investigating, the one your client is involved in, is the biggest thing on the FBI's plate right now. We're calling witnesses to testify before a grand jury in Washington, and the process is long, boring, and time-consuming. If I say the word, a subpoena will be issued for you to appear, and you'll sit in the grand jury room, doing crosswords or whatever, until they call your name. Sometimes it takes all day. Sometimes it takes more than a day. My own personal record is one week. That's how long I was able to keep a witness waiting before the grand jury was ready for them."

"That sounds petty, Agent Chandler. You'd drag an old woman across the country because she didn't want to talk with you?"

"Try me. And while you're gone, I'll get a search warrant for this house, and surround the place for a day or two with crime scene tape and FBI agents in raid jackets. Maybe tip off the media that you were aiding and abetting a fugitive. I'm sure you can imagine how that would impact your business."

"My, my. Your pettiness knows no end, does it? What if I call your bluff?"

"Lady, in the last twelve hours I've been shot at, had my ass ripped open by an FBI assistant director, and missed the chance to arrest my main target by hours, maybe minutes. I'm in no mood for negotiations. We'll play it your way. See you soon." He stood and moved toward the door.

"You're not a believer, are you?" she asked as he began walking away.

"In this nonsense? Hardly," he answered over his shoulder.

"Well, I can tell you this much. His name isn't Stephen Davenport."

Bryce stopped in his tracks and turned to face Madame Marie again. "How do you know that?"

She was smiling now. "You know it, too."

"So what's his real name then?"

"That's not how it works, Agent Chandler. I'm a psychic, not Google. When I work with a sitter, I can feel their energy, and I can tell if they're keeping something from me. Secrets."

Bryce narrowed his eyes. He would never be what she called a "believer," but she had managed to balance his senses of skepticism and curiosity. He pulled out a chair and sat down next to her.

"What secrets was Mr. Davenport keeping?" he asked.

"Bad ones. He had a powerful energy. Negative but powerful. Even when he left my home, I could feel it. I knew he lived somewhere close by, probably here in Fort Collins. His energy was that strong. But it's gone now."

"When you say a 'negative energy,' what do you mean?" Bryce asked.

"Your Mr. Davenport, or whatever his name is—he has a dark heart, a black soul. He's done horrible things. And he knows his day of reckoning is coming." She shook her head and sighed deeply as a look of resignation washed over her face. "This is between you and me, right?" she asked.

"If you tell me what I need to know, yes."

"He said someone was looking for him. A woman who claimed he fathered her child years ago. He said she wanted decades of child support, more than he could afford, and she had an army of private investigators on his tail. He wanted to know if they were close to finding him. If he was about to be caught. I knew there were people coming for him, but it had nothing to do with child support."

"How long had he been coming here?"

"About a year. And over that time, I could sense his fears were coming true. Whoever was after him, they were getting closer. But I never told him that. I got the feeling his pursuers were on the side of right, and he needed to be caught."

"And when was the last time you saw him?"

"Three days ago. His negative energy was higher than I'd ever seen it. And when we finished our session, I knew I would never see him again. To be honest, I was relieved."

"Do you remember any details from that session?"

"He was more agitated than usual. I sensed a conflict with a male family member. We'd done tarot readings in our previous sessions, and he asked for another one."

"Forgive my lack of knowledge, but explain how that works."

"Tarot is a form of cartomancy, which is a fancy way of saying fortune telling with cards. They date to fourteenth century Europe. A standard deck has seventy-eight cards with symbols that, if used properly, tell a story about the sitter's past, present, and future."

"And what story did it tell about Mr. Davenport?" Bryce asked.

"We decided on a simple three-card reading. I shuffled the cards, and he drew them. The first one was the tower, which means danger, crisis, or sudden change. The second one was death, which doesn't always mean someone has died, by the way. In this case I took it to mean a major transformational period in his life. But it was the third card that got his attention. When I turned it over, I could see the fear in his eyes."

"What was the third card?"

"Justice."

Bryce nodded. "And I assume that card is self-explanatory?"

"It is."

"You said you're certain he's no longer nearby. Do you know where he went?"

She shook her head. "Like I said, dear, I'm not Google, and I'm not Google Maps. I wish I could be more help. I'm just glad he's out of my life."

"Well, thank you for your time, and before I go, is there anything else I need to know? Anything I forgot to ask?"

"About Mr. Davenport? No. But I have a question for you."

"Ask away."

"What is this burden you're carrying? This intense sadness? Where does it come from?"

Bryce shot her a look of incredulity. "I'm not sure what you're talking about."

"Agent Chandler, I see people from all walks of life, men and women who have endured every hardship you can imagine. Unspeakable, some of it. And every one of them brings with them the energy they've developed as a result of their life experiences. Yours is one of unimaginable sorrow. And I'm curious as to why."

Bryce shook his head. "There's nothing remarkable about me. I've had my ups and downs just like everyone else."

She smiled and drew her chair closer to his. "Then will you do an old woman a kindness?" she asked.

"That depends."

She reached toward him. "Give me your hands."

He drew back instead. "Marie—excuse me, Madame Marie—this really isn't my thing."

"Do you believe more now than when you walked through that door?"

He nodded. "I'll admit there are things going on here I can't explain. But I'm still a long way from believing in crystal balls and palm readings."

"None of that. Just give me your hands."

He leaned forward and did as she asked.

"Now close your eyes."

It made him uncomfortable, but he relented. They sat for a minute, but it seemed much longer to Bryce. When she finally spoke, her voice was softer than before.

"Your demon has haunted you for many years. You told everyone you were all right, didn't you? The doctors, your wife, your friends. And you tried to drink the demons away. Until you lost it all."

The hairs on the back of Bryce's neck bristled as his heart raced. He wasn't sure how she knew, but she knew. He opened his eyes and loosed his grip. "I think we should stop now."

She clamped down on his hands and pulled him closer. "Close your eyes."

She smiled, her eyes closed yet somehow seeing into his soul. "Your demon is no demon at all. It's an angel. It's a—it's a child, isn't it? She's older now. She's a young woman in the next world. She's beautiful. But she was a baby when you found her. You found her—"

The smile left Madame Marie's face in that instant and was replaced by an expression of sheer horror. She drew in a prolonged gasp and let out a bloodcurdling scream. Her nails dug into the flesh of Bryce's wrists, and even through closed eyes he could see the lights in the room dimming. He opened his eyes but was too afraid to look at her, and so he closed them again. There was a terror building in him as well, one he hadn't confronted in years. He wanted to run, but was frozen in place.

Her voice lowered to a raspy whisper. "Oh, dear God, what did they do to her? She's crying—she's screaming—she's *burning*!" Madame Marie was crying herself now, rocking from side to side as she anguished, her hands clamped down like vises on his. She writhed in pain, as if she herself were the one on fire. "Who did this?" she moaned.

Bryce was no longer in the room. As the old woman wailed, he was back in Lamar County, Georgia, in the meth cook's trailer, on his hands and knees in the kitchen, crawling through the smoke and chemical fumes to close the oven door. It was happening again in real time, and he saw it all. He saw *her*. He let out his own scream and sprang to his feet, knocking the chair to the floor behind him.

She broke the grip, not him. When she did, he was back in her parlor, ten years and a thousand miles away from his nightmare. She was still in her chair, her eyes burning holes in him. The stare was almost accusatory.

She repeated her question. "Who did that to her?"

Bryce's answer came between measured breaths as he tried to compose himself. "The people who called themselves her parents."

"And where are they now?"

"On death row in Georgia, waiting for their appeals to run out."

Madame Marie nodded. "Normally I oppose capital punishment, but in this case I think an exception is warranted."

"You and me both. They're not even human beings in my book." He pushed the chair he had been sitting in back to the table. "I have to go."

"I understand, Agent Chandler, but there's one more thing I need to tell you."

"Ma'am, no offense, but I've had about all the psychic drama I can handle for one day." He was still shaking and sweating. His heart raced.

"This isn't quite so dramatic. There's another presence in your life. An important one. Did you remarry?"

"No."

"Do you have a girlfriend? This presence I'm feeling, it's a romantic one."

"I have a girlfriend. Or had one. To be honest, I'm not sure. We had a falling out. We haven't spoken in a week."

"You need to remedy that. There is a dark hole in your relationship, deeper than any lover's spat. If you don't fix it, you will regret it for the rest of your life. She needs you, and time is of the essence."

"I'll keep that in mind," Bryce said as he fished a business card from his pocket and handed it to Madame Marie. "If anything about Mr. Davenport comes up, or if you hear from him again, please call me."

"I will. One last thing, Agent Chandler."

"Yes?"

"The little girl. She knows it was you who found her. And she's at peace now."

———————

If he were being truthful, Bryce would have told Madame Marie that he and Ashley hadn't spoken in a week because neither had made the first move toward repairing the damage from their fight. On the short drive from Fort Collins to Loveland, Bryce called Ashley's phone and got no answer. Both of them found voicemail to be cumbersome and outdated, and they had agreed early in their relationship that a text would do when they couldn't get ahold of one another. He left her a simple one.

Call me. Important.

He lay awake that night, replaying the day's events in his head. He had killed a man, narrowly missed another, and been drawn by a psychic into reliving the most horrific event of his life. All in less than twelve hours.

But the heaviest burden on his mind and heart was Ashley. He thought of what she meant to him. How they had left it. And the ever present yet never resolved "I love you" situation. It would be his first order of business when he saw her again.

She hadn't returned his call or text, and he couldn't blame her. He had been ugly toward her, and since that day he had replayed the argument over and again in his head, imagining the more understanding and compassionate approach he could have taken. He promised himself he would never make that mistake again if she took him back.

And he worried. Madame Marie's vague yet ominous warning could have meant any number of things, including a threat to Ashley's personal safety. The Network knew her; they knew where she lived and worked. And if they saw her as being uncooperative, or a threat to their security? Even with Sal Pinti dead and Sonny on the run, the remaining partners might consider Ashley a loose end that needed tying up. It was all conjecture, and not enough to get a protective detail assigned to her, but enough that the silence between them was no longer an option. He needed to speak to Ashley, to tell her what he knew and ask her forgiveness. And he needed to make sure she was safe.

It was 2:00 a.m. in Colorado when he dialed Harley, who was two hours ahead. It could have been four hours later and it wouldn't have mattered; Harley was never up before ten. Still, he sounded happy to hear from his friend.

"Morning, boss," Harley said through a yawn. "Where you at?"

"Colorado."

"Good grief, what time is it there? Do you ever sleep?"

"Harley, I'm sorry to bother you at this hour, but I need a favor."

Harley guffawed through the phone. "The last time you needed a favor we almost got killed by those dudes up in Tavernier."

"This one's a little less dangerous. I need you to run by Ashley's place, knock on her door, and tell her to call me."

"Not to tell you your business, Bryce, but usually that's accomplished by just calling her yourself. You know, cell phones and all."

"We had an argument. She's not returning my calls. I'd rather not go into it all, but some things have come up, and I need to speak to her. At the very least, I need you to lay eyes on her and let me know she's all right. I won't be home for another day or two."

"Is everything okay? You seem concerned for her safety."

"I am. Really, Harley, I can't go into details. But you know what's been going on in my life for the last year. I don't want any of it to spill over into her life."

"Okay. Want me to try and catch her before she heads to work?"

"That would be great. She leaves around eight thirty. I'll text you her address."

"Sure thing. I'll be there."

Harley's promise to help was comforting, but still Bryce's insomnia raged. The Ashley situation consumed his thoughts while he was awake and invaded his dreams during a few fitful periods of sleep. There was no doubt she had conspired with the Network; she admitted as much. But he was convinced now, more than ever, that she did so under duress. More importantly, she was not the leak, the mole he feared she might have been. She knew nothing of the bureau's abrupt pivot from San Antonio to Fort Collins, yet Sonny had somehow been given enough advance notice of their arrival to escape. It had to be someone else.

He fixed himself a cup of coffee from the cheap drip machine in the bathroom. As he sipped it, he remembered Ashley's side of the story from their blowout. How she was forced into betraying his trust, and how she struggled to balance their relationship with their safety. Feelings of guilt swept over him as he remembered his anger, his tone, and the words he threw at her like weapons. The more he thought about what she must have gone through, the worse he felt.

CHAPTER 33

ASHLEY MADE A HABIT of getting to work early, at least an hour or two before her first scheduled client of the day. She found the alone time to be therapeutic as well as productive, and on most mornings, hers was the only vehicle in the parking lot when she pulled in between 7:30 and 8:00. On this Wednesday, the black Lincoln Navigator was there when she arrived, parked three spaces over from the slot she used. Ashley had a strict "no walk-ins" policy, and her first appointment of the day wasn't for several hours. For this reason alone the Navigator registered on her suspicion meter, but only mildly so, not at an alarming level. Had she known the identity of the driver and the purpose of his visit, she never would have gotten out of her car.

———————

The Law Offices of Ashley Oliver, Esquire, sounded more impressive than the actual space she occupied to ply her trade. The six hundred square feet of retail space was a Supercuts before the discount hair salon chain pulled out of the Florida Keys some five years ago, leaving a vacancy between a pet supply store and a Monroe County DMV satellite office. It was anything but glamorous, and when she signed the lease she told herself it would do until she got herself established. So she hung out a shingle, advertised her services as a criminal defense attorney, and began picking up all the DUI, drug possession, and petty theft cases she could handle.

And she was good at it. In a sea of shysters, quick-buck artists, and bottom-of-the-class legal hucksters, Ashley was an attack dog who used every means at her disposal to fight for her clients. She got confessions tossed for the slightest of procedural missteps. She crucified officers on the witness stand, especially when she caught them embellishing the probable cause they used to pull her clients over. She learned everything there was to learn about Florida's toxicology protocols and garnered countless DUI acquittals based on non-compliance on the part of either the arresting officer or the state laboratory. Word of her courtroom skills spread, and Ashley Oliver became the go-to name for Monroe County's ne'er-do-well community.

But there wasn't much money in representing the scourge of Florida Keys society, and after two years she was barely making ends meet. When the father of one of her clients stopped by the office to pay his son's retainer, he said he needed a will and asked if she could help him. She said yes without hesitation, went home, and broke out her old Wills, Estates, and Trusts reference material from law school. She supplemented it with a night's worth of internet research, and the next day pocketed two hundred dollars from the first of her clients to contact her from somewhere other than a jail cell. She added estate planning to her business cards, and it wasn't long before her white-collar revenues surpassed the money she was making as a criminal court streetfighter.

Three years into her law career, everything changed. A client who was battling breast cancer hired Ashley to prepare her will.

Not long after, she called in tears from the hospital, where she had just undergone a double mastectomy. As she was waking from the anesthesia, her husband, a doctor himself, served her with divorce papers. It seems he wanted to get on with his new life (with his new girlfriend) and had grown tired of waiting for her to die. She was a mess, and Ashley was the only attorney she knew. Within twenty-four hours, Ashley had a private investigator and a forensic accountant on retainer. The pair uncovered a pattern of philandering and a stash of hidden assets in offshore accounts exceeding ten million dollars. It was a pair of silver bullets that would spell his doom in the trial phase of the coming divorce. She got court orders freezing his bank accounts and encumbering him from selling any of his assets, including his lucrative medical practice. She compelled his testimony in a series of depositions during which she laid bare the entirety of his mistreatment of his wife and his efforts to defraud her of her rightful share of the community property. In the end, the wife was awarded two-thirds of the marital estate and half of all the future earnings from his practice. A week after the verdict, the good doctor put a gun in his mouth, but in his despair did so without amending or super-seding his own will. His now-ex-wife got everything. A shrewdly written retainer garnered Ashley two million dollars of the overall recovery, and her days of catering to drunks and shoplifters were over.

Subsequently, Ashley's practice consisted solely of family law and estate planning, with far more of the former than the lat-ter. Despite her windfall, she held on to the humble office, hav-ing grown comfortable there. She hired a legal secretary to come in three days per week and handle administrative matters. She stopped advertising, as all of her business by this point came from word of mouth. Ashley still carried the gunslinger reputation from her early days, only now she was on hire to the well-heeled denizens of paradise whose marriages had died and who were willing to pay whatever it took to make it official. Life was good.

Neither the pet shop nor the DMV would open for another hour. Ashley stared at the Lincoln, perhaps a bit too hard, as she locked her Mercedes and walked the twenty feet to her office. She saw the SUV's door open in the reflection of the storefront's glass facade. As she fumbled with her keys, she saw the driver step out and heard him call her name.

"Miss Oliver?"

Ashley turned to face him, and put her hand inside her purse where a registered, loaded .25-caliber pistol lay alongside her wallet and cell phone.

"Whoa, whoa, whoa," he protested and held his hands up in front of him as he smiled. One of them clutched a small manila envelope. "Whatever you're reaching for, there's no need. I'm not here to hurt you. I want to retain your services."

He was a hulking beast of a man, six feet plus and well in excess of three hundred pounds. He looked to be in his late fifties, maybe sixty. His hands were giant meat hooks with fingers the size of sausages, and his head seemed directly affixed to his shoulders. He wasn't what she would call fat, but he wasn't a bodybuilder either. More like a pro football player who had retired and stopped working out. His olive complexion, slicked-back hair, and gold chain screamed Guido mobster, and she made her mind up in that instant that he would not be her newest client.

"I don't take walk-ins," she said. "Call my secretary and set up a time to come in for a consult."

"I'm only here in town for the day. Maybe you could give me five minutes of your time."

"Sorry, no." She turned away from him just enough to eye the lock and insert the key.

For a big fellow, he was fast. Before she had a chance to react, he closed the distance between them, grabbed the wrist of the hand she had buried in the purse, and squeezed it so hard she thought it would break. She tried to scream, but little more than a whimper came out. He pulled her hand from the purse and made sure it was empty.

"Lady, I told you, I come in peace," he said with a bearish grin. "But if you scream, I swear I'll kill you right here and now. Now open the door and let's go inside."

There was something about his voice that made her understand, as terrifying as the moment was, he was telling the truth. He wasn't there to hurt her. He also wasn't there to hire her as his divorce attorney, but whatever his intent, she decided playing along was her best option. She opened the door and they stepped inside. He threw the lock behind them.

"I'll keep hold of this for the time being," he said, taking her purse with his free hand. "Sit down." He motioned to a side chair near her desk, one reserved for clients. He pulled Ashley's high-backed leather chair from behind her desk and sat down himself, putting about three feet between them. He leaned forward as he spoke.

"Like I said, I need to retain your services. No heavy lifting, and I'm sure what I'm offering is fifty times your hourly rate." He raised the envelope as he spoke. "It's also completely legal."

"Then why the strong-arm tactics?" Ashley asked.

"Well, for one, you looked like you were reaching for a gun," he replied, glancing down into her purse. He pulled the tiny pistol out with just his thumb and forefinger, held it in front of his face, and gazed in amusement. "And I'd say my instincts were correct." He put the gun back in the purse and kept ahold of the bag in a gargantuan hand that nearly swallowed it.

"I used to deal with a lot of scumbags," she said. "You can never be too careful."

"Tell me about it. Anyway, I need you to be a courier of sorts for a friend of mine who is a guest of the government in Miami. Like I said, no heavy lifting. Just take him a letter, ask him a few questions, and get the answers back to me. How hard is that?"

"And why me?"

"Because as an attorney, you can come and go as you please in the system, and they can't record your conversations or search your papers."

"No," Ashley continued. "Why *me*? Why not some other attorney?"

"Lady, there's twenty-five thousand in cash in this envelope. It's yours. Stop asking so many questions."

Ashley folded her arms across her chest. "Sorry, but the answer is no."

He winced as if stricken by a migraine and rubbed his temples as he pondered his next words.

"Okay, I was hoping to avoid this. Two months ago, there was a double murder at your boyfriend's house. The retired G-man. He was supposed to be there, but he wasn't. Instead, a couple of drug-cartel goons ended up dead. Sound familiar?"

Ashley's face betrayed her as it went ghostly white, and her breath began to come in short gasps.

"Anyway, the guy you're gonna take this letter to is the shooter. He was there to kill your boyfriend, but as we all know by now, that didn't happen." He smiled. "It still can."

The room was spinning. She would have fainted if she weren't already sitting down. Her vision began to narrow, and it felt as if her lungs were being squeezed from within, making it nearly impossible to breathe. It took all her strength to form the simple reply, which came out as a whisper.

"Okay." She nodded her head in staccato time to accentuate her agreement.

"There's more. First, you're not going to mention this to Mr. Chandler. But if he tells you anything about the people who came after him, you're going to get on the phone and let me know. The FBI is going to try and flip my friend, make him an informant. If you hear anything about that, you're going to get on the phone and let me know. Screw this up, and one of our people will be back to finish the job. Understand?"

She nodded. "You know he's retired, right? How would he know what the FBI is doing with your friend?"

"Let me worry about that. Those FBI guys are never really retired. Kind of like the men in my line of work. You just do what you're told. Get it?"

She nodded again.

"No, sweetheart. I need to hear it from you. Do you understand everything I just said?"

"Yes."

"Good." He stood and dropped the envelope on her desk. "The details are in there, including the very specific way in which you will introduce yourself to my friend. Read it carefully and don't screw it up. There's also a number you can use to call me. Someone will answer the phone 'McNair Industries.' You ask for Mr. Jackson. Got it so far?"

"Yes."

"Don't open the sealed envelope. It's for my friend's eyes only. I'll expect your first call right after your visit. And buy yourself something nice with the cash." He let himself out the front door, got back into the Navigator, and drove away.

As soon as he left, Ashley sprung from her chair and locked the door. She hurried to the bathroom as the bile began to rise in her throat, barely making it before retching her breakfast into the sink. When the spasms finally stopped, she splashed cold water on her face, stared at herself in the mirror for a minute, and made her decision.

CHAPTER 34

RANDALL FITCH had accepted the job just three days earlier, from Sal Pinti himself. There were only two conditions: Get it done quickly and don't leave a body or a messy scene behind. Easy enough.

He drove from his home in Mobile to Miami, where he parked his car at a long-term off-airport lot and took the shuttle to the terminal in the pre-dawn darkness. Inside, he walked past the ticket counters, took the escalator downstairs to arrivals, and boarded another bus to the rental car lots. By 6:00 a.m. he was headed south on Route 1 in a newer model minivan, twenty miles south of Florida City as he made his way toward Key Largo. Marathon was still an hour and a half away, and he hadn't decided if he was going to take her at her condominium or her office. In either case, he would strangle her inside and wait until after dark, then put her body in the back of the minivan. He would dispose of her in the Everglades, where the alligators would take care of the evidence.

He stopped at a hardware store in Islamorada, where he paid cash for a twelve-foot-square plastic tarp and thirty feet of marine-grade nylon rope. Self-conscious about the optics of his purchase, he made a lame remark to the sales clerk about needing to cover a couch he was buying on Craigslist. The clerk, a pimply faced eighteen-year-old making minimum wage, would not have noticed or cared if the customer had added a shovel and a bag of lime to his cart.

He pulled into Marathon at 7:45 and cruised past her work address just to have a look. As he expected, there were no lights on and no cars parked in the spaces out front. The website advertised her office hours as 9:30 a.m. to 5:00 p.m. Monday through Friday, and her home was only ten minutes away, so it was reasonable to assume she wouldn't be at work this early.

The DMV office next door concerned him. Driver's licenses and vehicle registrations were issued by the state and used by law enforcement agencies for all manner of criminal investigations. It was not uncommon to see a highway patrolman or a sheriff's deputy frequenting these places on official business. Since her work hours matched those of the motor vehicle office, there was no way to guarantee a nosy cop wouldn't see something suspicious and decide to have a look.

Upon further reflection, the DMV was more than a concern. It was a non-starter. He would kill Ashley Oliver in her home.

Harley set an alarm for six thirty, and it took every ounce of energy to rouse himself when it sounded. He went to bed well past midnight, and subtracting the time he spent talking with Bryce, had less than five hours of actual sleep in the tank when he stumbled into the kitchen for a cup of coffee. He downed a cup black, then another, before returning to his bedroom to throw on a pair of board shorts and a clean Waylon Jennings t-shirt. He had a job in Vaca Key later in the day, a simple lower-unit service on a three-hundred-horsepower Yamaha outboard, and so the stop in Marathon to see Ashley wasn't really that much of an inconvenience. It was just so damned early.

He gathered his tools and put them in the trunk of his car, then headed north along the Overseas Highway, stopping for one more jolt of caffeine at Mamacita's Cuban Coffee on the south end of Marathon. This time he opted for the café con leche, which was equal parts sweetened condensed milk, sugar, and espresso. It was sickeningly sweet to some, but Harley had to have one every time he passed through town. It wasn't as if he worried about packing weight on his 160-pound frame.

It was about ten minutes to eight when he pulled out of Mamacita's parking lot, and Ashley's house was only five minutes away. He decided he would park near her condo, enjoy his coffee, and wait for her to come outside rather than ringing the bell while she was getting ready for work. It seemed like the polite thing to do, and he could relay Bryce's message just as well in the parking lot as he could at her front door.

Randall pulled into Ashley's complex at 8:15. He parked fifty feet or so away from her building, in a spot marked *Visitor* in white painted block letters on the asphalt. He had a clear view of the outdoor hallway and stairs leading to her unit, but not to the front door itself. That, according to the numbered signs pointing toward the individual units, was around the back of the building. All the better for him to get inside without being noticed.

He scanned the area and liked what he saw, much more so than the office in the strip mall. First and foremost, it was quiet. Nobody was milling about. There were only a few cars in the resident spots, and one of them was a black Mercedes sedan in the space marked with her apartment number. She was home.

If he could get her to open the door, even a crack, he'd force his way in and it was game over. He could kill her straight away, wrap her body in the tarp, and wait for nightfall to finish the job. Or he could just knock her out, tie her up, and make a day of it. From the photographs on her website, she appeared to be quite the looker. The possibilities were endless.

Whatever he decided, he needed to move before she came outside. The tarp and rope were stowed in a backpack on the passenger seat, and he double checked the pistol in his waistband one last time. It wasn't part of today's plan, but it was always better to have a gun and not need it than to need one and not have it.

As he grabbed his backpack and reached for the door handle, a car passed in front of him and pulled into another visitor spot about thirty feet away and pointed in the same direction as him. It was a beater, either a Cutlass or a Malibu, at least forty years old, with a beige hood that stood in stark contrast to the wrinkled and rusting maroon body.

The driver looked like a typical Keys local. He was in his mid-forties, rail thin, with a patchy beard and a ponytail that disappeared behind the headrest. He waited for the interloper to shut off his car and go somewhere, anywhere but next to him in the parking lot. He was the only possible witness to what was about to happen, and Randall was running out of time.

Instead he sat, eyes focused on the same building, sipping coffee from a paper cup. Who the hell was this guy? Not a resident, judging by his choice of parking spaces. Was he picking someone up? Meeting somebody? Surely there was no connection between him and Ashley Oliver.

Screw it. Her doorway was around the corner and out of sight, but she could leave at any moment. If the mystery man got in the way, Randall would take care of him, too. He remembered the words of his Ranger school instructor: "No plan survives the first ten seconds of contact." If everything went to shit and he had to kill Ashley Oliver in the parking lot, so be it. Sal Pinti's wish list notwithstanding, this was a paid hit. It was getting done, and it was getting done now. He opened the door, got out of the minivan, and walked toward the building.

Harley noticed the minivan with out-of-state plates as soon as he pulled into the parking lot. Bryce's remark about Ashley's safety flashed through his head, and he picked a spot where he could keep an eye on both the minivan and her Mercedes at the same time. There was nothing threatening about the driver, other than the fact that he was parked outside a condo building at 8:00 in the morning for no apparent reason. *So are you,* he told himself. But still, twenty-plus years in the drug dealing business and another five as Bryce's informant had given him a set of observation skills on par with most street cops, and there was something about this guy that just didn't look right. He alternated between sips of coffee and side-eyed glances at the stranger as he waited for Ashley to emerge.

He didn't have to wait long. The minivan driver stepped out just as Ashley came into view from around the corner.

Harley saw the driver drop a backpack to the ground and reach for his waistband, all the while continuing to close distance with Ashley. He had seen the move enough times to know what he was reaching for. From his open window, Harley screamed in her direction.

"Get down! He has a gun!"

Ashley looked up just in time to see the muzzle flashes. The first bullet grazed her neck, and the second pierced her chest and dropped her to the pavement as Harley watched in horror. The gunman had fired from about thirty feet away, and now he was walking toward her crumpled body.

Harley knew his only option. Bryce had shown him the tactic in this very car, a little more than a year ago, just up the road in Tavernier. He dropped the shifter into drive, floored the gas pedal, and aimed straight for the gunman, who by now was walking past the front of Ashley's car, less than twenty feet from where she lay bleeding.

The squeal of the tires made the gunman turn his attention from her and toward the maniac barreling down on him from across the parking lot. He raised his pistol in the direction of the approaching car and began firing. The first round passed through the windshield and out the rear window. The second and third hit Harley in the middle of his chest and his right shoulder. It felt as if someone had hit him as hard as they could with a baseball bat. He ignored the pain, let out a mighty war cry, and hurtled toward his assailant.

He was doing twenty miles per hour when he sandwiched the gunman's legs between the front ends of the Oldsmobile and the

Mercedes. He saw the shock of the devastating impact in the man's eyes, then watched it turn to horror and pain as he bore down on the accelerator, as if trying to push it through the floorboards. The Cutlass roared, the tires smoked, and the Mercedes stood its ground as a combined three tons of rolling steel competed for the same space, crushing bones and ripping flesh in the process.

They lost consciousness at the same time, Harley's foot falling away from the accelerator just as the assassin collapsed in a limp heap across the hood of Harley's car. It was over in less than thirty seconds, and the parking lot went still. Crickets chirped in the humid morning air.

The neighborhood may have been quiet, but it wasn't deserted, and it didn't take long for a half dozen of its residents to call 911 and report the sound of gunshots and an automobile accident. Monroe County sheriff's deputies were on the scene in minutes, and a trio of ambulances followed them from Mariner's Hospital, the level-one trauma center just a few miles away.

The deputies secured the scene and began rounding up witnesses and taking statements. The paramedics set about treating the victims. The cops and the medics worked together often and well, and it was standard practice for each entity to keep the other apprised of what they were doing. The senior deputy on scene was the shift sergeant, and he was writing on a notepad when one of the paramedics approached.

"That one was dead when we got here," the medic said, pointing toward a heap on the ground covered by a white sheet. "The other two are in bad shape, but we'll see what the docs can do for them. We're ready to transport." Behind him, a pair of gurneys were being wheeled toward waiting ambulances.

The shift sergeant gave his colleague a thumbs-up and called the on-duty detective who would be taking over. The shots-fired call was now a murder case.

CHAPTER 35

BY THE TIME the FBI jet took off from Loveland it was 8:00 in Florida, and Bryce hadn't heard from Ashley or Harley. He was more worried than ever but forced himself to divert his attention to another pressing matter. Just before takeoff he received a text from Hannah Drummond, the San Antonio evidence team leader, asking him to call.

"Good morning, Bryce," she answered. "I hope the rest of your day went well."

"As well as it can go when you're after a fugitive and hit a dry hole," he answered.

"Sorry to hear that. Maybe I can cheer you up."

"You've already had time to go through everything from the house?"

"Most of it. The stuff with the shooting I won't bore you with. We're not supposed to talk to you about that anyway. And CART is imaging the computers and cell phones as we speak, so I'll let them fill you in on those details. But we did make an interesting find."

"I'm listening."

"So from what I hear about this Network of yours, they're all supposed to be a bunch of tech-savvy dark-web dudes who encrypt everything and leave nothing to chance."

"That's their reputation. But I've already spoken to one of their operators who said they're not all that advanced. At least not to some James Bond level."

"Well, this Pinti guy is a dinosaur. He's the first person I've seen with an AOL email address since my mom and dad got rid of theirs twenty years ago."

"Yeah, I noticed that."

"And that's not all. He kept a ledger. A freaking ledger, Bryce. It's got transaction dates, amounts paid, true names and account numbers of who he paid, how he paid them, you name it. It's about thirty pages thick. If he wrote all this stuff down, I can only imagine what's on his computer."

"You're right, this is cheering me up. How soon can you get everything to the Miami office?"

"Wait, I'm not done. There's a three-ring binder full of paperwork that looks like dossiers. Fifty in total. All men except for one woman. There are photos, credit reports, addresses, phone numbers, and more. There are even little handwritten notes in the margins of the pages. Do you think these are the Network's victims?"

"What's the woman's name?"

"Hang on." Bryce could hear her rustling through papers on her desk.

"Mary Katherine Reading. Thirty-two years old, from Huntsville, Alabama."

"I knew one of the Network's female victims. Her name was Julia Martinez. Check and see if there's a dossier for someone named Vincent Kamara."

More rustling, then, "Yep, here he is. Scottsdale, Arizona."

"Those aren't dossiers on the victims. They're the hit men and the partners who run the organization."

Hannah let out a surprised gasp. "Why would anyone keep that sort of information just lying around?" she asked.

"Why does any company keep employee files in their human resources office?" Bryce countered. "To vet them during the hiring process. To know where they live and how to contact them when a need arises. To pay them. Sal Pinti was the Network's chief operating officer and apparently their HR manager, and I'm sure he wasn't expecting to be raided and shot to death with that stuff sitting in his house. Like you said, he was a dinosaur, and that's a win for us."

"Good points. Anyway, I'm glad we could be of help. CART said they'll be done imaging the computers this afternoon. We'll get you electronic copies of all their data right away, and you'll have the actual computers and phones in Miami tomorrow morning. The SAC is having our pilots fly it all over on our aircraft. We're not leaving this one to FedEx."

"Thanks, Hannah. And thank your people for me. Nice job."

Bryce hung up, called Abbie Bishop, and relayed the news from San Antonio.

"Wow," she gushed. "You really know how to make a girl's day." Bryce knew from her tone and from her previous work products that her sentiment was genuine.

"I thought you'd like it," he said. "If everything is what Hannah says it is, let's start building a target list. Match ledger entries with the names and faces in the dossiers. Separate the operators from the partners, keeping in mind that Vincent Kamara told me some partners are former operators themselves. Once we know everyone's true identity, we can look for DNA and finger-print records and start matching those against unsolved homi-cides across the country. Hell, maybe even around the world."

"I love it," she said. "If you get me the electronic versions later today, I can start right away."

"I'll see what I can do. And Abbie, there's one more thing."

"What's that?"

He walked toward the back of the plane where he would be alone. There, he lowered his voice and explained his theory to the superstar analyst, along with a plan he wouldn't even be sharing with Donnie. When he finished, there was dead silence on the other end.

After a moment, she spoke. "Bryce, are you sure about this?"

"Nope. That's why I need you to look into it."

"No, I mean are you sure you even want to go down this road? If you're wrong and we get caught—"

He stopped her. "If you're uncomfortable with it, I under-stand. You don't have to do it."

"Oh, no, mister. Don't you dangle something that juicy in front of me and then yank it away. Let's do this."

CHAPTER 36

THE DARKNESS FADED, then there was a pinpoint of light that grew broader and brighter until the shapes became visible. They were fuzzy, moving left and right, closer and farther away, and they made sounds that were impossible to understand. As the minutes went by, the shapes became blurry faces, and the sounds became their voices. One of them reached down and touched her shoulder.

"Miss Oliver? Can you hear me? Ashley? Can you hear me?"

She managed a groan and a weak nod in response. Her eyes darted around the room as her vision cleared. She took in the bright lights, the tubes, the machines, and the crew of masked nurses and doctors moving around her bed. Her frightened look asked the question she couldn't form with her mouth.

Where am I?

"Miss Oliver, you're in the intensive care unit at Mariner's Hospital in Marathon. Do you remember being shot?"

Another groan, and this time a slow head shake.

"It happened about four hours ago. You've just come out of surgery. One bullet went through your lung, and the other nicked your trachea. The surgeons fixed everything. Are you in any pain?"

She reached up with her right hand and touched her neck.

"You have a breathing tube in your throat for now. It's just a precaution, because of the injury to your throat. The doctor will decide when it can come out. It's going to be hard to talk, and maybe impossible, until then. I can bring you a whiteboard if there's something you need to tell me, or somebody we can call."

Ashley nodded, more forcefully this time, as she continued to emerge from the fog of the anesthesia. The nurse brought a magazine-sized whiteboard and a red dry-erase marker to her bedside, pulled the cap from the marker, and held the board in front of Ashley. It took her three attempts in her weakened state, but she managed to write "Bryce" on the board before her hand gave out.

"Is Bryce your husband?"

Ashley shook her head.

"Your boyfriend?"

She nodded.

"And do you know his number?"

She nodded again.

"Okay, honey, we have an easier way to do this next part." The nurse took the marker from Ashley and wrote the numbers zero to nine in large print on the whiteboard. "Just point and I'll write it down."

Ashley used the last of her strength to spell out Bryce's phone number with her finger, then drifted back into the darkness, where she would remain for the next several hours.

CHAPTER 37

THE GULFSTREAM was needed back in DC for the attorney general, so there was no time to stop along the way to let Donnie and Bryce off. They worked on their commercial flight reservations in the air. As soon as Bryce finished booking his flight from Washington to Key West, his phone rang. It was the nurse supervisor from Mariner's hospital, calling with the news about Ashley. Donnie watched his friend's face go ashen as he excused himself to continue the call in the empty forward cabin. When Bryce returned, he looked as if his entire world had come crashing down around him.

"What happened?" Donnie asked.

Bryce told him everything he knew from the nurse's call.

Donnie wrapped his friend in a bear hug. "Thank God Ashley's going to be all right," he said as he pulled away. "Did the nurse know any details about the shooting?"

Bryce shook his head. "I haven't been able to get Harley on the phone. I sent him there, Donnie. If anything happened to him—"

His friend cut him off. "It's too early to play guessing games. Let's get the sheriff's office on the phone and see what they can tell us."

Donnie called the main switchboard and asked to be put through to the detective's bureau in Marathon. He handed his phone to Bryce as the call was transferred. A detective named Simons answered the phone, and Bryce introduced himself.

"Pleased to meet you, Agent Chandler," Detective Simons said. "How can I help you?"

"I'm calling about a shooting in Marathon earlier today. In the Ocean Breezes condominium complex."

"Oh, yeah. We just cleared that scene. It was a bloodbath. What's the FBI's interest?"

"Full disclosure, Detective Simons. My girlfriend is Ashley Oliver, and she was one of the victims."

"Oh, man, I am so sorry to hear that. How's she doing? All I heard was she went to Mariner's and was headed to emergency surgery."

"She was lucky, thanks. Can you tell me if there was another victim named Harley Christian?"

"There was. He was also transported to Mariner's, but he didn't make it. Did you know him?"

Bryce's heart sank. "Yes," was all he could manage. He sank into a leather seat as tears formed in the corners of his eyes.

"Again, I'm very sorry. It looks like Mr. Christian drove his car into the shooter and crushed him up against another vehicle. He bled out on the scene from two severed femoral arteries. But in the process, Mr. Christian took a couple of rounds to the chest. I don't know if he died at Mariner's or en route. Either way, I hate to be the one to tell you."

"I appreciate that. Do you have an ID on the shooter?"

"Minnesota driver's license says he's Jerome Pettibone, aged thirty-three, from Saint Paul, Minnesota."

"It's a fake," Bryce offered. "Get me a copy of the DL photo and I can compare it against some true-name documents we just uncovered. This was a paid hit, and Ashley was the target."

"Holy cow, are you serious?" the detective asked. "That's a new one, and I've been on the job here twenty years."

"I'm serious. What else can you tell me about the shooter?"

"He was driving a minivan that he rented at the Miami airport early this morning. The gun was a Glock nine-millimeter, and we found a backpack on the ground with a tarp and some rope inside. Sorry, I know that's not something you want to hear, with this being your girlfriend and all."

"No, tell me everything. We've been after these guys for a long time."

"Are you sure? Because there's one more thing, but it made my skin crawl."

Bryce braced himself. "Go ahead."

"So, in the shooter's back pocket there was a pair of dental forceps. Like for pulling teeth. I didn't even know what they were at first."

Bryce was silent for a moment as the grotesque image of the killer using those forceps on Ashley bombarded his brain. He shook his head violently, as if to clear the thoughts from his head.

"We know this guy. After we have his DNA and prints, we'll be able to tie him to at least three more murders, maybe more," Bryce said.

"That's good to hear. Once Miss Oliver is well enough to talk to us, we'll be by to see her in the hospital. Hope you and I get a chance to meet then."

"I'm sure we will. Take care, and thanks for all the information."

The call ended just as the pilot announced the Gulfstream was thirty minutes out of Manassas. Bryce fastened his seatbelt and didn't talk to anyone for the rest of the flight.

It took seven excruciating hours to get to Key West, and another ninety minutes to get from the airport to Mariner's. Ashley was still in the ICU when he arrived, and there was an armed sheriff's deputy sitting outside her door, reading a magazine. The breathing tube had been removed and she was sleeping. A Styrofoam cup almost filled with a chocolate milkshake sat on the bedside table next to a plate of untouched green Jell-O cubes. Bryce leaned over the bed and kissed her forehead, then pulled up a chair and lowered the safety rail to get closer to her. He laid his head alongside her shoulder, put his hand on hers, and closed his eyes. And then Bryce Chandler did something he hadn't done in decades.

He talked to God.

He had accepted a higher power as part of his twelve-step Alcoholics Anonymous program, but it was just an acknowledgment for the sake of progress; a ticked box on his sobriety checklist. This was different. He bared his soul in silence, asking God to forgive the mess he'd made of his life and thanking Him for saving the one good thing in it. When he finished, he watched her chest rise and fall and listened as the EKG signaled her every heartbeat. No symphony had ever sounded sweeter, and he fell asleep to its rhythm.

He woke to a hand on his head, stroking his hair. Ashley was awake, and she had adjusted the bed to a sitting position. A clock on the wall read 2:30 a.m. Bryce sat up and looked at her. The woman had been shot, cut open, and sewn back together. Her hair was dirty and matted, she had no makeup on, and there were more tubes running in and around her body than he could count. Still, she was a vision of pure beauty.

"Hey," she whispered with a smile.

"Hey yourself. How are you feeling?"

"Like shit. How do I look?"

"Like an angel."

She managed a sleepy eye-roll. Her words came slowly and with obvious effort. "Yeah, I bet. They said I was shot. I heard someone yell something about a gun, then—nothing. Was it them?"

Bryce nodded. "The man who came for you is dead. He can't hurt you anymore. None of them can, baby. It's over."

"Was anyone else hurt?"

"Let's just worry about you for now. Get better so we can get out of this place."

She shook her head. "No, Bryce, I want to know. Was anyone else hurt?"

He sighed and looked at the floor, then back up at her. "Harley came to your house to warn you. I sent him. He saw the gunman and rammed him with his car. He killed the man who shot you, but he got shot, too." He paused, not wanting to say it, but knowing he had to. "Harley's dead."

"Oh, Bryce. No. No." She began crying, and Bryce reached forward to cradle her head next to his. "This is all my fault," she sobbed. "Getting mixed up with those people. And not telling you. And ignoring your calls and texts. Oh God, that's what you were trying to tell me the other night? That I was in danger? And if I had listened to you, Harley would be alive—"

Bryce shook his head. "No, Ashley. We're not playing the blame game. This might have gone so many different ways. You could have died and I could be talking to Harley right now. You could have both died. The 'what ifs' will drive you crazy. Here's one: What if you and I didn't end up spending the night together at your place after I got shot? I would have been back at my house when Vincent Kamara showed up to kill me. But I was with you instead. Was that your fault?"

She shook her head. "No."

"So we accept our fates, the blessings with the curses, and we're thankful we still have each other. That's all that matters. Do you remember our fight?"

"Of course."

"The last words I said to you have been haunting me since I got the call. I told you to leave me alone. And that almost happened. Baby, I don't want to be alone. Ever."

She nodded and wiped her eyes. "Are you saying you still want me? After everything?"

"I'm saying more than that. I love you, Ashley."

The crying began anew, and Bryce repositioned himself so he could wrap his arms around her. She buried her head in his chest and went on for a solid minute while he rocked her back and forth. When she stopped, she looked up at him and she was smiling.

"I guess I should say something too, huh?" she asked through watery eyes.

"Not if you don't want to."

"Stop it," she said. "And kiss me."

He leaned forward, mindful of the tubes, the wires, and her delicate post-surgical state, and planted a soft kiss on her lips. As he pulled away, she put her hands on his and gave him his answer.

"I love you too," she said. "More than you know."

CHAPTER 38

SONNY ROLLED OVER and glanced at the ancient blinking red LED display. It was 2:30 in the morning. His sleep was coming in fits and starts on the lumpy mattress in the dingy off-brand motel on the outskirts of Kearney, Nebraska. He lit a cigarette, found a water glass in the bathroom to use as an ashtray, and set it down between the clock radio and the no-smoking sign on the nightstand. The last twenty-four hours raced through his mind.

He got the warning call with minutes to spare, and though he couldn't be sure, he swore he drove past a motorcade of FBI agents making their way to his house on Interstate 25 as he fled town. There were fifteen or twenty of them, all late-model sedans, not too flashy and not too plain, sporting dark tinted windows and the dead giveaway curlicue antennae on their trunk decks. They were headed north from Denver; he was headed south to freedom, wherever that ended up being.

There was just enough time to throw together his go-kit, a carefully curated assembly of essentials he would need to escape, evade, and begin again in a new locale. Central to the kit was an array of false identity documents, twenty in all. And these were no ordinary fake IDs but legitimate, government-produced forms bearing the names of long-dead souls whose identities Sonny had plucked from gravestones and obituaries over the years. The key was the birth certificate. It was the genesis document that most states would send in the mail for a simple request form and nominal fee. Once you had the birth certificate, obtaining a driver's license was easy. Then a passport. And so on.

He had cash, nearly a hundred thousand dollars in all, but that was by no means his only financial security blanket. Millions more were scattered across the country and around the world in a bevy of overt and covert accounts, each tied to one of his assumed personas. There were ten burner phones, eight still unopened in their boxes, and he would pick up new ones as he traveled, disposing of used ones every few days.

He tossed the first phone after using it to contact a Craigslist seller in North Platte about a 2015 Ford F-150. They met at a public park on the city's north side, where Sonny counted off the full asking price in hundred-dollar bills to the delighted owner, who was happy to leave the tags on the truck until his buyer had a chance to get to the DMV. Sonny stripped the plates from his own car and left it parked under a sign reading *Absolutely No Overnight Parking, Violators WILL Be Towed*.

A small arsenal rounded out his travel bag. There were a pair of suppressed nine-millimeter pistols and a noisy Colt model 1911 for close-in work. And there was the heavy hitter, a scoped Nemesis Arms .308-caliber folding sniper rifle capable of delivering a lethal shot over as much as a thousand meters, depending on the skill level of the shooter. He would need to dispose of them all before he left the country. But not yet.

The news carried the latest on his brother's scandal and the resulting effect on his poll numbers. To the surprise of nearly everyone, Frank's approval rating among his party's faithful had gone up, not down, since the *Washington Post* story broke. Rather than turning the electorate against the senator, the scandal had galvanized voters who saw the whole thing as a dirty trick, a conspiracy of power brokers and their lackeys in the mainstream media. With Iowa just days away, Frank's seventeen-point share of likely voters grew to twenty-two. He seized on the momentum and used it to whip his base into a frenzy, vowing to press on, to fight the baseless charges against him, blah, blah, blah. No surprise there. Sonny's little brother had always been an arrogant, ambitious little prick.

And he had finally made up his mind what to do about him.

Bill Connell surveyed the ballroom, noting the emergency exit points, the placement of the metal detectors, and a myriad of other factors that were second nature for an agent with his years of experience. He downed three Excedrin with his last swig of Red Bull, hoping his days of insomnia were almost over. The energy drink had been fueling him for the past sleep-deprived month, but it wasn't just a lack of rest giving him migraines. This detail had been one giant-sized pain in the ass from its inception, and the latest developments only compounded matters.

To start, Senator Frank D'Angelo was one of the most entitled, class-conscious, self-promoting career politicians it had ever been his misfortune to protect. Thirty years ago as a rookie, he had served on the detail for a first lady with a reputation for being one of the most vile human beings in Washington. Frank D'Angelo was worse. He treated Secret Service agents like day laborers. He groped every decent-looking woman who wandered too close. He was foul-mouthed, short-tempered, and devoid of self-awareness. That is until he stepped in front of a camera or worked a room of supporters. He could turn on charm as if with a switch and turn it off just as quickly.

Ten days earlier, Bill was summoned to Secret Service head-quarters, to a meeting in the office of the director himself. If there was any doubt as to the gravity of the occasion, it was erased when he walked into the room and saw the FBI director sitting along-side his Secret Service counterpart.

There were ten of them, five each from the service and the FBI, and before the meeting began they all signed nondisclosure agreements, acknowledging that what they were about to discuss was top secret and would not be shared outside the room. Once the administrative chores were done, an FBI supervisor from Atlanta took over. Before he started talking, Bill wondered if the security measures were being overblown. When the FBI agent finished, he asked himself if what he had just heard could possibly be true.

There had been a threat on the life of Senator D'Angelo. The threat, which the FBI had on tape, came from his own brother, a Philadelphia thug turned hit man who presided over a dark web-based network of hired assassins. To muddy the waters further, the threat was in retaliation for Frank's own ultimatum to his brother, whom Frank wanted to hire in order to kill a witness. And the cherry on top? The witness was poised to testify against Senator D'Angelo, claiming that he had orchestrated the Griffin

Air Force Base poisoned-water disaster for his own financial gain. They played the tape of the threatening phone call as the meeting's participants listened in stunned silence.

The discussions on how to handle it all were above Bill's paygrade. He was only in the room because he was the agent in charge of the security detail. In the end, it was decided the Secret Service would continue protecting Senator D'Angelo, as he was surging in the polls and represented a legitimate target for a crackpot who wanted to ink his name in the history books. The FBI would continue its investigation and present their case to a federal grand jury no later than the day before the Iowa caucuses. If the grand jury returned an indictment, the senator would be arrested before the denizens of the Hawkeye State met to choose their presidential nominee. And since the senator was already aware of the threat, having heard it with his own ears, there was no need to discuss the rest of the matter with him.

Then, five days after the meeting in DC, the *Washington Post* story broke, adding a fourth circle to what was already a three-ring circus. Bill watched as his protectee's demeanor became even more unbearable, and he saw the effect it was having on his agents. He wanted to tell them it would all be over soon, to hang in there, but of course he couldn't. He took solace in knowing that, whether they realized it or not, their time with the senior senator from New York was almost at its end.

The crowds in Dayton and Wheeling were double what they had come to expect, in the wake of the 24/7 news coverage of Senator D'Angelo's alleged crimes. Frank reveled in it and motored on as if he had done nothing wrong. Bill realized that it was because, in his mind, he hadn't. The man had no shame. At each event he repeated the same fierce denials, the counteraccusations against nonexistent deep-state bogeymen, and the promise to clear his good name for the sake of Americans who needed him now more than ever. The crowds lapped it up, and Frank grew bolder by the day.

They made camp in Des Moines on this, the final morning before the caucuses. The event would be held in the grand ballroom of the Regal Palace, the city's oldest and most luxurious hotel. It was an art-deco masterpiece that had hosted receptions for every president from Herbert Hoover to Barack Obama, and it was chosen for its political symbolism and historical significance. The ballroom portion of the rally was for deep-pocketed donors only, and it was where Frank would deliver his pre-victory address. After his speech, as was his custom, he would work the crowd outside the hotel, pressing the flesh and scouting for photo ops to polish his image. The best subjects were babies, the handicapped, and the rabid faithful who dressed in regalia either supportive of the senator or critical of his enemies.

As his agents finished up their advance work in the ballroom, Bill wandered outside to the front of the hotel where the senator would end his night. It was set well back from the main thoroughfare, with a large circular driveway three-cars wide that allowed room for guests checking in and out, valets, and luggage attendants all to go about their business without bringing everything to a standstill. An hour before the senator made his appearance, all vehicular traffic would stop, and velvet ropes would go up on either side of the massive entrance doors to keep the crowd at bay. Foot traffic would be redirected to side entrances while Frank D'Angelo pandered to the masses.

The street itself was a sniper's dream and a Secret Service agent's nightmare. The Regal Palace was built in the 1920s, and since then every building within six city blocks had been demolished and replaced with mid- and high-rise condominiums, office buildings, and newer hotels. If the senator was the actual nominee, there was no way he would have been allowed outside the hotel without the protection of a robust counter-sniper team. But it was too early in the process for a clear front-runner to emerge, and there weren't enough assets to offer a presidential-level protection package to everyone in a seven-candidate field. Bill would repeat his admonishment to the senator to stick to the ballroom, and it would be a waste of breath.

He pulled a cigarette from his pocket and lit it. The first draw was sweet and satisfying, but the enjoyment was tinged with guilt as he thought of the promise he had made to his wife. He would make good on it, starting tomorrow. And then he would finally get some sleep.

It was just over three hundred miles from Kearney to Des Moines, and Sonny made the drive in four hours. Check-in time at the Marriott Marquis, across the street from the Regal Palace, wasn't for another five hours, but that gave him plenty of time. He had requested a high floor away from the elevator, and Marriott confirmed his selection in their online app.

He parked in a public lot two blocks from both hotels and donned a baseball cap and a pair of dark sunglasses. It wasn't much of a disguise, but then he wasn't planning on getting up close and personal with anyone who might be looking for him. He walked between the hotels, taking note of the angles and elevations from either end of the Marriott to the center of the Regal Palace, where the grand entrance was located.

When he got to the end of the block he turned left, following signs pointing to the Marriott parking garage. As expected, entry was via the guest's room card, so there was no attendant to stop him from ducking under the mechanical arm and walking into the structure. He took his time scanning the area, noting the locations of the elevators, the stairwells, and the service lift. The entire garage was four levels high, and he calculated that, in the fog of confusion after the assassination, it would take the Secret Service and local police at least two minutes to determine where the shots came from and another minute or so to take action and seal off the exits from the Marriott.

He planned for the worst case scenario, and assumed his car would be parked on the lowest level of the garage, furthest from the top floor of the hotel. The Marriott topped out at the fourteenth floor, which meant thirteen flights of stairs (hotels don't have thirteen floors out of respect for their superstitious guests). Then there would be three more flights to navigate once he reached the garage levels. He began at the bottom and trudged up the stairs, in no hurry because his escape would be from top to bottom, not the other way. When he reached the top, he gathered his breath in the stairwell before stepping into the hallway of the fourteenth floor.

He found himself in the center of the building, near the elevator bank. He could see the ends of the corridor in the distance in each direction, so it didn't matter which side of the building his room was on. The timing would be the same. He turned to his left and walked to the end of the hallway. When he got there, he pulled his phone from his pocket, set the stopwatch, and pressed "Start" as he began walking with a purpose back toward the stairwell entry.

When he was through the door, his quick walk turned into a full-on sprint down the stairs. He almost lost his balance twice, and by the time he got to the bottom, he was wheezing, and needed a moment to catch his breath. He bent at the waist, his hands on his knees for a few seconds, then stood and jogged to the furthest parking spot from the stairwell entry, still thinking in terms of having to deal with Murphy's Law at every turn. When he got to the empty space, he checked his stopwatch, and it read three minutes, forty-five seconds.

Maybe he could run faster. Maybe the police and the Secret Service would be slower than he anticipated. He pondered those and other variables as he walked back to his car. And he considered the most important question of all: Was he willing to make this, likely the final hit of his career, a suicide mission? He had no intention of going to prison, and if that meant shooting it out with the cops, the Secret Service, or anyone else who tried to stop him, so be it.

In the final analysis, Frank's betrayal drove his decision. Sonny had lived his entire life by a code, and to have his own brother so wantonly disrespect their family's honor was more than he could bear.

Game on.

CHAPTER 39

AS SONNY WAS conducting his reconnaissance mission, Ashley was being moved from the ICU to a private room. Her doctors were happy with her progress, but she would still need to spend two or three days in the hospital before being released. Bryce called the Monroe County Sheriff's Office and told them the armed deputy outside her room could stand down. With its CEO on the run and its dispatcher dead, the Network was crippled, at least for the time being. And the day of reckoning was coming for all the players after Abbie Bishop had a chance to work her magic on the trove of information seized from Sal Pinti's home.

Still, Bryce refused to leave Ashley's side, and the nurses brought a reclining chair and a folding bed into her room to make his stay more comfortable. As they left the room, Donnie called.

"How's Ashley doing?" he asked.

"Better. Sleeping right now."

"Glad to hear it. And I have good news for you. They moved Norma Whitehurst to the federal building this morning. As we speak, she's in front of the grand jury. They're going to indict Frank D'Angelo today. One less corrupt politician."

Bryce snorted. "Uh-huh. One down, a couple hundred to go. Let me know how it all turns out."

Over a thousand miles away, the federal grand jury shuffled into their assigned space at the federal courthouse building on Constitution Avenue. Grand juries were different from trial juries, the main difference being, as the name implied, size. There were twenty-three jurors in all, and sixteen had to be present in order to hear a case. As prosecutors presented the only evidence and there was no defensive rebuttal, the odds were overwhelmingly in the government's favor, and the old saying among courtroom lawyers was that you could indict a ham sandwich.

Two jurors had called out sick for the day, and the remaining twenty-one took their seats, not knowing what the day held in store. They brought with them their lunches, their paperback novels, and other distractions to while away the time between (and sometimes during) deliberations. While cell phones were prohibited in the grand jury room, it wasn't uncommon to see jurors knitting or working a crossword while the prosecutor droned on, especially during more tedious presentations.

On this day the United States attorney himself, not one of his assistants, would run the show, owing to the gravity of the charge and the celebrity of the accused. By the end of his opening statement, there wasn't a sudoku in sight, and all the jurors were laser focused and leaning forward in their seats. Norma Whitehurst took the stand and told her story. The agent who intercepted the phone call between Sonny and Frank D'Angelo was next, and he detailed the facts the FBI had used to get the wiretap on the senator's phone. When he finished, the US attorney played the recording of the call. They listened to Frank D'Angelo imploring his hit man brother to kill Norma Whitehurst and threatening retaliation if he didn't.

It all took about three hours, and when they were done, the US attorney asked the jurors to return a true bill on a single-count violation of Title 18 of the United States Code, Section 373: Solicitation to commit a crime of violence. A hand shot up in the rear of the room.

"Question?" he asked.

"Yes," the elderly woman replied. "Why are we only indicting him for making a threatening phone call? What about all those people he killed in New York?" Several of her fellow jurors nodded their heads in agreement.

The US attorney smiled. "I understand your concern, ma'am. We are still building that case, and it will require much more than Miss Whitehurst's testimony to get it to the level of proof necessary to win in court. Today's charge is a serious one, a felony, and it allows us to take the senator into custody, where he can't be a threat to anyone."

The old woman wasn't done. "Well, I'm ready to charge the son of a bitch with the whole thing. He should rot in hell, poisoning people like that. Goddamned lawyers." Then, realizing her gaffe, she added, "No offense." The room erupted in laughter.

The US attorney flashed another smile. "None taken. I appreciate your enthusiasm. And on that note, ladies and gentlemen, I leave you to your deliberations." He walked out the door, and instead of returning to his office, took a seat in the hallway outside the grand jury room. He didn't plan to be waiting long.

He was correct. Five minutes later, the door popped open and the foreman beckoned him inside. The vote was unanimous, and he took the charging documents two floors up to the magistrate's office. There, a pair of FBI agents was waiting with an arrest warrant in hand, needing only the court's signature. At 4:15 p.m., Judge Dennis Hagy, who had days before issued the search warrant for Sal Pinti's house, signed his name twice more, and Frank D'Angelo was a wanted man.

Bill Connell crushed out his cigarette on his heel, flipped the butt into a trash can, and walked back inside the Regal Plaza's ballroom to check the final security details. His phone rang, and he recognized the number as that of his special agent in charge, who had been one of the ten attendees at the meeting in the Secret Service director's office.

"Connell."

"Bill, it's done. The bureau guys have the warrant. I just came from a meeting with the director, and they're going to hold off until tomorrow morning to arrest him. They don't want to look like they're showboating, so no press, no perp walk. They'll meet you at five a.m. in the parking garage at the hotel. I assume you have access to the service elevator?"

"Of course."

"Use it. Take them up to his room, let them do their thing, and take them back down to their vehicles. Keep everything as quiet as possible. And once they leave with him, my friend, you and your people are relieved."

"Music to my ears, Dave. Thanks for the call."

It was finally over. One more night with Senator Asshole.

"Checking in, sir?" the pretty young blonde asked.

"Mm-hmm."

"Great, I'll just need your driver's license and a form of payment." He slid them across the counter and watched as the clerk hunted, pecked, and swiped her way through the check-in process.

"Here you are, Mister McCoy," she said as she returned his cards. "I have you in a king standard room, high floor away from the elevator. Is that correct?"

"Yes."

"Super. Checkout time is eleven a.m. Will you be needing a late checkout?"

"No."

"Awesome. You're all set then. Do you need any assistance with your bags?"

"No thanks," he smiled. "I'll get them."

CHAPTER 40

THE MEDIA was on hand for Frank's rally, not only because he was a legitimate threat to win the presidency, but also to hound him about his involvement in the Griffin disaster. As he strode to the ballroom's podium at 7:00 p.m. sharp, cameras flashed, video rolled, and the usual flurry of questions was shouted in his direction.

"Senator, what do you have to say to the families who've lost loved ones?"

"Senator, do you know who's making these accusations against you?"

"Did you poison the water at Griffin Air Force Base?"

"Senator, should your law firm recuse itself from representing the victims?"

He ignored them all, stepped to the microphone, and delivered his speech, opening as usual with a string of denials and a promise to clear his good name. The rest of the address was a blistering attack on his rivals, some of whom had dared to reach across the aisle and support legislation that, while good for the middle class, had been authored by the enemies from the opposition party. They were all traitors, and he was his party's only path to salvation in November, at least to hear him tell it.

Bill Connell and three other agents emerged from the wings as the senator wrapped it up, and they walked with him, two in front and two behind, down the center aisle as he made his exit from the ballroom. Two more colleagues were monitoring the situation outside, and they gave the go-ahead for the inside team to bring the principal through the lobby and the hotel's front doors.

The crowd, numbering in the thousands, erupted in cheers when their man made his appearance. He responded with a wave and a fist pump, eliciting still more emotion from the throng of faithful. Frank turned first to his right and made his way toward the velvet rope holding them back. He walked the line, shaking hands and trading thumbs-up gestures. Every time he moved, Bill Connell and another agent moved with him. The official campaign photographer was on orders to get the senator in frame with something snappy they could use for that evening's website update. But the crowd, though large, wasn't well stocked with the usual subjects. There were no disabled veterans wearing D'Angelo buttons, no millennials crossing generational lines to throw their support behind the old White guy. Just a bunch of people who looked and sounded angry, like Frank.

As he moved toward the other side, Frank spotted a contender. He was two deep in the crowd, waving an angry fist in the air, chanting "Run, Frank, run!" along with the others. And he was wearing a white baseball cap with black lettering that read "A.N.N. LIES."

Of all the cable news outlets covering the Griffin disaster, ANN had been the most relentless. Their reporters camped outside the senator's home and office. The story dominated their news cycle, and the coverage itself went beyond reporting straight to accusation. In the court of public opinion, ANN had already tried and convicted Frank D'Angelo.

And so Frank made a beeline for the man in the hat, motioning for the photographer to follow him. When he got to the rope, he gestured to those in the front row to step to one side and allow his new friend through. And when his Secret Service followers got in the shot, he shooed them away so as not to ruin the photo.

———————

Sonny had been following his brother through the scope on his Nemesis sniper rifle from the moment he emerged from the hotel lobby. The Secret Service agents were smothering him, and while it wouldn't have bothered him to take one of them out in the process, Frank was the only one with whom he had an axe to grind. He watched the senator as he moved along the ropes, gladhanding and whoring it up for the crowd. He followed him as he acknowledged the faithful at the other side of the entrance and moved toward them. He saw the crowd part, and he saw a supporter in a white baseball cap make his way to the front. He saw his brother wave away his detail and turn toward the cameras, his arm around the man in the hat, his unshielded face pointed in Sonny's direction for just the few seconds he needed.

Sonny inhaled deeply, let half of it out, and held his breath. He centered the crosshairs on his brother's face. As he pulled the slack out of the trigger, his world exploded in a flash of blinding light.

———————

It was fifteen pounds of TNT, and the bomber knew it would be overkill when he built the device. The explosives were hidden in a fishing vest under his coat, individual one-pound blocks linked together with detonating cord that had a loop fashioned at one end. In the loop, a pair of blasting caps were secured by a dozen wraps of electrical tape, and the detonator leads ran through the bottom of the vest, inside the waistline of the bomber's pants, and into his front pocket. There, a simple push-button switch and a nine-volt battery completed the device's triggering system.

The baseball cap proved to be just the decoy the bomber needed, and the senator walked toward it like a mouse toward a cheese-laden trap. He left one hand in his pocket and detonated the device just as he felt the senator's arm on his shoulder. The last pictures ever snapped of Frank D'Angelo and his killer would show a broad smile on one man's face and a look of solemn determination on the other's.

The effects were devastating, and not just for the two of them. Both Frank D'Angelo and the bomber were blown to pieces. Another two dozen spectators closest to the explosion were spared that grisly fate but ended up just as dead, as a blast over-pressure on the order of four pounds per square inch ran through them, crushing their internal organs and separating their brains from their spinal cords. Those who survived the blast wave were subjected to horrendous burns and fragmentation damage from the bomb, which turned everything from rope stanchions and camera tripods to window glass and even human bones into flying projectiles. Everyone within fifty meters would suffer temporary if not permanent hearing loss.

In a strange twist of fate, Frank D'Angelo's last act on Earth was to spare the lives of two of his Secret Service detail members, whom he waved away in order to get his precious photo op. As they acquiesced to his demands, it put space between themselves and the senator. That space was then filled by selfie-seekers who wanted in on the action, and it was the mass of their bodies that absorbed the brunt of the blast energy. Bill Connell and his assistant team leader suffered burns and shrapnel wounds, and both would later be diagnosed with traumatic brain injuries, but they survived the day.

In all, thirty-four people, including Frank D'Angelo and the bomber, were killed immediately or died at the scene. In the coming days, another ten would succumb to their wounds in the hospital. Over two hundred were injured, ranging from third-degree burns and broken bones to multiple amputations of upper and lower limbs. Ten were permanently blinded. Frank D'Angelo's dying legacy, as in life, was one of incalculable human suffering.

As it turned out, Sonny didn't need to hurry down the staircase after all. He repacked his rifle and the small bag of clothing and toiletries he'd brought to his room and rode the elevator down to the parking garage. There was no police interest in the Marriott or anywhere else other than the crime scene, which by now covered several thousand square feet of bloodstained sidewalk and city street. He drove away, watching the red and blue strobes disappear in his rearview mirror, and followed the signs to Interstate 235 West, then 35 South.

He made it as far as the outskirts of Kansas City before stopping for the night. The next morning he began again, his plan no more specific than to keep driving south. He listened to news radio as he drove, where the big story was still Frank D'Angelo, but of course for a different reason.

He made an entire day of the drive, pulling into Fort Worth near nightfall. As he searched for a hotel, the news broke that the FBI had identified the bomber responsible for the carnage in Des Moines. According to sources, he was a veteran—a former explosive ordnance disposal specialist from Griffin Air Force Base.

His name was William Joseph Newberry, but his friends and family called him Joe.

CHAPTER 41

FOR TWO WEEKS after the Iowa bombing, the entire weight of the FBI's investigative machine was thrown into its latest major case. Lesser matters, including the Network investigation, took a back seat as the bureau focused on determining who was behind Frank D'Angelo's murder and why they did it. In these cases, the most burning question was whether the assassin was a lone wolf or part of a conspiracy or, worse yet, a tool of a foreign government. In the end, the FBI's official position was that Joe Newberry acted alone.

The time outside the headquarters spotlight was a blessing for Abbie Bishop, who used it to put the finishing touches on her latest analytical masterpiece. Bryce also took full advantage, tending to Ashley around the clock as she recovered in the hospital and at home.

He only left her alone a few times, and it was for the grimmest of tasks. He inquired with the county coroner's office, and as he suspected, nobody had come forward to claim Harley's body or take care of his final affairs. After a half day's administrative wrangling, he convinced the county bureaucrats that he was the closest thing Harley had to next of kin, and they allowed him to send the remains to a funeral home for cremation. The hospital released the only personal items they had: Harley's cell phone, a key ring, and a brown leather wallet with a large marijuana leaf embossed on the outside and four hundred dollars in twenties inside.

The car was a total loss, and after taking possession of the tools in the trunk, Bryce signed a release at the sheriff's department impound yard so it could be scrapped. All that was left was to go through his house, though Bryce wasn't sure what he would do with Harley's belongings. Donate what he could to charity, he figured, and take the rest to the dump.

Bryce picked up Harley's ashes at the funeral home, placed them in a backpack on the front seat of his truck, and drove south. When he pulled up to Harley's house, there was a newer-model Jeep parked in the middle of the driveway. Bryce had a twinge of investigator's paranoia, but it subsided as quickly as it arose. It was broad daylight. Whoever had driven the Jeep there was making no effort to hide it. And the front door was wide open, with just a screen door between the inside and outside of the house.

He knocked on the screen door, and a woman appeared from the kitchen. She was younger than Bryce by several years, blonde and pretty but rough around the edges. She had full-sleeve tattoos on both arms, and there was a cigarette dangling from her lips. Bryce couldn't help but think he knew her from somewhere.

"Can I help you?" the woman asked, standing inside the door and making no attempt to open it.

"I'm not sure. I'm here to take care of Harley Christian's affairs. Did you know him?"

"What's your name, mister?"

"I'm Bryce."

She pulled the cigarette out of her mouth and stared in amazement. "Holy shit. You're Bryce Chander, aren't you? I thought I recognized you." She opened the screen door and stood to one side to let him in.

"I'm sorry, ma'am, but you're going to have to remind me where we've met," Bryce said as he stepped inside.

"I'm Rebecca Calley. Becky. I used to tend bar at the Chart House. You were a regular back in the day."

The cobwebs cleared and the memories came flooding back. "Oh my gosh. I'm sorry. I remember you now. I apologize for forgetting. Most of those years are still a haze."

"I'll bet they are. You were a two-fisted cowboy. I heard you got a DUI leaving our place one night. Never saw you again."

Bryce nodded. "It was my wakeup call. Are you still working there?"

She shook her head. "I finally scratched together enough money to buy a few places, and renting them out is a full-time job."

"So you were Harley's landlord?"

"And wife number three. We divorced seven years ago, and since I had just bought this place, he became my first renter. I have to say, he was a helluva better tenant than he was a husband."

They moved to the living room, and Becky sat down on the couch. A bottle of Don Julio Anejo was sitting open on the coffee table in front of her, next to a nearly empty glass.

"I'm going to refresh this," she said. "I don't imagine you care to join me?"

"No thanks," Bryce replied, taking a seat in an easy chair across the table from her. "But tell me, how did you hear about Harley?"

"Are you kidding?" Becky replied. She took a sip from the glass. "You've lived here long enough. The Keys is a tiny community. Everyone knows everyone else, especially the locals. I heard about it the night he died."

Bryce stared at her, incredulous. "And you just let him lie there in the morgue? Did it occur to you to claim his body, maybe to have some sort of memorial for him? You two were married, for Christ's sake."

"Don't judge me," she snapped. "You don't know anything about me, or about me and Harley. It was complicated. We were bad for each other, you know? I don't think I laid eyes on him ten times in the last few years, and when I did it was because we bumped into each other down in Key West. And a memorial service? Who would have gone to that? His doper pals? His weed customers? You're the only friend he had."

The last statement stunned Bryce, and it showed in his face.

"Yeah, that's right," she continued. "I know about you, and not just as a customer. When Harley and I did see each other, we'd chitchat for a few minutes, how's it going, that kind of stuff. And every single time he managed to work your name into the conversation. Bryce and I are doing this and that. Bryce took me fishing on his boat. Bryce has a girlfriend. Harley cared about three things: boat motors, dope, and you. And trust me, you were the most important thing in his life. He idolized you, mister FBI agent."

Bryce had never been so humbled. He sat quietly while Becky sipped her tequila and lit another cigarette. An awkward moment stretched into minutes as neither one of them said a word. Finally, he broke the silence.

"Look, I'm sorry. You're right, I had no business judging you. I came here today to do what I could for Harley, so tell me, how can I help?"

She shrugged. "He didn't have much. I rented the house furnished, so all the stuff you see is mine. I've boxed up his clothes in the bedroom, and I went through the place top to bottom looking for his weed supply. I found a few ounces and threw it away. The last thing I need is the next renter finding it and turning my ass in to the cops."

Bryce nodded his understanding. "Would you like me to take his clothes to Salvation Army?"

"That would be nice, thanks."

"I have a bag from the hospital with his belongings. There's not much in there, but there is four hundred dollars in a wallet. Do you have any idea what I could do with it?"

She thought for a moment. "Harley liked dogs. Never had time for one, but he always wanted one. He used to feed strays every chance he got. Maybe donate the money to the ASPCA?"

"That's a great idea. One last thing. I have his ashes in my truck. Do you want them, or a portion of them?"

"No. Not to sound like a heartless bitch, but I'm not connected to Harley that way anymore. You were his friend. I'm sure you'll do what's right. Let's go get those clothes."

They loaded the boxes into Bryce's truck, and he dropped them at a Salvation Army thrift store on Big Pine Key. It was a short distance from there to his house, where his boat was perched on its lift above the canal waters. With the backpack slung over his shoulders, he hopped on board, lowered the boat into the water, and idled away toward Pine Channel, where he could turn south toward the Atlantic Ocean or north to the Gulf of Mexico.

He turned south. The vast expanse of ocean lay before him as he opened the throttle, put the boat on plane, and got his speed up to forty knots, scanning between the open water and his navigation screen, where a pin he had dropped over a year ago was getting closer and closer.

The pin brought him to a reef he hadn't fished since the last time he was there with Harley. It had been a great day on the water, and between the two of them they took the legal limit for yellowtail snapper in just a couple hours before returning to Bryce's house, cleaning their catch, and grilling it on the back porch. To Bryce it was just another good day of fishing, and his newfound knowledge of what it may have meant to Harley filled him with guilt.

He cut the engine, let the boat drift, and reached inside the backpack. The ashes were in a plastic bag, which in turn was in a cardboard box. Bryce pondered the indignity of the humble packaging for a minute before assuring himself that Harley, as humble a man as he ever knew, wouldn't have minded. He undid the twist tie holding the bag closed, stepped to the side of the boat, and tried to think of a prayer, or at least something worthy of the moment. He came up empty, and so as he slowly turned the open bag toward the sea, he just whispered two words on repeat until it was empty.

"I'm sorry."

He put the bag aside, reached into the backpack, and retrieved the bottle of Jack Daniel's he had stowed away after the fight with Ashley. The plastic sheath was still in place over the bottle top. Bryce removed it, twisted off the cap, and brought the bottle to his nose. The smell was sweet and beckoning. He walked back to the side of the boat, where some of Harley's ashes were still floating on the surface. He reached over the side, held the bottle over the ashes, and turned it upside down until it was empty. One final drink for his friend.

The last stop was at the Marathon animal shelter, where Bryce donated Harley's cash to a surprised and appreciative staff. He tossed Harley's empty wallet onto the passenger seat when he got back into his truck. He started the engine and reached for the shift lever, then stopped. He picked up the wallet, turned it over, and opened it to examine the inside. It was made of high-quality, full-grain leather, and both the embossing and stitching were top-notch in terms of craftsmanship. More importantly, it was all of Harley he had left.

Bryce pulled his own wallet from his pocket and emptied the contents into the center console tray. He tossed his wallet into the back seat, picked up Harley's, and began filling it with his driver's license, credit cards, insurance cards, and cash. He smiled, then started laughing at the irony of it all. A career federal agent carrying a wallet adorned with a huge pot plant. It would raise eyebrows for sure, not that he cared.

He couldn't wait to get home and show it to Ashley.

CHAPTER 42

WHEN ABBIE CALLED to say the work was done, Bryce invited Donnie to join them in the Key West office for the unveiling.

Abbie led them to the same conference room where just a month earlier she had laid out the telephone analysis that led to Sal Pinti's house. As before, the long table was filled with binders, boxes, and folders, all arranged into stacks according to subject matter. Glossy eight-by-ten photographs topped several of the piles, with a name inked at the bottom of each picture in black marker. A map of the world was taped to the wall, and hundreds of colored pushpins dotted locations inside the United States, Europe, South America, and Southeast Asia.

"You've been busy, Miss Bishop," Donnie quipped.

"Well, before I begin," Abbie replied, "keep in mind, everything you see is just for the last three years. That's as far back as Pinti's records went, at least on the computer we analyzed. And he was a stickler for details. There was a spreadsheet for everything, starting with the requests that came in from clients through the Network's dark-web site." She pointed to the largest of the binders in the center of the table.

"Once a job was approved," she continued, "the fee was collected, and the details went out to the hit men in a coded email message from the Network. As soon as one of the operators accepted a job, it was assigned to them. And documented on yet another spreadsheet."

"When did everyone get paid?" Bryce asked.

"When the job was done. The call was made to McNair Industries, and Sal Pinti, as the Network's chief financial officer, distributed the funds. And that made it easy to identify who was who in the zoo, so to speak."

"How so?"

"Let's say an average job cost the client a hundred thousand dollars. Some were a little less, most were more, but we'll use a hundred grand as a nice round example. Of that amount, the hit man got paid fifteen percent. Sonny and Sal took five percent each off the top. The remainder was divided into equal amounts that went to the same ten people every time, including Sonny and Sal. Those are your partners, and each one of them made close to a million dollars every year for the last three years. There are dossiers on seven of them, but not for Sal or Sonny. I guess seniority has its privileges."

"Seven dossiers, plus Sal and Sonny. That's nine," Donnie interjected.

"I'm getting there. Bryce asked me to hold one until the end."

Donnie made his way around the table, taking in the volume of Abbie's work while she spoke. "I can't believe you got all this done in such a short period of time," he said.

"Thank you," Abbie beamed. "But if you look carefully, you'll see there's one glaring omission in our cast of characters."

Bryce spoke up. "The clients."

"Exactly. For whatever reason, Pinti kept detailed records on everything except who was paying for the jobs. Probably because he didn't know. My best guess is the Network guaranteed anonymity to their customers, so as long as they got paid, the company policy was no questions asked."

"And if all those pins on the map mean what I think," Donnie added, "the people who paid for all this are getting off scot-free."

Abbie shrugged. "For now. And the map's not done. A red pin means a confirmed kill. Yellow is for a location where the Network's records show a job was completed and paid out, but we haven't linked it to a known murder yet. Those are going to take a while, while we coordinate with state and local police and INTERPOL. Green means a request was made, but it looks like the Network declined the job. Still, we have the names of the intended victims, so we can query our law enforcement partners to see who among them is still with us and who isn't. Maybe the client found someone else to take care of their problem."

She walked around the table, scanning with her eyes until they lit up. She reached down, grabbed a folder with a photograph on its cover, and handed it to Bryce.

"This will make you happy," she said.

Bryce opened the dossier and scanned it while Donnie read over his shoulder. Both of them broke into wide smiles at the same time.

"We get dibs on this one, don't we?" Bryce asked Donnie.

"You better believe it."

"Good. Where do we go from here?"

"The short answer is, we lock their asses up," Donnie replied. "It will take at least a week to coordinate everything between DOJ, FBI headquarters, and all the field offices. And we want to pick them all up at the same time. Once the word gets out, every one of them that can run, will run."

Bryce nodded and turned toward Abbie. "Time to talk about the other thing?" he asked.

She nodded her head. "It's all I have left."

"Okay then. Donnie, you may want to sit down for this. I'll join you." Bryce nodded toward Abbie and took a seat next to his friend. Abbie picked up an unmarked folder, took a position at the head of the table, and began her speech.

"As I said, we identified seven of the partners by linking the payments in Sal Pinti's spreadsheets to their dossiers. There were no files on Pinti or Sonny, but it was easy to see they were among the ten partners getting paid. That left one. Our mystery man."

She opened the folder and read aloud from her notes. "Bryce called me a couple weeks back with his theory. The nameless payments were going to a bank in Grand Cayman, so I went through FINCEN to get the account holder's information." The Financial Crimes Enforcement Network was a department within the United States Treasury that tracked suspicious bank transactions around the globe.

Abbie continued. "The account holder is one Peter Coffee of Annandale, Virginia."

"What do we know about this Coffee guy?" Donnie asked.

"Well for starters, he's dead. For about seven years, in fact. But he was a real person with a real address, and he sold his house about a year before he died. I'll get to why that's important in a minute. Anyway, since we knew the account holder name was fake, we asked for a copy of the identification documents he used to establish the account." She reached into the folder, pulled out a color photocopy of a United States passport, and laid it on the table in front of Donnie, whose jaw went slack as he realized what he was seeing.

"Is that who I think it is?" he asked.

"Yep," Bryce answered.

Donnie never looked up, his disbelieving eyes fixed on the photo. "How? When?"

"It started when the Network got to Vincent Kamara's place in Scottsdale the day before I did. It really stuck in my craw, and that was the point where I began to think we had a leak, maybe an outright mole. But I didn't know who it was."

He made no mention of his suspicions regarding Ashley.

"Then," he continued, "we hit Sonny's place, and it's a dry hole. We missed him by what—an hour, maybe less? Sal Pinti couldn't have warned him; he didn't have time. So same question: Who's the mole? I had my suspicions at this point, but still not enough to point a finger."

"When did you become sure?" Donnie asked.

"In the house in Fort Collins," Bryce replied. "When that son of a bitch made the snide remark about Sonny running to Las Vegas. It didn't dawn on me until hours later, when we were on the plane back to DC."

Donnie looked perplexed. "I'm not following."

"We knew Sonny spent time in Vegas because Vincent Kamara told me and I told you. But I had Abbie check, and it's not in my 302 of the interview. It's not anywhere in the case file. There was no way for AD Caine to know of any connection between Sonny and Las Vegas unless—"

Donnie completed the sentence, staring at Bryce through eyes as wide as saucers. "Unless he knew Sonny."

"Yep. And there was one more thing. Caine knew about Scottsdale. He knew about Fort Collins. He didn't know about San Antonio, because you forgot to tell him. And Sal Pinti was the only one we caught by surprise. So there's your mole," he said, pointing toward the table.

"Ho. Lee. Shit," Donnie said, staring at the photograph.

"That's one way to say it. Abbie put the rest of it together from there," he said and motioned toward her to take over.

"The banking authorities in Grand Cayman are fussy about giving out customer information," Abbie said. "Almost as bad as the Swiss. FINCEN got us the account holder's name, but Bryce had to reach out to one of his National Academy buddies to get me a copy of the passport that was used to open the account. And he was also able to find security video of Peter Coffee, who is of course Sullivan Caine, accessing a safety deposit box at the bank on three different occasions. The last time was just two months ago. And we have it all on this thumb drive." She held it up for Donnie to see.

"And you can open an account in a different name than what's on your passport?" Donnie asked.

"Yep," Abbie said. "It's like their version of the Swiss numbered account system. As long as they know who you really are, what name you put on the account is up to you. They see it as a form of privacy protection, and that's what keeps illegal money coming into the Caymans. It's their number one source of revenue."

"So how did he choose his alias?" Donnie asked.

"Remember I told you the actual Peter Coffee sold his home in Annandale a year before he died? Well, guess who bought it," Abbie answered.

Donnie shook his head. "This is surreal. I'm still trying to wrap my head around how Sonny and Caine even knew each other."

"Caine was a first office agent in Las Vegas from 1997 until 2010," Bryce answered. "Back when that was Sonny's stomping ground. And he was working organized crime matters. Maybe he ran a case against Sonny or one of his associates. Hell, maybe he had Sonny as a source. Nothing would surprise me at this point. But at the end of the day, one thing is for certain. Sullivan Caine is a full-share partner in the Network. Now we have to figure out how to put everything together without spooking him."

"We'll wall it off," Donnie said. "Caine will see everything we have except the info on him. I'll take that straight to the deputy attorney general. She can run it up to the AG and then over to the director. I just pray we can keep everything quiet until roundup day. One more question: Why did you two keep this to yourselves?"

"Partner, we were accusing an FBI assistant director of being a member of an international murder-for-hire conspiracy. If we were wrong and it got out, it would have been everyone's ass. The last time you went off the reservation it almost cost you your job. Abbie's KMA, and I've been playing with house money since you dragged me back in, so we had nothing to lose." FBI employees who had reached the minimum years of age and service for retirement eligibility were deemed to have achieved KMA status, or "Kiss my ass."

Donnie laughed. "I don't know whether to be flattered or terrified. But sincere thanks to both of you. Let's do this."

CHAPTER 43

ALBUQUERQUE, NEW MEXICO

He was Phil to his wife, Mr. S. to his eleventh-grade geometry students, and Coach to the defensive linemen on the Raul Garcia High School varsity football team. Phillip Shearer was also a decorated veteran of the first and second Gulf Wars, where he served in the 75th Ranger Regiment and the 3rd Special Forces Group. Armed with a degree in secondary education and a chronic case of PTSD, he embarked on his teaching career soon after separating from the Army in 2006.

In 2008 his wife left him, and in 2009 his youngest son, thinking he could fly, took a header off the top of his bunkbed and broke his neck, leaving him a quadriplegic for life. Social workers estimated the boy's care costs would run several hundred thousand dollars annually, of which Phillip's insurance would cover 20 percent. His teacher's salary at the time was forty six thousand dollars per year.

He had heard whispers about the "extra work" a few of his former colleagues were doing, and it only took a few calls before he was offered his first job. The target was a real scumbag, a schoolteacher himself, but one who had knocked up a fifteen-year-old student. A week after she made a tearful confession to her parents, she disappeared, and her body was never found. The police found love letters and texts from the teacher, but little more. In the end, there was no conclusive proof of an affair or a pregnancy, much less a murder.

The girl's father had all the proof he needed, and so it was that Phillip was dispatched to West Memphis, Arkansas. He found the lecher in a dark, seedy strip bar on the outskirts of town, getting a lap dance, not surprisingly, from a dancer wearing a school-girl outfit. He waited until nature called, then followed him into the bathroom, where he rammed a six-inch icepick through the man's medulla oblongata and left him lying face down in the floor urinal.

His first foray into the world of murder for hire netted him ten thousand dollars. In the process, he discovered that it mattered not whether his prey was Iraqi soldiers, the Taliban, or middle-aged perverts. Killing was easy, and Phillip was good at it, so he took on as many jobs as he needed to pay for his son's round-the-clock nursing care and physical therapy. He didn't always know who he was murdering or why, but he learned to make up stories in his head as to why his victim deserved their fate. Between that and his noble use of the proceeds, Phillip Shearer slept soundly at night.

In 2021, he accepted a position as a partner with the Network. No longer on the street, his new duties including vetting clients and operators, approving and disapproving jobs, and putting out fires wherever they popped up. It paid just as well as the wet work, with far less risk. It also allowed him to spend more time with his son, who had grown into a teenager and regained some movement in his hands and arms. All in all, Phillip's life had turned out far better than he would have predicted fifteen years prior, and he had a guarded sense of optimism for the future.

Still, when the front door of his house came crashing in at 4:30 in the morning, his first instinct was correct. He sat bolt upright in bed, reached for the pistol in his nightstand, and trained it on the closed bedroom door with a single-handed grip. He waited as the sound of stun grenades split the air downstairs. The explosions were followed by the unmistakable sound of combat boots beating across the floor as the men who came for him cleared the house, room by room, shouting orders as they went. For a split second he felt a twinge of envy for them, brothers in arms, doing what he had done so many times in his former life, when killing made him a hero.

As the boots pounded up the stairs, he had a moment of clarity, and the last two decades of his life flashed in front of him. The violence. The misery. The human suffering caused in his name and by his hand. He turned the muzzle and placed it against his temple as the boots reached the landing and came his way. A second later, the crash of the bedroom door and the roar of the pistol made a single, thunderous sound.

Mobile, Alabama

The SWAT team stacked four deep on either side of the door to Randall Fitch's two-bedroom condominium. It was go-time, and under ordinary circumstances the operators would be adrenaline-ridden, laser-focused warriors welcoming the danger on the other side of the threshold. But not today. The owner was dead, his legs nearly severed in a Florida Keys parking lot a month ago, and they all knew it. Some of them wondered why they were even there. It was a simple search warrant, and there was nobody home. Easily within the skill set of their non-SWAT qualified colleagues.

The decision wasn't theirs to make, nor was it within the purview of the executive management team in their office. The word had come down from FBI headquarters. Every search and arrest warrant would be served with the full force of the FBI's tactical teams. The director wasn't taking chances.

The door crashed, the stun grenades roared, and two minutes later the empty apartment was cleared and released to the evidence response team. The entire residence was photographed from top to bottom. Fingerprints were lifted from every surface that might hold one. Beds were overturned, drawers rummaged, and carpets vacuumed for hairs and fibers. Toothbrushes, nail clippers, and any other implements that might produce a DNA sample were bagged and tagged.

As the search was winding down, a rookie evidence technician found a large mahogany jewelry box hidden behind a pile of clothes in Randall's closet. When she opened it, she was hit by simultaneous waves of shock and nausea and almost fainted. She gathered herself and called for a photographer to document her discovery.

As she changed lenses and readied her flash, the camera-woman was also struck by the gruesomeness of the find. She was a veteran of some of the grisliest crime scenes the FBI had to offer, but still, this was something new.

The box was filled to the top with human teeth. Some were gleaming white, others yellowed, and many were cracked or fractured by the instrument that had been used to extract them.

Whoever had removed the teeth hadn't bothered to clean the roots, where the blood had dried to varying shades of dark red, brown, and black.

The team leader came for a look, and the young technician's day got even worse. The contents of the box were designated as human remains, and the handling protocols were clear. Each tooth would be placed in a one-inch-square clear ziplock bag, labeled, and annotated with a unique inventory number. The boss assigned three more technicians to assist, and between the four of them it still took three hours to complete the task. When they finished, the tooth count stood at 327.

Clarksburg, West Virginia

Timmy Reese parked as far from the building as possible, mere feet from the black wrought-iron security fence that ringed the FBI's Criminal Justice Information Services complex. Not because he wanted the exercise, but because he took up two spaces to park his car. If he pulled a stunt like that in the premium spots, it would be only a matter of time before somebody keyed his baby.

And if that happened, he just might have lost his mind. The Corvette ZR-1 was the center of his material world, an inaugural year C8 model, and the first in Corvette's legendary seventy-year history to sport a mid-engine design. Fire-engine red with a tan calfskin interior, it was the most expensive thing he owned or ever would own. It should have set off alarms during his five-year security-clearance renewal, but he was never questioned as to how he could afford a six-figure sports car on a salary of eighty thousand dollars a year.

He chirped the alarm, stuffed the key fob into the rear pocket of his jeans, and left the Corvette-logo keychain dangling behind him as he made his way through the mass of lesser vehicles dotting the parking lot. He swiped his badge at a turnstile, the first of two between the lot and the building that held the FBI's massive library of fingerprint and DNA files. He cleared the second turnstile, then badged his way into the building's lobby, where another swipe and a six-digit PIN granted him elevator access. As usual, his 6:30 a.m. arrival made him one of the first employees in the building.

He got off at the sixth floor, stowed his cell phone in a bank of lockboxes, and touched his badge to one final keypad to gain entry to suite 604, home to the division's team of fifteen information technology specialists. When he turned the corner toward his cubicle, he saw them. One was sitting in his chair, another at the desk next to his. They were wearing dark suits, white shirts, and the serious expressions of men on a mission.

"Good morning, Timmy," Bryce said.

The computer geek stared at him. "Do I know you?"

"Not yet. I'm Special Agent Bryce Chandler, and this is Supervisory Special Agent Donald Morris. Take a seat." He reached, without standing, for a nearby swivel chair, and rolled it toward Timmy, who sat and stared in bewilderment.

"Do you know why we're here?" Donnie asked.

Timmy responded with a shrug.

"Okay," Donnie continued. "We'll play it that way. Timmy, you've been doing some side work for the past several years. For some very bad people. Well, we raided their offices a month ago, and guess what? There was a file on you and all the other scumbags you worked for, and as we speak, they're all being taken into custody."

It was a bone-chilling sixty-eight degrees in the room, and sweat broke out across Timmy's brow. He rocked back and forth in his chair, his hands gripping his knees, and blurted out the only words his mind and mouth could form.

"I don't know what you're talking about."

"Sure you do, Timmy," Bryce said. "How else could you afford that midlife-crisis-on-wheels you just rolled up in? Which, by the way, we'll be seizing as soon as we're done with you. If it's any comfort, though, the car didn't do you in. You just picked the wrong bunch of contract killers to call your friends."

Timmy's senses returned, and he managed a more useful statement.

"I want a lawyer."

"I'm sure you do," Bryce said. "Now stand up." He cuffed Timmy and gave him a quick search while Donnie advised him of his Miranda rights.

"Let's go," Donnie said as he pointed toward the door.

"Wait," he said, squirming in the cuffs. "I can give you somebody. Somebody big. The one who set it all up. But I want a deal. Full immunity, or you can both go to hell." He said it with an air of defiance, as if their case hung on his cooperation.

"Mighty bold demands, Timmy," Bryce said. "This Mister Big wouldn't be the assistant director of the criminal division, would it?" The deflated look on the subject's face gave them their answer.

"We're way ahead of you, Timmy," Donnie said. "Now let's go." They walked him out of the office and rode down the elevator, stopping at the lobby level.

A few more employees had made their way into the building, and they stared wide-eyed as their colleague was led out of the building by the two agents. About halfway across the lobby, Donnie turned toward Bryce, a mischievous look on his face.

"We're forgetting something," he said.

"What's that?" Bryce asked.

"Remember what the director said?"

Kicking and screaming.

"Oh, yeah," Bryce replied. "I did forget." As he spoke, he put one hand on Timmy's upper back and pulled upward on the cuffs with the other hand. It wasn't enough to cause any real damage, but it dug the metal into his wrists and put an enormous amount of pressure on his elbows and shoulders.

"Hey!" Timmy screamed. "Stop it! That hurts, you fucking asshole! Stop!" His legs flailed and his head bucked back and forth as he protested. Anyone who hadn't noticed before was now paying full attention.

Bryce looked at Donnie. "Better?"

Donnie smiled. "Better."

Washington, DC

"The director needs to see you." It was all the big man's secretary ever needed to say. There was never a why or a when. It meant now, and it meant you'll find out when you get there.

Sullivan Caine gathered his notebook and pen, threw on his jacket, and boarded the elevator for the seventh floor. The director's suite was at the end of the long hallway, and his mind raced as he walked it, sifting through the possible reasons for his summoning.

He got his answer when he turned the final corner and entered the director's outer office, where visitors waited their turn to see the nation's top law man. There were six of them in there, all standing, all eyes on him as he entered the room. He recognized the assistant director of the Office of Professional Responsibility, whose job it was to deal with agents who misbehaved and broke the law. He recognized the FBI's chief counsel, who advised the director on the most serious of legal matters. And while he didn't know any of the four uniformed and armed FBI police officers, he knew in that instant why they were there.

His knees went weak and his stomach flip-flopped as his situation became clear. He stood, a deer in the headlights for just a moment, then reached toward his pistol as his fight-or-flight reflexes kicked in. His right hand moved less than an inch before two of the officers were on him, one wrenching his arm behind his back while the other applied a death grip to the still-holstered gun. Seconds later he was disarmed, handcuffed, and being led away to a waiting car that would deliver him to the Marshal's Service lockup.

He was the last of the day, one of eight partners and twenty-three hit men the FBI had taken into custody. Besides the subjects, agents seized sixty million dollars in assets, including domestic and foreign bank accounts housing the revenues of the vast murder-for-hire enterprise. The victim count, which stood at two when Bryce put together the first pieces of the puzzle nearly two years earlier, was now over a hundred and rising every day. Counting Sonny, another nineteen killers remained at large, but the blow to the organization was devastating and final.

The Network was out of business.

CHAPTER 44

TWO WEEKS AFTER the mass arrests, Vincent Kamara died at the United States Federal Correctional Institution in Coleman, Florida. Shayna had been staying at a motel near the prison and learned of her father's passing via phone call from a prison staffer.

She knew he was getting close. There were increasing lapses in lucidity, a decline in appetite, and more frequent seizures during his final days. A week before he died, he stopped eating altogether, and was moved to the prison's hospice ward and placed on intravenous pain management. Shayna signed a do-not-resuscitate order and made arrangements for a local funeral home to cremate his remains. She would return to Scottsdale with her father's ashes, facing a mountain of debt and an uphill fight against her multiple sclerosis.

On her last morning in Coleman, she prepared a simple breakfast of microwaved oatmeal and instant coffee and glanced at the national news as she packed. Nearly six weeks after the murder of Frank D'Angelo, the networks were still milking the story for every ounce of ratings. The spin of the day was a spate of lawsuits filed by victims of the bombing against the Regal Palace, the city of Des Moines, and the manufacturer of the TNT used in the bomber's device. The story, as usual, was peppered with replays of the infamous three-second video depicting the senator's demise, beginning with him embracing the killer and ending with the explosion. It played no less than six times during the minute-long story. An unedited version, complete with the carnage-filled aftermath, was available across the internet.

Shayna sat down to eat in the hotel room kitchenette just as the commercial break began. The first advertisement caught her attention. It opened with a video of a cesspool, glowing bright green, with a vapor cloud rising from its center.

Did you or a family member live on or near Griffin Air Force Base in New York between 1993 and 2014? Have you developed any life-threatening or debilitating diseases? If so, you might be entitled to significant compensation.

The graphic switched to a government printing press with sheets of hundred-dollar bills passing through its rollers.

The United States government is paying billions of dollars to the victims of their malfeasance, but time is running out for you to file a claim.

Another graphic change, this one of an elderly woman sitting in her kitchen, wringing her hands and staring in bewilderment at a huge pile of papers on the table in front of her.

And you won't have to go it alone. We're with you every step of the way, to make sure you get the money you deserve. Call now!

The final shot was the toll-free number superimposed on a waving American flag. Shayna punched it into her phone.

Marge Greenfield was in her fourth year with ClientCare Services, and the trio of "Employee of the Year" trophies on her desk was testament to her productivity and longevity in an industry where the average employee stuck around for six months. Call screening was a grueling, monotonous business, and there was a reason the large corporations outsourced it. Time was money. Full-time employees meant salaries, health benefits, 401(k) matching, and human resources headaches. Paying a third party to gather and manage leads was a no-brainer.

And there was no shortage of leads. They called in response to flashy time-share advertisements. They called to inquire about dental implants. They called to see how much they could save by switching car insurance companies. And more than anything else, they called to see if they were eligible for a large cash award due to someone's negligence.

At any given time in the United States, there were in excess of three thousand class-action and wrongful-injury lawsuits of varying size and scope working their way through the courts. Most of them never garnered the public's attention. When a cable company got caught overcharging its customers for their pro-football package, they would simply reimburse the offended parties a portion of their subscription price or offer them the next season free of charge.

Then there were the monsters. It started with big tobacco, moved on to asbestos, then blossomed into an industry unto itself. Legions of law firms leveled the playing fields between greedy corporations and the everyday people whose lives they ruined for profit. It was David and Goliath meets *Law & Order*.

And for a personal-injury firm, there was no bigger and better target than the United States government, which the average American saw as oversized, overfunded, and out of touch. It was hard to feel sympathy for an entity that used its four-trillion-dollar budget to poison children. Even though that's not what the government did at Griffin Air Force Base, it happened on their watch, and they were left holding the bag when Earth Tech folded.

Marge's value lay in her ability to cut through the bullshitters, the window shoppers, and the delusional callers who had no business adding their name to a class action. She processed more calls than anyone at ClientCare, and her referrals ended up transacting business with the client 75 percent of the time. Her closest competitor averaged 40 percent. When Marge took your call, you had about a minute to convince her you were worth the time, or off you went.

The calls came in on a computer screen that displayed the caller identification, the toll-free number they had dialed, and the name of the client company. This one was coming from a low-rent hotel in a lower-rent city in Florida. Never a good sign. Probably another gold digger who had a cup of coffee near the disaster site and wanted their payday. Marge would make short work of it.

"Abbott Law Firm."

"Umm, yeah, hello. I just saw a commercial about Griffin Air Force Base. The water."

"And were you or someone in your immediate family harmed by drinking the water there?"

"Well, I don't know. I mean, I've never been tested."

Marge's patience was already wearing thin, and there were three more calls waiting. "Let's start with the basics. What was your connection to Griffin Air Force Base?"

"It wasn't really me. It was my dad."

"And what was his connection?"

"He was stationed there in the late nineties. In the army."

"Okay, and did he get sick?"

"He had brain cancer. But I can't prove it was from drinking any water."

"That's not important. Can I talk to him?"

"No. He died two days ago. In prison."

"Oh, dear, I'm sorry to hear that."

What Marge was actually sorry to hear was that the caller's father would be an unsympathetic victim. As the claims poured in and the payouts mounted, the government had begun to challenge cases where they believed they could win a jury trial. She hovered her mouse over the disconnect tab and readied her "Sorry we couldn't be of more help" speech.

"Thank you. And I have MS," the caller added.

"Oh, no. I'm sorry to hear that too." Last chance. "Did you live with your dad at Griffin?"

"I was born there."

Jackpot.

CHAPTER 45

THEY MET AT AN out-of-the-way dive bar on Laredo's south side. M.K. got there first and found a booth in the back near the kitchen. She smiled warmly when Sonny slid in across from her, and he noticed the scar on her left cheekbone right away.

"What happened there?" he asked, pointing to her face.

"A customer got a little frisky," she answered. "He paid for it."

"You still using a knife?"

"When it suits me. I was trained by the best, you know."

Sonny scowled. "A blade is *one* of the tools of the trade. It was never meant to be the only one. One day all that martial-arts shit is going to get you killed."

She reached across the table and took his hands in hers. "Nice to see you, too. Wish it was under better circumstances."

Sonny shrugged. "We all knew it was going to end someday. The smart ones like us had escape plans."

"Yeah. Speaking of that, I appreciate the call. Did your friend warn you?" she asked.

"He did. Then I saw on the news he got popped. They raided Sal's house, so there must have been something there that led the feds to our FBI friend. I cleaned my place out."

"Me too. Have you seen any news recently?"

"Not for the last few days. Other than the assassination of a presidential candidate and all our people getting picked up, what have I missed?"

A waitress came by, and they ordered two beers. M.K. watched her walk away and lowered her voice.

"You made the big time. The FBI added you to their top ten most wanted fugitives list this morning. They had a press conference in DC to announce it. There was a huge picture of you next to the FBI director while he was talking, and they even used your real name. How did they get that?"

"It's a long story. What did they say the charges were?"

"A whole buttload of murder-for-hires, conspiracy, and something called interstate flight to avoid prosecution. Like you're supposed to just sit and wait for them to come get you."

Sonny smiled. "Not gonna happen. If they want to chase me, I'll give them a chase."

"Oh, yeah, that reminds me." She reached into her pocket and slid a small white envelope across the table. "He's expecting you."

"Thanks. You can vouch for this guy?"

"I've never laid eyes on him. But a friend had her boobs done there. And he's discreet."

"Does he do good work?"

She laughed. "We're not that kind of friends. What's next for you?"

"Well, I think it's time for me to find somewhere else to live. As in another country. My luck's run out here. So I'll go see the good doctor and make a plan from there. What about you?"

M.K. shrugged. "It's not like I have a client list. The only steady work I ever got was through you. I may have to go legit."

Sonny chuckled. "Trust me, you're not suited for it. Too many rules. Keep doing what you do. Just do it smarter, will you?"

Their beers came and they drank them slowly, reminiscing on old times. When their bottles were empty Sonny left a twenty on the table and they walked to his truck. He opened the rear door and handed her a duffle bag.

"There are four of them," he said. "Melt them or run them through an industrial shredder, whichever is easier."

"I'll handle it," she said as she took the bag from him. She leaned toward him and they embraced. Sonny gave her a kiss on the cheek, climbed into his truck, and started the engine.

"Be careful down there," she said to him through the open window. "And wherever you end up."

Sonny smiled and nodded. "Take care of yourself, kid."

The drive to San Luis Potosi took another two days. He had exchanged twenty thousand dollars for pesos in Nuevo Laredo, and he parted with the Mexican equivalent of five thousand of those dollars at the clinic's reception desk.

The doctor was about sixty years old, overweight but not obese, and still blessed with a full head of jet black hair that he combed in a slicked back 'do that reached his collar. He wore a pair of khaki pants and a loud electric-blue flower print, and much to Sonny's surprise, he spoke perfect English. He offered Sonny a seat and got right to business.

"From what my assistant tells me, you're trying to beat facial recognition, am I correct?" he asked.

Sonny was taken aback. "I never said anything like that."

"Mr. Holloway, I've been doing this for thirty years. My clients have included some of the most infamous cartel bosses from Mexico and Colombia. I would never tell you or anyone else their names, just as your name will never leave my lips when we are done here. But this is my business, and there's a reason I can't practice in Mexico City, or even north of the border."

Sonny noticed the diploma on the wall behind the doctor. It was from the University of Iowa.

"You went to med school in the States?" he asked.

"Carver College of Medicine," he said proudly. "Undergrad at Tennessee. Go Vols. But back on point, I understand why you're here, so let's get down to it, shall we?"

Sonny nodded.

"There are things we can and can't do to fool the AI algorithms that make facial recognition work. We can't change the distance between your pupils, for instance. We can't change the basic geometry of how your eyes, mouth, and nose are arranged on your face. But we don't have to. Here's what we can do."

He got up from his chair and walked around to where Sonny was sitting.

"May I?" he asked, reaching for Sonny's face.

"Sure."

"We can raise these eyebrows and change their angle," he said, touching each facial feature as he described his plan. "We can make your nose wider or narrower, your choice. You have otapostasis, which is a fancy way of saying your ears stick out. We can pin them back. And you have a good deal of wrinkling around the mouth and eyes, which we can get rid of. That may or may not help, depending on what image of you the facial recognition software is using as a baseline."

"I think the only one they have is a driver's license photo," Sonny said. "It's about three years old."

"Perfect. If we take care of all those issues, you'll be unrecognizable. Plan on four hours of surgery, a couple of weeks to heal, and another ten thousand dollars for me to work my magic."

"When can you do it?"

"Day after tomorrow, if that's not too soon."

"See you then."

CHAPTER 46

AS ASHLEY HEALED, she and Bryce spent nearly every waking hour together. They passed the time with card games and Trivial Pursuit while she was on bed rest. When the doctors gave the go-ahead, they started taking walks that grew in length from around the block up to several miles. And through it all, they planned their trip.

Bryce had first floated the idea of a getaway while Ashley was still in the hospital. She was on board from the inception, and they spent the next several weeks brainstorming locations and activities. In the end, they decided on a two-week tour of the Pacific Northwest, California wine country, and Las Vegas. After ten days in Washington, Oregon, and Napa, they drove to Sin City and checked into a suite at the Bellagio.

Neither of them were serious gamblers, but that didn't matter. They were happy spending their days with each other, waking up late, taking in the sights, and enjoying the food scene that made Vegas one of the world's top culinary destinations. They also spent a fair amount of their vacation in bed, making up for lost time.

The day before their flight home, Bryce made dinner reservations at Sinatra, the Wynn's signature Italian eatery. They dressed for the occasion, he in a dark suit and she in a red evening gown.

Even in a city where the beautiful people were a dime a dozen, Ashley was a standout, and Bryce swelled with pride, watching heads turn toward the woman on his arm as they walked through the casino.

They spent two hours at Sinatra and had just paid the check when they heard the uproar behind them. It came from the hallway, and it was getting louder. There were whistles from the crowd, applause, and flashes of light as cameras popped. When the noise reached its loudest point, they saw the subject of the celebration. A bride and groom had just tied the knot, and were making their way through the casino. They wore casual beach attire, and a white boutonniere identified him as the lucky man. She clutched a bouquet with one hand and fussed over a long bridal veil with the other. They were accompanied by a raucous wedding party of ten similarly dressed celebrants. Vegas being Vegas, the mass of casino patrons, nearly all strangers to the newly betrothed, had joined in the festivities. They raised drinks, cheered, and toasted the couple as they passed.

"Looks like fun," Ashley said.

"It does. Is that what you always pictured, though?"

"What do you mean?"

"Don't little girls dream about traditional weddings? Big church, bunch of bridesmaids, long white dress, the whole thing?"

She twirled a ringlet of hair. "I guess, maybe when I was a kid. When you hit forty, you adjust your expectations. It's not about the day. It's about the life. What about you?"

"I never dreamed about my wedding as a little girl," Bryce joked.

"Stop it. You know what I mean."

"Truthfully, after my divorce I promised myself I was never getting married again. But if there's one thing I've learned, it's to never say never."

"So you're open to the idea?" Ashley asked.

"Sure, if I ever find the right girl."

She slapped his hand playfully, smiling all the while, and took his hands in hers from across the table. "You're terrible, you know that?"

After dinner they walked hand in hand through the Wynn complex, browsing the stores and watching the action at the high-stakes blackjack tables. As they gawked at the gamblers playing ten thousand dollars per hand, the bride and groom walked by. Ashley and Bryce saw them, offered their congratulations, and were surprised when the couple stopped to chat. They were David and Elizabeth from Sacramento, and they had been planning a huge ceremony back home for months.

"Three hundred guests," a tipsy Elizabeth said, touching Ashley's hand as she slurred her words. "And the whole thing turned into one giant shit show. His mother and mine were at war over every detail. The budget was out of control. My best friend disowned me because I picked my sister as my maid of honor."

David, who was just as drunk as his bride, if not more so, joined in. "And so I said, you know what? Screw it. You grab your bridesmaids, I'll get my groomsmen, and we'll go to Vegas and do this thing. And here we are!" He raised a bourbon glass in a toast to nobody in particular.

"That's amazing," Bryce said. "You two look very happy."

"Best decision we ever made," David replied. "And it was so easy. The marriage license place is open 'til midnight, and the chapels are all 24/7. We got here yesterday afternoon, and here we are!" he shouted, repeating the toast from ten seconds earlier.

"Well, congratulations again, and best of luck to both of you," Ashley said as she took Bryce's hand and led him away.

"That was interesting," he said.

"If you're into that kind of thing, yeah, I guess." They were each trying their best to be as nonchalant as possible.

They meandered through the casino and shops for another half hour. They were mostly silent, exchanging glances, sizing one another up as they ran through the dinner table conversation and the chance meeting with the newlyweds in their heads.

When they reached the casino entrance, a bellman hailed a taxi. Bryce opened the door for Ashley, who slid in behind the driver. He then walked around the car and got in on the passenger side. As he closed his door, the cab driver turned toward them and smiled. He asked the question every cabbie asks every customer, but still, it caught them off guard.

"Where to?"

EPILOGUE

THE AIRBUS A-380 touched down at 2:30 in the morning, fourteen hours after it had taken off from Mexico City. The planeload of weary travelers gathered their belongings and waited for the slow debarkation process to take its course. Sonny was in business class and exited the plane along with the first-class section as the flight attendants held the coach passengers at bay.

The airport was nearly empty, and that wasn't in Sonny's favor. He needed to be in a crowd, and he certainly didn't want to be first in line for a border agent starting a new shift. He ducked into a bathroom and spent twenty minutes using the toilet, brushing his teeth and freshening up from the flight. When he finished, he stared at himself in the mirror and liked what he saw.

The surgery was a success, and when the bandages came off in San Luis Potosi, Sonny barely recognized himself. He looked ten years younger, with different eyes, a wider nose, and ears that no longer looked like they could help him fly. The wrinkles around his mouth were all but gone. The surgeon had been true to his word. Sonny thought about killing him to cover his tracks, but in the end he opted not to. Had he wanted to turn Sonny in, there were plenty of opportunities to alert the authorities before the surgery. Sonny decided the doctor was trustworthy; still, he switched motel rooms every couple of days, stayed out of sight, and slept with one eye open.

When he left the bathroom, he found himself right where he needed to be, in the middle of the six-hundred-strong crowd making their way to immigration control. He worked his way through the rope maze for thirty minutes before being called forward. As he handed over his passport, Sonny was encouraged to see the immigration officer looking bored.

"Stand at the line, take off your glasses, and look straight ahead at the camera," the officer instructed in a thick accent.

Sonny did as he was told, realizing this was the moment of truth. After a few seconds that seemed like an eternity, the officer spoke again.

"You can put your glasses back on. What is the purpose of your visit?"

"Business."

"What type of business?"

"I'm a cyber security consultant." Sonny had checked, and it was the number one in-demand occupation in his new home.

"And where will you be staying?"

"The J.W. Marriott."

The officer looked at Sonny, then back down at the passport twice more. Finally, he reached for an entry stamp and brought it down with a loud thwack. He handed the passport back to Sonny and motioned toward the exit.

"Welcome to Dubai."

ABOUT THE AUTHOR

STEVE LAZARUS is an author, a retired FBI Special Agent, and a United States Air Force veteran. He served twenty-two years in the FBI, spending the first half of his career investigating drug trafficking organizations and violent street gangs. Later, he became a full-time bomb technician, an assignment that led him to Iraq, Kuwait, and Afghanistan as part of the Global War on Terror. After retiring from the Bureau, he spent several years as a national security consultant in Abu Dhabi, United Arab Emirates. Steve lives in South Carolina with his wife Susan and their amazing wonder dog, Aspen.

Learn more about Steve and keep up with his writing at
stevelazarusbooks.com.

Made in the USA
Las Vegas, NV
17 July 2025